Mrs. Tipperwillow's Afterlife Adventures

Robyn & Bruce!

New Friends

well met!

♡ Krista

Mrs. Tipperwillow's Afterlife Adventures

Krista Markowitz
Illustrations by Jenny Markowitz

iUniverse, Inc.
New York Bloomington Shanghai

Mrs. Tipperwillow's Afterlife Adventures

iUniverse books may be ordered through booksellers or by contacting:

iUniverse
1663 Liberty Drive
Bloomington, IN 47403
www.iuniverse.com
1-800-Authors (1-800-288-4677)

Because of the dynamic nature of the Internet, any Web addresses or links contained in this book may have changed since publication and may no longer be valid.

This is a work of fiction. All of the characters, names, incidents, organizations, and dialogue in this novel are either the products of the author's imagination or are used fictitiously.

ISBN: 978-0-595-44671-1 (pbk)
ISBN: 978-0-595-49079-0 (cloth)
ISBN: 978-0-595-88994-5 (ebk)

Printed in the United States of America

To the best family dancers,
Hal, Tim and Jenny!
I love you forever.

To sweet friends

Hal

Contents

Book Three From Here to Earth And Back Again

Acknowledgments

Thanks to all the dear friends who supported Mrs. Tipperwillow's flight to Earth and into these pages. Cheers to author Jean Bartlett who helped me with my beginning manuscript set-up and first reading. Balloons of appreciation are drifting to Kalei Ching, Joy Gardner and to Valentina Zeff for their fine editing and ideas, and to Bill Brencze for his last minute scanning help. A warm aloha is traveling across the ocean to Norm Goody in Kona, Hawaii, for taking time in his too busy schedule to design my colorful web page. The computer and photo shop help of Tim Markowitz, Michelle Jarvis and Ryckje Wagner saved the day more than once. And thanks again to the very creative Ryckje for knitting me my very own Snoody!

Hooray to Jenny Markowitz for capturing so well the characters of the magical sort of cow and her family of children! Her fanciful illustrations helped to bring these stories to life. Thanks also to Emma, Dante, Justin and David for allowing their images to become the faces of Jamie, Gino, Wallace and Aaron, and to all my other friends, seen and unseen, who previewed and commented on these stories as they took shape over the last seven years.

Finally, there are no adequate words to describe the depth of my gratitude to my most supportive husband, Hal Markowitz, who helped me every step of the way with ideas, proofreading, formatting, and hour upon hour of trouble shooting on the computer.

Book One
Jamie Takes Flight

1

Remembering

She was soaring through the air, arms spread out like wings. Wind pushed against her face and her clothing as she looked toward the rising sun. Thin clouds filled the sky with hot pink and orange stripes and touched the curved Earth below. Gazing down at the green patchwork fields beneath her, she did a double take. The ground was coming up fast! Quick! She fumbled for the ripcord by her shoulder, grabbed hold tight … and pulled.

With a start, eight-year-old Jamie Reed opened her eyes. Morning sun slanted through the hospital window forming a patch of light on her covers. She moved her hand over to feel its warmth and sighed. *I'm back here again … room 408.*

Jamie turned her head to look at her mother, who was still asleep on the small bed that folded back into a chair during the day. Mom's curly brown hair which was exactly the same shade and texture as her daughter's flopped over her eyes as she slept. Jamie loved her mother's soft brown eyes, which were so different from her own "big blues," as Daddy called them. For five nights now, either Mom or Dad had slept next to her in the hospital.

Four of Jamie's marker pen pictures brightened the pale yellow wall near her bed, each of them illustrating a story she had written. Her stories were always about a girl traveling by plane or boat or rocket ship to some magical far-off place. Mom and dad were so proud. "A born artist and writer" they called her time and time again.

Jamie's most recent poem was about a cat that climbed high into a tree but was afraid to come down. She had typed the poem all by her-

3

self on Dad's new computer. He had shown her how to make the lettering fancy and how to add a border of leaves. He even scanned in her drawing of a cat sitting on a tree branch.

Jamie remembered painting watercolor pictures with mom at the kitchen table before she got so sick. Her younger brother, Bobby, wearing his red felt cowboy hat, would gallop around them, whinnying.

Bobby was going to be a doctor *and* a cowboy when he grew up, and he could hardly wait for the first grade. He loved playing school with his big sister, and he *always* had to be Teacher. And what a bossy teacher he was!

Bobby would pull Jamie into his room and write on his blackboard and make up lessons as she sat on his bed doodling in her "workbook." Her brother would tap-tap-tap his chalk loudly if he noticed Jamie wasn't paying attention.

Jamie's thoughts drifted to her grandparents, whom she loved more than just about anything. She remembered the day Mommy had come into her room and told her sadly that Grandpa had something called "Alzheimer's" and couldn't remember so well anymore. They would drive across town to her grandparents' home, and Jamie would sit on Grandpa's lap and tell him her stories. He would laugh and laugh, even though the stories were not *that* funny, and that would make Jamie laugh, too. Soon they would both be laughing so hard that no sound would come out, and they would gasp for air with tears streaming down their cheeks.

Whenever the children would come for dinner, Grandma called Jamie and Bobby her "special guests." She would set a table with flowers, her best China dishes and sparkly crystal glasses. Jamie remembered the night Bobby accidentally broke Grandma's favorite water glass and the look of horror on his face. Grandma had taken Bobby onto her lap and told him not to worry, that it was only a thing. Jamie loved her grandmother especially for that.

In her mind's eye, Jamie saw Grandma pushing through her swinging kitchen door with a big smile on her face, carrying a plate of her famous chocolate chip cookies, still warm from the oven. Jamie's mouth watered as she remembered the taste of those cookies.

The eight-year-old sighed. *I've had a good life,* she thought, *but I wish I didn't have to leave so soon. Are there really angels in heaven? What will I do there? Will I make new friends?*

There it was again, that tingling on her cheek. Someone was touching her gently, so very gently. *It's you,* she thought. *Thank you. Thank you for being here with me.* A familiar tune began in Jamie's head and worked its way down to her toes. It always reminded her of bubbling water and singing birds and fresh, fresh air. At last, with a trill of soft tinkling notes, the music faded.

Jamie felt a sudden burst of happiness and glimpsed a large striped tent standing in the middle of an impossibly bright green field speckled with wildflowers. The image faded.

Jamie turned painfully onto her side and adjusted her pillow. Then, hoping the dream would return and she could fly again, she closed her eyes.

2

Summerland

Puffy clouds moved slowly across the sky outside of Jamie's hospital window. She felt so tired. Tubes connected her to machines that were humming … humming … white tubes, looking almost like tree branches. The humming became louder. Jamie felt a bit dizzy and closed her eyes to see trees with white bark, birches just like those in Grandma's yard. Eyes open, tubes … eyes closed, trees. Eyes open … trees! Golden light was everywhere. Jamie's eyes opened wide. Birch trees! A whole forest of birch trees, leaves rustling … rustling in the warm breeze. But this wasn't Grandma's yard. This was even better, brighter and more real, somehow.

Jamie watched the leaves and understood. She was glad she had already said her 'just in case' goodbyes and "I love you forever."

I love you forever, she thought again to her family. There was a soft beeping sound coming from far away and some other noises. Then they stopped.

Jamie watched as a beautiful red bird landed in the branches of the nearest birch and turned to look at her. There was another rustle coming from behind the trees and another flash of red. Suddenly a creature in a short, red polka-dot dress was standing before her.

She looks sort of like a cow, the eight-year-old thought as she looked from the creature's head to the dress to the two thin cow legs and finally to the small round hooves, which floated slightly above the ground.

Jamie's gaze moved back up to the creature's face. *Yes, she's mostly like a cow, but she has that small antler stuck to the middle of her forehead … and what a goofy smile!* As if the creature knew *exactly* what Jamie was thinking, the smile got even bigger.

"Hello, Jamie. My name is Daisy Tipperwillow," said the sort of cow in a musical voice, "but I am usually just called *Mrs. Tipperwillow*. I will be your guide here in Summerland."

A long, furry white creature appeared curled around Mrs. Tipperwillow's shoulders. It stared at Jamie with sleepy eyes.

"And this is my friend Snoody." Mrs. T. reached up and petted the creature with one small hoof. His eyes closed. "You could look and look, but you would *never* find a snoode on Earth, Jamie," the sort of cow continued. "He is my special creation, you see. But he does look a little like a mink or perhaps a ferret. Don't you think so?"

Tipperwillow glided over and touched the tie of Jamie's hospital gown with one hoof. She muttered, "This will *never* do." Jamie's eyes opened wide. She was now wearing a yellow flowered sundress. "There, that's better. Come along!" A sparkly golden path opened through the forest and not knowing what else to do, the girl moved forward following the bouncing, dancing cow.

I'm following a cow, she thought. *How very strange.*

They moved into a clearing of the softest bright green grass Jamie had ever seen. Suddenly Mrs. Tipperwillow was standing twenty feet further away than she'd been the moment before. She turned, and Jamie noticed a pink rubber ball between her hooves.

"Catch!" trilled the magical sort of cow. As the ball rolled through the air it began to take on a fuzzy look. When Jamie closed her hands around it, it was soft and sticky. Cotton candy!

Jamie stared at the ball of spun sugar and then into the large brown eyes of Mrs. Tipperwillow who had drifted closer and was motioning for her to take a bite. "I couldn't eat this when I was sick," the girl said, popping some into her mouth.

"I know dear, but here in Summerland you can eat anything you want, and it will *always* be good for you." Jamie finished slowly, licking her fingers to get the last sweetness.

Jamie shook her head in confusion as the magical cow disappeared and reappeared further away and called, "Now catch this!" Jamie raised her hands as a white volleyball rolled slowly through the air toward her. Again at the midway point it changed, turning lumpy … and feathered! Two wings unfurled revealing a snowy white dove. Jamie reached for the bird but missed as it quickly lifted out of range and flitted around her head sending silvery sparkles fluttering down into her brown curls.

"*I've* always wanted to fly," the eight-year-old said, flapping her arms up and down like wings. A surprised "Oh!" escaped Jamie's lips as her feet left the ground and she found herself floating above Mrs. Tipperwillow. She stretched her arms wide and wiggled her fingers. Letting out a whoop of delight, Jamie lifted higher until she was over forty feet in the air. The magical sort of cow floated up to join her and turned two graceful somersaults in the sky.

Realizing just how high she was above the meadow, Jamie felt a stab of fear. She looked at the ground, and just like that, she was once again standing on the soft green grass. Sensing something behind her, she turned. Four balls of light were rolling toward her. *What's this?* Jamie took a step backward as the balls of light swirled upward to become ... children!

"Can we play?" asked the nearest one.

"Yes," said Mrs. Tipperwillow landing next to Jamie. "Join us, Children.

"Jamie, may I present Lateesha, Wallace, Yoshiko, who goes by the name of Yoshi, and Gino."

Each hopped forward as Mrs. Tipperwillow said their names. Lateesha was a girl near Jamie's age with a wide smile, chocolate brown skin and tiny, dark braids all over her head held in place with colored stars. Wallace was older and skinny with blond hair, pale skin, and a serious expression. Yoshi was small with long black hair, almond-shaped eyes, and a shy smile.

Gino was a bit shorter than Jamie. He had glistening green eyes and light brown hair which went this way and that way, part slicked down and part sticking up like it couldn't decide which way to go. To Jamie he looked like one of those silly boys in school who were always playing jokes and laughing.

Gino bowed low. Lateesha jumped high into the sky and swirled around in mid-air. Yoshi came over and took Jamie's hand. "It's really okay, Jamie. It's fun here. You'll see." Wallace smiled knowingly and rose into the air doing slow loops. He looked like he was imitating a hawk, as he flew majestically with arms widespread.

"Why can we fly, Mrs. Tipperwillow?" Jamie asked, tipping her curly head to one side. "I couldn't do that at home."

"This is your home now, Jamie, until you choose to return to Earth and a new life. Here in Summerland, everything is created instantly by thought. So balls can turn into birds and cotton candy, and you can fly. There are houses and schools and libraries, beautiful flowers, lakes, rivers, oceans and forests here. All of it has been created by someone's thought, someone's memory and wish, just as your flying is created by your wish. What do you want to do or see or be? Anything at all, that's how we play!"

Jamie played in the golden sky with her new friends for what seemed like hours. She practiced flying higher and higher until she was no longer afraid even at one hundred and then at two hundred feet in the air. She copied her new friends and got the knack of doing loops and twirls and back flips and long glides.

Finally setting down on the grass the children watched as Mrs. Tipperwillow began creating things with her thoughts. Hats in crazy shapes with feathers stuck in the brims appeared one by one between her hooves. Each child took one, giggling and making faces as they plopped the silly looking hats on their heads.

"Mrs. Tipperwillow loves to dress up," Lateesha explained, as she helped Jamie adjust the rounded pink hat with its two red feathers. "And she *especially* loves hats and feathers."

Jamie's mouth opened in surprise as giant flowers more than ten feet tall slowly materialized in a circle surrounding them. Daisies, tulips and daffodils bobbed down their flower faces to look at the group. They were followed by a swarm of butterflies made of *butter* and *flies*.

The sort of cow chuckled, and the children squealed "Eew!" when the butterflies fluttered down and landed on pieces of toast which had appeared next to them.

"Would you care perhaps for a small snack?" Mrs. Tipperwillow's grin was full of mischief.

"No thank *you*," replied Wallace, making a face.

Gino's eyes narrowed, and he licked his lips. "That looks d-e-e-licious!" he said. Quickly grabbing a piece of the toast, he leaned toward Lateesha and ran it over her arm butterfly side down. He moved on to Yoshi and was making a move toward Wallace before Mrs. Tipperwillow could intervene.

"Hmmm," was all she said, and the butterflies and toast disappeared followed by the giant flowers.

"Yuck!" snapped Yoshi rubbing her arm which was immediately clean. Gino's eyes were still gleaming with mischief.

Lateesha stuck out her tongue. "You just wait, Gino!"

The sort of cow laughed. "My young friends, it's been a long and a lovely day of play, but now it is time for quiet. Let's all show Jamie how we dim the lights until morning."

She raised her arms, and the children copied her. "Evening come, quiet, quiet," they chanted softly. The light in the sky began to fade.

"Now, let's take Jamie to our home."

As a group they lifted softly into the air and their hats disappeared as they floated over bright green fields. They landed in a flower-speckled meadow next to a large striped tent.

This is the tent I saw, Jamie thought. She peeked through the tent flap and noticed lighted lanterns and bunk beds on one side and a cozy fire burning brightly in a grey stone fireplace on the other side of the tent. Somehow the tent looked bigger on the inside than it did on the outside.

"All of us helped build this tent house," Mrs. Tipperwillow said. "I imagined the tent. Lateesha made it red and white striped like a candy cane. I helped Wallace build the fireplace with his thought. And a good solid look it has, too!

"Gino wanted bunk beds, like the ones he used when he visited his aunt and uncle's cabin in the woods. Yoshi chose a soft rug for the floor the color of peaches, which are her favorite fruit. And soon, Jamie, you can think of what you want to add here. I'll show you how to create it yourself.

"Now before we tuck in, let's say our blessings and turn the dusk to nighttime."

The children and Mrs. Tipperwillow held hands and hooves together. Jamie listened closely as they said: "Blessings to all we've ever been and to all we'll ever be. Blessings to all we've ever loved, to the Earth, to spirit, and to dreams."

"And now," continued the sort of cow, "the last part, please."

And they chanted: "Softly, softly into night, softly, softy goes the light. Good night! Good night! Good night! Good night!" The sky dimmed further until it was almost dark.

"We always leave a little night light on," said Mrs. Tipperwillow with a wink of her large brown eye.

As they entered the tent one by one the children's clothing was replaced by soft pajamas, which were each midnight blue with pale yellow stars. Wallace, Yoshi, Lateesha and Gino got settled in their own bunks, while the sort of cow floated to an empty upper bunk, pulled back the covers, and motioned to Jamie. "This one is for you, dear."

Jamie smiled at Lateesha as she climbed up past her new friend and slid into her own bed. Mrs. Tipperwillow gently tucked the soft blue blanket around her.

"A new golden day will be here soon, Jamie, and new adventures. Now nighty-night and sleep sweet!"

Jamie's lips curved to a smile as she closed her eyes and snuggled into her fluffy pillow. "I flew today," she said softly.

"Yes, my dear," replied Mrs. Tipperwillow. "You most certainly did."

3

Her Tale

"Today, Children, is an exciting day!" Mrs. Tipperwillow was wearing a ballooning yellow dress and an impossibly large hat of the same color. "Today we take Jamie on her first visit to the Library of Lives." The sort of cow turned to Jamie. "You've been to a library, of course. What did you find there?"

"Books," replied Jamie, "many books, everywhere."

"Yes! And this is a very special library because it contains the stories of your lifetimes on Earth … every single one of them."

"I only remember one lifetime with Mommy, Daddy and my little brother Bobby," Jamie said, shaking her head.

"Yes, Jamie. That would be the life you just finished. But before we leave for the library, I thought you all might like to hear a bit about my last lifetime on Earth."

Out standing in your field! Moo-oo, piped Gino, doing a fair imitation of a cow.

Jamie chuckled, Wallace raised his eyebrows, and Lateesha laughed out loud. From the way Lateesha looked at Gino, Jamie suspected that her new friend *always* laughed at Gino's jokes, whether they were funny or not.

Mrs. Tipperwillow chortled, "That's a very clever pun, Gino. But you know I only take this form because it pleases me."

"I don't get it." Yoshi whispered, but Gino heard her loud and clear.

"That's okay, Yoshi," he said. "You're only just seven, so you're too young to understand jokes. She's out there standing in her field, see? That's what cows do, they *stand* in *fields*. And being outstanding at something means you're really good at it, and a field is what you're good at. Get it?"

Yoshi's eyes glazed over. "I guess. Thanks."

"I got that joke from a book, so I know it's good."

Yoshi shrugged.

Lateesha looked over at Mrs. Tipperwillow. "We'd love to hear your story now, Mrs. T.," she said. The other children nodded.

Their teacher turned to look at the empty fireplace. There was a puff of smoke, and a blazing fire appeared. Jamie shook her head. *This all takes some getting used to*, she thought as she sat down with her new friends before the warm fire.

Mrs. Tipperwillow began. "Once long, long ago in the thirteenth … or perhaps it was in the fourteenth century, I lived in a castle in the Lake District of England. And cold and drafty that castle was, too!

"Now it was a time of brave knights and fair maidens, and the castle was a-bustle day and night with the comings and goings of petitioners seeking a boon from the king and with visitors come from other kingdoms.

"Because they were so busy, you see, the king and queen had little time for their children. I'd grown up in the castle. My father was the stable master, and I'd taken care of my own brothers when they were little. So I was hired when barely fifteen years of age to be nanny for the king and queen's two children; Prince Gerick and his younger sister, Princess Gwendolyn.

"Oh, they were my darlings, to be sure they were," said Mrs. T., suddenly speaking in a heavy English accent. "One year when Gerick was six and Gwenny was four, I remember dressing them in their finest clothes and taking them hand-in-hand to the Harvest Faire. It was little Gwen's first faire. And her last, too," added Mrs. Tipperwillow with a sigh.

"Now the Harvest Faire was the biggest celebration of the year. People who lived in the castle and in the villages and farmlands all around prepared for months.

"Some women spun wool and dyed it using crushed berries, tree bark, mosses and such to create beautiful colors. From this they made soft clothing and fine blankets to sell at the faire. Others gathered herbs to dry and hang with colorful ribbons, while still others made scented soaps and candles to sell. Men crafted finely worked saddles for the horses or forged sharp knives and swords or carved wooden toys for the children.

"A few days before the event, exotic people came from faraway lands to set up *their* booths. They brought spices, flowing pieces of silk, fine wood carvings, and gold jewelry to sell.

"The morning before the faire, fruits and vegetables were harvested and placed in large baskets.

"The big day finally arrived. There were pennants flying and booths lined up all along the narrow, dusty streets. The smell of apples, flowers, and fine pastries filled the air. There was music and dancing.

"Gwen and Gerick laughed with glee as I led them in their first dance that beautiful autumn day. We found a place to sit in the shade and ate apple pastries while we listened to a bard play his small harp. As I recall, he sang a popular ballad concerning a dragon and the brave knight who conquered him.

"Afterwards, we walked to the edge of the village to watch foot races, horse races and contests of strength. I remember that by midafternoon Little Gwen was so tired I had to carry her home.

"On the final day of the celebration, I finally had some time to myself. I wandered alone through the winding streets looking in all of the booths. Gerick and Gwen joined the king and queen on the castle balcony as they presided over the final event of the faire, the jousting tournament. Do any of you know about jousting?" Mrs. Tipperwillow asked, looking around.

"I know! I know!" answered Gino, before anyone else had a chance to speak. "Jousting was where men rode toward each other on horseback and tried to knock each other off their horses using long poles."

"That's right, Gino." Mrs. Tipperwillow smiled. "Such a time it was!"

Her smile faded. "But soon after the festival, little Gwen came down sick. There were no medicines in those days to make her better, and in a few short weeks she passed away. Two more little ones were born later, but I never forgot my little Princess."

Mrs. T. stared into the fire. "Gwenny simply *loved* the cows. We would often watch them together as they grazed in the hills and valleys all around the castle. We would marvel at the cows' gentleness, and at the way they kept us all alive with their milk and even with their flesh nourishing ours. Gwen's favorite cow was named Daisy," Mrs. Tipperwillow added with a sigh.

"After my little Princess died, I wondered what had become of her spirit. I wondered if she was lonely. I imagined that when I left Earth I might become some sort of magical cow and greet boys and girls when they came to the spirit world. And here I am." She looked warmly at each of the children.

"You sure are a good storyteller," Jamie said as Mrs. Tipperwillow's large brown eyes met hers.

"It takes one to know one," replied Mrs. T. with a wink.

"So, is there a *Mr.* Tipperwillow hiding somewhere?" Lateesha asked.

"No, dear, I simply thought it a cozy name. I suppose in your day I would properly be called Ms. But to me this sounds like so many angry bees stuck in a bottle."

"Mzzz … mzzz … mzzz," buzzed the children.

"What about this?" Gino asked, pointing to the small antler on Mrs. T.'s forehead.

"My boy, to me an antler represents strength. And it's on my forehead so I won't forget where I put it."

There was dead silence. Wallace repeated in a soft voice, "… So I won't forget where I put it." A chuckle escaped his lips. Suddenly the tent exploded with laughter.

"So she won't forget where she put it!" squealed Gino and laughed so hard that he started to hiccough, rolled over on his belly and beat the rug with his fists.

Jamie's face was bright red. Her mouth was open, but no sound came out, and tears were running down both cheeks. Yoshi and Lateesha thought this was hilarious. They laughed even harder until tears were running down their cheeks as well.

At last the hilarity faded to an occasional chuckle. The magical sort of cow licked a tear of laughter that had made its way to her mouth. She put her hooves on her hips and said in a serious voice, "Well, I don't see what's so funny about *that*."

4

The Library of Lives

"Now it's time for you to experience some of *your* lifetimes," Mrs. Tipperwillow said cheerfully. She clicked her hooves together twice. Instantly, the children were dressed in thick, cream-colored ankle-length robes, with cloth belts tied around their waists and running shoes for their feet. Jamie looked down.

"This is what we usually wear to the library, Jamie," Lateesha explained as they floated out of the tent.

"Now," said their teacher, "shall we fly or take the train?"

"The train! The train!" the other children yelled.

Jamie thought flying would be more fun, until she saw what happened next. The sky turned dark. A circle of pulsing orange light appeared, floating just above the ground next to the children and their teacher. They moved out of the way quickly, Yoshi taking Jamie's hand to pull her back, just as the circle expanded.

Through the glowing circle pushed a reddish-orange fountain of light, which reached high into the darkened sky. Plumes of blue, yellow, and green emerged from the fountain and billowed like smoke until the whole sky was alight with color. And high above, through the colors, Jamie could just make out the headlights of a train emerging. She heard the whoosh of steam being expelled as the train came to a shuddering halt.

"All Aboard!" called a booming voice. Jamie felt herself lifted high into the air with the others, through the colored lights and into the door of the passenger car where they quickly found seats.

"And away we go!" trilled Mrs. Tipperwillow. The train began moving slowly, gradually picking up speed and altitude. It chugged along, sounding just like a real train. But Jamie noticed as she looked out the window that there were no tracks beneath the wheels ... only sky.

Through the rainbow lights they flew. One color bathed the children in yellow, and they felt happy and confident. Coming into orange light, they felt excited. As they passed through red, they felt strong and safe. When purple passed over them, they were enfolded in a feeling of peace. The train stopped with a lurch.

"Hall of Records! Hall of Records!" yelled the conductor and without any notice, they were standing on the ground in front of a big brick building.

"This is it, Children," said Mrs. T. softly. "Each of you may visit your Life Books. There will be a guide for each of you. But what is the rule in the library?"

Speak quietly and don't disturb others?" Yoshi tried.

"That's right, my polite child. And since this is new to Jamie, I'll go with her this time."

With a nod of Mrs. Tipperwillow's head, the big double doors opened.

Wow! Jamie thought. *I never imagined a library could be this big.* She stared at the rows and rows of magenta-colored, leather bound books, going back so far that she couldn't even see the back of the library as it dissolved into mist.

"All lives ever lived on Earth are recorded here," whispered the sort of cow. "Imagine Jamie, how many people have *ever* lived on Earth. Amazing, isn't it?"

"Yeah, it sure is," the girl whispered, looking around. "Where is my Life Book?"

A tall robed woman drifted toward them, and Jamie heard the words *this way* in the center of her head.

"Her lips didn't move," Jamie whispered. There was no more time to think about this. Mrs. Tipperwillow and Jamie were whisked away on a little wind and pulled down one of the rows.

They stopped suddenly. *Here you are,* said the guide, again in Jamie's head. *Jamie Reed ... soul name, Jayla.*

Jamie shivered. *That's familiar ... Jayla.*

"Everyone has a soul name, Jamie," Mrs. Tipperwillow said softly. "All of your lives are part of the bigger you called your higher self or soul. And all of the lifetimes you have ever lived are recorded *right here.*" Mrs. T. pointed a hoof at a book nestled on the shelf between "Jaykeba" and "Jaymek." "Jayla" was engraved on the binding.

"My book is really fat," whispered Jamie. "I must have lived a lot of lives."

The sort of cow nodded. "There will be more trips to the library for you, Jamie. But for today, let's look at your last lifetime."

The guide removed the large book from the shelf. She placed it on one of the heavy wooden tables lined up between the rows. She motioned them over.

Mrs. Tipperwillow touched Jamie's arm with her small hoof. "This book may surprise you, Jamie. Here, open it at the marker."

"Oh! The pictures move."

"They do indeed, Child. This book contains the memories of all your lifetimes on Earth. Notice the first page of this life ... your birth."

"Oh, Mommy's pushing, and I'm squeezed trying to get out. I can *feel* this book, Mrs. T. Look! I am born and crying and breathing for the very first time. Mommy and Daddy look *so* happy. Now I can feel Mommy's warmth as I lie on her tummy."

Jamie turned the pages one by one. She formed her first word. She felt her first steps, and how it felt to fall back down on her padded bottom. She started toddling and then getting bigger, she was running. She could see and feel the brightly colored plastic blocks as she played with her friends in nursery school. It hurt when she got pushed down by that new boy in kindergarten, and she shook with rage.

Next she experienced her first trip to the hospital with all the tests and needles. She saw the looks on her parents' faces and felt her own confusion as the doctor explained to her about her illness and what they would do to help her get better. It still hurt, thinking of all that happened.

"*Why*, Mrs. Tipperwillow?" the eight-year-old asked, quickly closing the book and looking through her tears into the caring brown eyes.

"Only your higher self knows the answer to *that* question, my dear."

An overstuffed armchair appeared in the aisle, and Mrs. Tipperwillow sat down, motioning the girl to sit next to her. "Often the timing of a child's death is decided even before she is born, Jamie. This is what happened in your case."

"Mommy said God was calling me home."

"Your soul chooses, Jamie, but yes, in a way what your mother said is true because your soul or higher self is part of that loving energy of God. And that makes you a part of God, too.

Look here!" A large woven rug with an intricate design appeared floating in the air before them. Mrs. Tipperwillow took hold of one corner and pulled it close. "Notice the weave, Jamie, how these threads form a pattern. One lifetime is like this thread moving through the rest."

"I can't see the pattern if I only look at this one thread."

"Exactly, my dear! Your higher self knows the pattern formed by all of your lifetimes and that each added life will make that pattern more complete and beautiful. As you get accustomed to being here, you will begin to feel and understand your pattern and the reasons you passed to spirit when you did. Then you will merge with your higher self to decide what will come next.

"Even though it seemed short, I want you to understand that your life was important, Jamie, and not just to you. Shall we look in some other books?"

They spent the rest of the morning first in one row of the huge library and then in another. Jamie saw in her brother's book that he would grow up to be a scientist. She stared in wonder as her grown brother peered into a microscope and scribbled notes on a little pad next to him.

But Bobby is only six years old, she thought. *How can I see him as a grown-up?* Jamie turned a page of Bobby's book and spied a newspaper article taped to the middle of one page. She read that at age thirty-eight Doctor Robert Reed discovered the cure for a rare type of cancer. Jamie remembered the name of *that* disease. It was the very same disease that had ended her life.

Before she thought better of it, Jamie raised her arms in the air, and her voice exploded with a loud "Yes!" She looked around quickly and felt relieved that no one else in the long aisle seemed to notice.

Jamie was still smiling from her discovery as she drifted with Mrs. Tipperwillow to another section of the library to peek in her mother's Life Book. Jamie saw that soon after her passing, her mom had begun doing oil paintings in soft pastel colors, and that this had seemed to comfort her. Later, these paintings were displayed in art galleries around town, and her work became popular. People somehow seemed to feel better about *their* lives just by looking at them. Next Mom began teaching a class called "Art as Healing." She worked with many sad people, and they started to feel better, too.

When Jamie looked in her father's book, she saw that he'd had an especially hard time dealing with her death. Dad had buried himself in work and stayed at the office after hours. Finally at Mom's urging, he saw a therapist who helped him talk about his feelings. Her father quit his old job, and following a lifelong dream, he started his own computer company. He also volunteered with a hospice, and he became a trusted friend to many.

"Life is magic, isn't it?" whispered Mrs. Tipperwillow, as she placed an arm around Jamie's shoulders. "The things you do are constantly creating the play you live in, and they are constantly affecting other people. Your family went on to live in new ways, different from what they would have if you had stayed. Look how important you are to your parents and to your brother. Look how their lives changed because of their love for you.

"All of your family found ways to heal themselves, Jamie. Then they decided to honor your memory by living well and helping others."

The girl looked into Mrs. T's large brown eyes and nodded her head in understanding. Thank you for showing me, Mrs. Tipperwillow," she said softly. "I feel a lot better now."

5

Sharing

The morning ended with everyone gathering again outside of the library door. They drifted over a path to a grassy park directly across from the large building. Mrs. Tipperwillow spread a blue and white plaid blanket on the lawn, and they sat down to enjoy a picnic with everyone's favorite foods.

Lateesha shared her grilled cheese sandwich with Jamie, and Jamie shared her peanut butter and banana sandwich with Lateesha. Gino couldn't sit still for long. He hopped on one foot as he popped his third hot dog into his mouth. Then he stuffed olives on all his fingers and floated over to wiggle them in Yoshi's face.

"Stop that, Gino," she complained. Yoshi offered some of her sushi to Wallace. He took a piece.

"Thanks. Do you want some taco?"

"No thank you," Yoshi replied politely.

Wallace studied the insides of a flower which had popped up next to him and began explaining to Yoshi about the parts of the flower. She peered inside and touched what he called "an anther." Yellow pollen came off on her hand.

Licking peanut butter off her fingers, Lateesha turned to Jamie. "Wallace's parents were both teachers. I bet if he'd grown up, he would have been a teacher, too."

Jamie nodded. "How old is Wallace?"

"Wallace is the oldest of us," Lateesha replied, looking over at the boy, who was now explaining the process of pollination. "He's twelve, and he thinks he knows just about *everything*. Well, he does know a lot.

25

Wallace acts like a big brother to Yoshi, who is the youngest in our family. She turned seven just before she came here. I'm nine and Gino's eight."

"I'm eight, too," added Jamie.

"So were you sick or in an accident or what?" The others turned to listen.

"I had this weird kind of cancer that children don't usually get," Jamie answered. "I had treatments, and sometimes I felt better, and sometimes I felt worse. My hair fell out, and when it came back in it was curlier than before. Mommy and Daddy said I was beautiful either way. I was sick a long time. What about you?"

"I was sick, too," Lateesha replied, "but only for about a week before I came here. Mrs. Tipperwillow told me the name of the disease. It's really hard to remember. Mema … mena…. What was that, Mrs. T.?"

"It's called *bacterial meningitis*, dear."

"Yeah, that's it. Thanks.

"Anyway, I love all kinds of sports, but I *especially* love softball and soccer. It happened at the end of soccer season. I'd been playing nearly every day with my two very best friends, Teresa and Megan. We were in the youth soccer league together, and our team had just won the regional championships. Even better, I kicked in the winning goal! We were *so* excited. Our picture was in the newspaper and everything.

"Suddenly I got really sick. I'd had an earache for awhile, but I didn't tell my parents because finals were coming up, and I was afraid they wouldn't let me play. Mrs. Tipperwillow told me the disease started with the ear infection."

Lateesha shook her head. "At first I felt really guilty about that. But Mrs. T. told me not to worry about it, because everybody passes to spirit at just the right time for them.

"Anyway, I felt really miserable with a fever and throwing up and a neck ache and a pounding headache … the worst headache *ever*. At first Nana and Mom and Dad thought I just had the flu, so they didn't take me to the clinic right away. They gave me lots of juice and medicine, but I kept feeling worse and worse. Mom was on the phone talking with my doctor when I fell asleep and just like that, I woke up in Summerland."

That was fast! Jamie thought.

"Yes it really was," agreed Lateesha.

Jamie almost jumped. "You heard my thought!"

That's the way it is here in Summerland, Yoshi thought to Jamie. *We don't need to talk out loud if we don't want to, and we can still hear each other.*

"So Lateesha," said a very impressed Gino, "you were a star soccer player. That is *so* cool."

"And it must have been really exciting to win the championship," Jamie added. She turned to look at the small seven-year-old. "So what happened to you, Yoshi? Were you sick, too?"

"It was a car accident," replied the girl in barely a whisper, looking first at Jamie and then down at her feet.

Jamie wanted to ask more, but she changed her mind quickly when she noticed Yoshi rub a hand across her eyes and shake her head in an angry way. And when the little girl put her balled-up fist into her lap, it was wet with tears.

Jamie shook her head in confusion. She turned to look at Gino. "What about you, Gino?"

"A dumb accident—my fault, and I was out of my body in a *flash*. But Wallace had the most exciting death," he said, quickly changing the subject. "Tell Jamie all about it, Wallace … okay?"

"Okay," replied the twelve-year-old, "but of course *death* is really the wrong word, eh? *Passing over* is more appropriate." (Gino rolled his eyes.)

"My father was a college professor. He taught botany—that's the study of plants, you know, and he studied ecosystems and how pollution and global warming are changing plant life—stuff like that."

"Well, maybe not *that* much detail," mumbled Gino.

Wallace shrugged his shoulders. "Anyway, my mother, my father, my older sister, Alice, and I were coming back on a plane from the island of Oahu, in Hawaii, where my father had given a talk at a big convention.

"We had a really great time. I learned how to snorkel and body surf, and we went to a real Hawaiian luau with traditional foods like *poi* which is made from mashed taro root, and roasted pig, called *kalua* pig, which is wrapped in ti leaves and cooked under hot stones in a pit called an...."

Gino fluffed his hands in the air, as if to say "get on with it."

Wallace gave Gino a crooked smile. "As I was *saying*," he continued, "we were on the plane heading home. The 'Fasten Your Seatbelts' sign went off, so I got up to go to the bathroom. On the way back to my seat the plane started shaking real bad. The captain came on the intercom and told everyone to sit down and fasten our seat belts. I got to my seat and was trying to get my belt fastened, but the plane was shaking like crazy. I couldn't do it. Suddenly a giant hole tore out of the plane right above me. Just like that I was pushed out into the sky!"

"Oh, my gosh!" Jamie exclaimed. "How did that feel?"

"It felt sort of like it does when we pull up into the air fast to fly in Summerland. But I never felt anything like that before. I was *really* surprised!"

"Did you hit the ground?"

"No I didn't, Jamie, not that I remember, anyway. First I saw pictures of my life pass in front my eyes, and I heard this loud whirring sound. Then I was speeding down a long tunnel. I could see light at the end of it, and when I came out, I was standing at the edge of a steep cliff. I figured it must be a long way down, but the golden fog made it hard to see. I could just barely make out land on the other side of the cliff. And the only way across was a bridge made of *flowers*. What was I supposed to do about that?

"Just then my guardian appeared next to me. I remembered him from my dreams, and it seemed like I'd known him forever. He took my hand, and together we walked out onto the bridge. I couldn't believe it. It held our weight!

When we got to the other side, my favorite grandma and grandpa and one of my aunts who died when I was little were there to greet me. There were some other people, too, that I *almost* remembered. We talked for awhile.

"Then a sort of cow appeared nearby and came over to say hello. You all know who that was! I said goodbye to the others and followed Mrs. Tipperwillow into the grassy meadow. After I got the knack of flying, Mrs. T. took me on a tour of Summerland and showed me how she creates things with her thoughts. Then we met Gino and moved to the tent house that Mrs. Tipperwillow imagined for us in the meadow."

"Wow, that's a *really* exciting story, Wallace. Did the rest of your family pass over at the same time?"

"Yep, and we got together later for tea. Mrs. Tipperwillow told me that we all have new things to do when we come here, so people don't stay with the same families they had on Earth.

Jamie thought about this. "I guess that makes sense, as long as we can still see the people we love sometimes." The twelve-year-old nodded.

"But what about the tunnel and the whirring sound?" she asked. "I didn't have anything like that happen to me. Wait a minute! I remember the humming from the machine at the hospital. It got louder at the same time I started to feel dizzy. That was right before I came here. But I don't remember any tunnel. Do the rest of you?"

"Nope," said Gino. "This is what happened to me. I opened my eyes, and I was standing at the entrance to Playland. I thought it must be some kind of trick."

"What do you mean ... a trick?" Jamie asked, scratching her nose.

"Well, you see I love going to amusement parks more than just about anything. And I knew I must have died. And Mom always said the same thing when she got mad at me, that the devil would sure be happy to see *me* coming. And Grandpa told my brothers and me stories from the time I was little about how sneaky the devil is, almost giving you something you *really* want and then snatching it away at the last second. So I was sort of looking around and waiting for the Prince of Darkness to show up and take me to the fiery depths. That's what Grandpa called hell … *the fiery depths*, Gino repeated in a spooky voice. He shivered.

"But a cow appeared instead. She was standing on two legs and wearing jeans and a flowered sweatshirt. She didn't seem scary, only different and friendly. Mrs. Tipperwillow said hello and invited me to go into the park with her.

"For awhile I was still scared, because it looked like we were the only ones there, and I kept thinking that something bad was about to happen. But it didn't. Mrs. Tipperwillow let me choose the rides we took. I started having fun, and then I forgot all about being scared.

"I was surprised because when we got onto the ride, the cars started moving all by themselves. They stopped the same way.

"After our third time on the Twister and our second roller coaster ride, Mrs. Tipperwillow was looking kind of wobbly. She asked me if we could try something *a little less exciting*, and she led me to the Ferris wheel. There's nothing more *boring* than a Ferris wheel," Gino added and rolled his eyes. "Anyway, a boy was sitting in the next car up. It was Wallace."

"That's sounds like a fun way to start your life here," Jamie said, as she stared into Gino's green eyes. "But I don't think you should have worried. Mom and Dad told me that the devil is just made up to scare people into being good and to have someone to blame when things go wrong."

Gino frowned and looked over at Mrs. Tipperwillow. "So what's the truth, Mrs. T.?"

"The truth is always what you make it, Gino."

"What do you mean by *that*?" asked the boy with a hint of anger in his voice.

"Remember all that you have learned about creation in the spirit world, Gino," said the sort of cow, kindly. "Now tell me, do you *want* a devil to exist?"

"No, of course not," he answered quickly.

"Then don't create one for yourself."

Gino let out a barking laugh and shook his head.

Jamie turned to look at Lateesha (who was at that moment holding two fingers above her head like horns and wiggling them at Gino). "What about you, Lateesha? What happened when you first came here?"

The nine-year-old lowered her arms. "I was in bed imagining daffodils. That's what I did when the headaches got really bad ... because daffodils are my favorite flowers, see? So I put them in my mind, and they helped me forget about how bad I was hurting.

"But all of a sudden, I wasn't just imagining anymore. I was sitting in a whole *field* of daffodils. I was surprised that they smelled so extra good, as if I'd never really smelled a daffodil before. On Earth they have such a tiny smell," Lateesha added. "And everything looked so bright and clear, clearer than I've *ever* seen on Earth.

"Finally I noticed this cow in a pretty blue dress sitting in the grass a little ways away. She seemed to be talking to the flowers. Mrs. Tipperwillow looked up at me and drifted over to introduce herself. I thought I was dreaming at first, but I wasn't. Soon Gino and Wallace flew in for a landing and showed me that I could fly, too. I remember how good that felt, flying for the very first time. We followed Mrs. T. to the tent house. Then I moved in."

Jamie nodded her head, and turned to look at Yoshi, wondering if the little girl would start crying again.

"It was totally different for me," Yoshi said, taking a deep breath and twisting a strand of her long, black hair as she launched into her story. "After the accident, I woke up in a bed in the nursery. It was warm and cozy in there, and the people who took care of me were *so* nice. They told me stories of fairies and magic, and they sang me beautiful songs until I fell asleep. I slept a lot at first.

"Then one day they opened the curtains, and beautiful golden light filled up the room. They said I was in this magic place called Summerland, and they said I could even fly if I wanted to. I was *so* excited. I was floating around the room getting used to how it felt when Mrs. Tipperwillow came. She took me to meet Gino and Lateesha and Wallace. And *that's* what happened to me."

"Why was it different for each of us?" Jamie asked, turning to look at Mrs. Tipperwillow.

"Your first experiences of the spirit world were different because you are each unique. So what you saw and felt was just right for each of you."

"And dying didn't hurt a bit, did it?" Jamie said as she looked around at her new friends.

"Nope," answered Lateesha, "it didn't hurt at all." The others nodded.

Mrs. Tipperwillow scratched the base of her ear with one hoof. "That's right, Children. Passing to the spirit world is as simple as finding yourself in a new place. And the change happens in the blink of an eye."

6

Running, Skating, Climbing

Mrs. Tipperwillow blinked her eyes and wiggled her broad nose. Jamie chuckled, thinking of reruns on T.V. where the witch with yellow hair did the very same thing.

A soccer ball appeared on the lawn and began rolling toward Lateesha. Laughing, Lateesha picked it up and bounced it from hand to hand.

"Why don't you show us some of your fast moves, dear," encouraged the sort of cow. With another blink of Mrs. T's eyes, the children were dressed in different colored sweat suits.

Lateesha jumped up and began moving around, tapping the ball between her feet and keeping it under tight control. Gino leapt to his feet and tried to knock the ball away from her. Then the rest of the children joined in. Lateesha kicked the ball to Jamie, who kicked it to Wallace, who kicked it to Yoshi.

"Hey! What about me?" Gino yelled, running to intercept the ball, which was again headed for Lateesha. Gino jumped for the ball, landing on his stomach with the ball trapped underneath.

"Tummy soccer!" yelled Yoshi, as Jamie and Lateesha knelt down and tried to bat the ball out from under the boy. The ball disappeared, and Gino collapsed to the ground. Everyone broke out laughing.

"You're really good, Teesh," said Gino, sitting up as the rest joined him on the grass. The girl grinned and took a deep bow.

Gino looked at the older boy: "So do you have a favorite sport, Wallace, or is it just science, science, science all the time?"

Wallace gave a snort. "Well you see, I'm Canadian, from near Toronto, Ontario. That's in the eastern part of Canada, eh? And for kids growing up in our area, the most popular game we play from the time we are little is...." Suddenly there was a crackling sound as the ground turned hard and glassy.

"Ice hockey," he finished, staring in amazement between his feet. The children and Mrs. Tipperwillow leapt up from the freezing cold ice which had just appeared and was forming a thick coating over the grass. With a click of their teacher's hooves, the children's running shoes disappeared, to be replaced by ice skates. A hockey stick materialized in Wallace's hand, and a hockey puck plopped down next to him. Wasting no time, he skimmed off over the ice laughing as the puck flew before him.

"Yes!" exclaimed Gino, looking down at his own skates. A hockey stick appeared in his hands, also. He took off chasing Wallace.

"I've never done this before," said Jamie in a worried voice as she looked at the boys in the distance. "I'm not sure I can balance on these thin blades." Yoshi nodded her head in agreement. Neither girl seemed to notice that they were balancing just fine on their skates as they *stood* on the ice.

"Why, of course you can, girls," said Mrs. Tipperwillow warmly. "Have you ever seen ice skating on television?"

"Sure," Jamie replied. "I loved watching figure skating on T.V., and last winter Mom and Dad took Bobby and me to see an ice show."

"I went to an ice show once." Yoshi added.

Lateesha nodded. "So did I!"

"Then merely remember what you saw, girls, and make a wish! That's all there is to it in the spirit world."

Jamie shut her eyes a moment and imagined herself skating beautifully. Moments later she was skimming out over the ice with Yoshi and Lateesha by her side. The girls skated backwards and performed fabulous leaps and twirls, as the boys continued to chase the puck back and forth across the ice which stretched out before them as they moved.

"This is great!" squealed Jamie, doing a double loop in the air before landing.

Finally as if a bell had sounded, the children all glided back and turned their feet expertly to stop in front of their teacher. At the same instant, their skates and the ice disappeared. They sat down laughing and soon were stretched out on the grass, wiggling their toes and staring up at the golden sky.

"That was fun," said Yoshi with a yawn. "It was almost like ballet. I *loved* my ballet class." She sighed.

"Did you take ballet for a long time?" Jamie asked.

"Yes. My best friend Lizzie and I took Mrs. Bronson's class since we were five. Our mommies got us matching pink leotards and tutus and ballet shoes," Yoshi answered, smiling up at the sky. "We practiced a lot together, 'cause we played at Lizzie's house or my house every day when one of our mommies was working." She paused, remembering the one day that was different, took another deep breath and continued.

"Last year at Christmas time we got all dressed up in our prettiest clothes, and then Daddy and Mommy took me and Lizzie and her mommy and daddy out to a fancy dinner. We had to act like little ladies, but I didn't mind.

"After we finished eating dinner, we went to this big building with a huge stage, and we saw the Nutcracker Ballet. It was *so* beautiful. And after that we went to see the giant Christmas tree lit up with gazillions of lights. We lived in New York City. Did I say that?" Yoshi yawned again, and all was quiet for awhile.

"What did you do for fun in your last lifetime, Jamie?" Lateesha asked, propping her head up on one hand.

"Well, I never got into sports like you did, because I was sick for so long." Teesha nodded. Jamie continued, "But I loved to read and to write my own stories and to draw pictures about them.

"One time my best friend Marabel and I made this scrapbook about two best friends who travel all over the world together. We cut out pictures from magazines showing the places they went and the crazy out-fits they wore. We wrote a funny story to go along with the pictures, too." She smiled at the memory.

"I liked making jewelry, too," Jamie continued. "I got a beading kit for my seventh birthday, and sometimes Mom or Dad would bring home special beads for me to use in my necklaces and bracelets. Other times, when I felt strong enough, we'd go downtown to the Saturday Market. One booth had lots of beads in all kinds of colors, and I got to choose my favorite ones. I liked the sparkly crystal beads the best. I made Mom a *beautiful* crystal necklace for her last birthday."

"I like jewelry, too." Lateesha rolled onto her back again and stared at the sky. "Where did you live?"

"We lived in Portland, just up the street from the Rose Garden. Oregon was a good place to live, except it rains a lot there." Jamie closed her eyes.

"So Gino," Wallace began in a sleepy voice, "what did you do on Earth with all that Gino energy?"

"Climbing trees and playing spy were my very favorite things to do," Gino said, turning his head to look at the older boy. "My best friend Jason would come over, and we'd jump the fence into Mr. and Mrs. O'Flaherty's yard when they weren't home. They lived next door, and they had the biggest tree in the whole neighborhood. We'd climb to the top of their tree, and we'd spy on everything that went on down below. And no one could find us!" Gino chuckled.

"Once we saw my oldest brother—he was in High School—walking home with his girl friend. When they got close to the tree where we were hiding they stopped, and he *kissed* her. It was *so* icky. I started making smacking noises, and Jason had to put his hand over my mouth to keep me from ruining our secret hiding place!"

Gino grinned at the memory and closed his eyes. When he reopened them he was staring up at a tall pine tree.

He sat up. "Hey look! That's it! That's the tree I was telling you about—the very same one!"

The boy was on his feet in a flash and began climbing the tall tree barefoot. Lateesha jumped up and scrambled right after him. Wallace was next, and Jamie and Yoshi followed close behind. Gino reached the top. "I am the King of Summerland!" he yelled and sat down on the nearest branch.

As his friends found places to sit, Gino gazed down upon the Library of Lives, at the grassy park, and over to a round stone building at the other end of the broad expanse of lawn. Nearby he noticed several more buildings, and in the distance he saw rolling hills with paths meandering through them.

Suddenly the scene blurred. Gino blinked his eyes in confusion and stared in amazement as a new scene came into focus. There below him was his old neighborhood with the O'Flaherty's house and his own house right next door.

People were walking on the sidewalks. Cars were driving by, and the school bus Gino took every day since kindergarten stopped at the corner. The door opened, and Jason walked down the steps, followed by … Gino.

The other children shared their friend's vision of himself, their mouths open in surprise. Below, Gino and his best friend were punching each other's arms playfully as they made their way down the street.

"It's good there are no flies buzzing about today, Children," chortled Mrs. Tipperwillow, who appeared on a branch nearby. "Otherwise, your mouths would be full of them."

They watched as down below, Gino entered his house with Jason right on his heels. It seemed that they could even hear him throw down his backpack and yell, "Hey, Mom, we're home!"

The scene blurred, and when their vision cleared, the children were once again gazing down at the library across from the green park where they had been playing all afternoon. They all turned to look at their teacher, and Gino brushed a tear from his eye.

"That was really something, Mrs. T. I didn't know you could do anything like *that*. Thanks so much."

"You are quite welcome, Gino. It was my pleasure."

The children and Mrs. Tipperwillow floated down to the grass. Gino's tree disappeared. Only a moment later they heard chugging and the hiss of a steam engine overhead.

"All aboard!" called the conductor as the Sky Train appeared, with white smoke puffing out of its smokestack. The children and the magical sort of cow floated up quickly and chose places to sit in the passenger car.

They were quiet all the way home.

7

To the Seashore

"Time to get up!" trilled the magical sort of cow. Up popped Gino out of bed in a flash. He floated down by Yoshi, who was already playing with the snoode and a ball of yarn by the fireplace.

"I wish a fire in that!" Gino declared in a loud voice as he pointed to the empty fireplace. *Presto Chango!* A single flame appeared … and went out.

"Focus!" said his teacher. "Put a clear picture in your mind and … *Alacazam!*" A blazing fire roared to life.

Gino frowned and looked at his feet. "I will *never* get that, Mrs. T."

"Of course you will, Gino. You've almost got it now. See the picture with your imagination. Smell the fire. Feel its heat. Remember all that a fire is, and it will appear.

"Today, Children" said Mrs. Tipperwillow as they gathered around, "I thought it would be fun to show Jamie our beach and go for a swim."

"Yes!" Jamie's new friends answered in unison.

"But won't we eat breakfast first?" Jamie asked. She noticed for the first time that the tent had no kitchen or dining room.

"Certainly my dear, we can have breakfast. We don't need to eat since we are spirit, but it *is* fun. Let's do it."

A long table appeared in the center of the tent. On it sat a platter stacked high with waffles, a bowl of strawberries and another bowl of golden pineapple slices. There was a big pitcher of milk and six glasses. Plates, silverware and napkins appeared next. And finally six chairs quivered into sight. Everyone sat down.

"Did you make *this*, Mrs. T?" asked Gino with a smirk. He leaned forward and wiggled his fingers in the milk. Then he pretended he was milking a cow.

"No Gino, not in the way you are suggesting, but thank you so much for asking."

They all piled into breakfast, talking and joking between bites. As the children finished and stood up, their teacher delicately blotted her wide mouth with her napkin and stood also. With a casual flick of her hoof, she dissolved the dining area. "It's time for the seashore. Today we fly! Is everyone ready?"

"We are!" proclaimed Wallace as a beach bucket appeared in his hands. "I am the King of Creation!" he proclaimed as he leapt into the air. Gino made a face.

Out of the tent floated the children and Mrs. Tipperwillow. They quickly lifted high into the golden sky, full of laughter that bubbled up through them. Over the fields they flew and over hills to the sea and a beautiful white sand beach.

Touching down on the glistening sand, the group was immediately dressed in colorful swimsuits. Jamie smiled, running one hand down her sunny yellow one-piece suit.

Mrs. Tipperwillow modeled her pink and black, diagonally-striped suit for the children. She twirled in a circle. "These stripes are so slimming, don't you think?"

Gino raised his arms and turned in a circle, too, wildly wiggling his hips.

Mrs. Tipperwillow removed the sleeping snoode from her shoulders and carefully placed him on the warm sand. She rose into the air, and the children followed as she headed for the ocean. The sort of cow looked back at the newest member of her family.

"Jamie! In Summerland we can breathe under water, so there is no need to hold your breath. And we can hear each others thoughts underwater, too. Now everyone … ready, set, *go!*"

They dove into the warm sea. As Mrs. Tipperwillow turned this way and that, the ocean was alive with tropical fish. A parrot fish appeared. Its green and aqua splotched body sparkled, as it swam along the ocean floor feeding on coral with its parrot-like beak. Three Moorish idols swam by. These diamond-shaped fish were brilliantly striped in yellow, black and white, with long, thin, wavy fins at the top and bottom and a shorter fin at the back. Their tiny pursed lips made them look like they were kissing. Gino sped toward them making a fish face. They scurried away fast.

Six bright yellow fish appeared near Jamie. *What are these round fish with the bump over their eyes called?* Jamie asked as Mrs. Tipperwillow floated near.

Clear as day she heard her teacher's voice. *They're called yellow tang, Jamie.* The girl reached out and almost touched one before it glided away.

Meanwhile Yoshi noticed a small spotted fish swimming near the ocean floor. It had white polka dots on a black background, little fluttering fins, and a strange shape. *Mrs. Tipperwillow, come look at this,* she said pointing. *See this tiny fish? It looks a little like a box.*

Good spotting, Yoshi, thought the punning sort of cow. *That's called a box fish.*

Mrs. Tipperwillow swam a short distance away and called the children over. They moved underwater to some large rocks, where they discovered a large purple starfish with many legs and a smaller orange one with fewer legs clinging to one stone. Wallace tapped Yoshi's shoulder to tell her that on Earth these types of starfish happened to live in different water temperatures than the tropical fish.

Now, suggested their teacher, *let's look on the other side of that biggest rock.* They swam around. A huge octopus was before them waving its eight legs.

Wallace stared in wonder, his mouth forming a surprised *Oh!*

Gino jumped back with a bubbly *Eek!* And the spot where the octopus had been was suddenly empty.

Lateesha turned to Mrs. Tipperwillow, her eyes wide. *Did you do that?*

Wallace interrupted. *She probably did because this is Summerland. But on Earth this would be normal octopi behavior. You see … an octopus can camouflage itself so well that it seems to disappear.*

Mrs. T. winked. *That's right, Wallace.*

The children began playing underwater turning somersaults and standing on their hands on the ocean floor. Gino and Lateesha popped out of the water at the same time. Gino pointed at his friend's head. "A star fell off, Teesh."

She pulled on the loose tuft of curly hair. "No problem. I'll ask Mrs. T. to create me a new one later."

Gino splashed Lateesha, who splashed him right back. They were in the midst of a tremendous water fight when the boy looked over his friend's shoulder. Five dolphins were leaping in the air.

"Look! Look!" Gino yelled. The pod of bottlenose dolphins glided though the waves and in moments surrounded the Summerland family. The animals raised their rounded heads out of the water and nodded and chattered in that dolphin way. The children petted their soft gray sides, and soon they were copying the creatures rolling over and over underwater.

Lateesha was floating on her back on the surface of the ocean when she felt something bump against her. She turned over to look just as a dolphin's head emerged. There, right above its mouth on its beak, was her missing red star.

"Thank you, Dolphin," Teesha laughed. She took the star and quickly re-braided her dark hair.

Meanwhile a sixth dolphin had appeared. Mrs. Tipperwillow, who was standing in waist deep water, seemed to be having a silent conversation with it. Gino swam up. "Mrs. T.," he asked, "do you suppose these dolphins would take us for a ride?"

"I have no idea, Gino," she replied as all the animals gathered around. "Why don't you simply ask them?" Gino looked from one dolphin to another and asked his question in a polite voice. Excitement filled his round face as he waited to see what would happen next.

As one, the dolphins raised the fronts of their bodies out of the water and began chattering again.

The boy clapped his hands. "Is that a *yes?*"

In answer, one dolphin glided up, rolled slightly toward Gino and presented a dorsal fin. With a laugh, the boy grabbed hold and pulled himself up to sit in front of the fin.

And they were off! Soon each child and one sort of cow were skimming through the water and leaping the waves, riding high on a dolphin's back. This play went on longer than long until one by one, the children and their teacher were deposited with a splash near the shore. With a chattering goodbye, the dolphins swam away.

"I hope all of you appreciate how lucky we are in Summerland to be able to ride on dolphins," said Mrs. Tipperwillow as she watched the beautiful animals disappear in the distance. "In Earth's oceans you might make a dolphin sick or get hurt yourself if you tried this." The children nodded their heads and followed their teacher to shore.

As her hooves touched the sand, the magical sort of cow was suddenly wearing a stylish flowered *moomoo*. [A mu'u mu'u is a loose Hawaiian dress.]

With a wink of her eye, buckets and shovels appeared on the beach. Each child grabbed a set, and together they began building a huge sand castle. Before long the castle was finished. It had turrets, doorways, windows, a drawbridge made of sticks, and a moat all around, which was filled with round beach stones. As a finishing touch, Wallace imagined two red flags which he placed above each side of the main doorway.

Mrs. T. clapped her hooves in appreciation. "My friends," she said at last, "it has been a fine trip to the seashore. Are you about ready to go?"

"Yes," Yoshi replied. What a great day we had!"

"I don't remember a better one," added Lateesha.

"Ta Dum!" shouted Gino as a smallish driftwood fire appeared on the beach.

"Nice creating, Gino," said Mrs. Tipperwillow.

"I'm King of the Fire!"

She smiled at the excited boy. "Then *you*, Gino, can make the next fire in our fireplace."

"You bet I will!"

Mrs. Tipperwillow picked up the still sleeping snoode and placed him gently around her shoulders.

Then back the family flew, over the hills and fields toward home. And this time when they drifted down for a landing, there were yellow daisies growing all around their tent.

Forming a circle on the soft grass, they called in the evening. Then in the dim light Jamie joined her new friends saying: "Blessings to all we've ever been and to all we'll ever be. Blessings to all we've ever loved, to the Earth, to spirit, and to dreams. Softly, softly into night, softly, softly goes the light. Good night! Good night! Good night! Good night!"

As the children glided through the tent flap, their clothing was once more replaced by soft pajamas. They floated into their warm bunks and were asleep immediately.

8

Jamie Goes Back

"Jamie, are you ready for a new day of play and exploring?" Jamie awakened and looked into the eyes of the magical cow she was beginning to love, who was floating beside her bunk.

"Yes!" the girl exclaimed, rolling back her blue covers, jumping into the air and bumping her head on the top of the tent. She stayed suspended above her bed. "It is so much fun here!" Jamie squealed. "Flying feels so free!"

Jamie's smile faded. "But, Mrs. T., I'm sort of worried about my family back on Earth. Do you think they are doing okay?"

"Our sense of time is different here, Jamie. You can play and relax and get settled in, and then you can go back to see your family whenever you choose. Even if you feel that you've been here for a year, very little time might have passed on Earth.

"And here is something that comes in *quite* handy for us in the spirit world. When we switch dimensions to be on Earth, we are able to travel *into* whatever time we choose."

"Do you mean that we can be *time travelers*, Mrs. T?" Jamie's teacher nodded her large head. Jamie laughed and clapped her hands. "Great! Then I want to travel to Earth and see my family *right now*! I want to go to the time right after I got here. Will you take me?"

"I will be happy to, Jamie." Mrs. Tipperwillow lovingly touched Jamie's hand with her small hoof. "Why don't you put on your favorite clothes, and we will head for Earth immediately."

A familiar closet appeared floating next to Jamie's bunk and settled on the carpet. As she landed beside it, Jamie glanced at the poster of the boy wizard riding a broomstick that she had taped to her closet door at home. Even the torn corner was the same.

Jamie laughed and opened the door. She put on her favorite jeans and t-shirt, but she changed her mind and grabbed out the light blue dress her mother had bought for her.

"I'll wear this," Jamie said, smiling. "It will make Mommy happy." Jamie quickly put on the dress.

"That is a very nice choice, dear. Are you ready?"

The eight-year-old nodded. They floated through the tent flap, rose into the sky, and flew off so fast that Jamie couldn't even see the land-scape beneath them.

Moments later they came to a sudden stop by a big wooden door floating in mid-air. The word "Back" was painted in large gold letters on the top of the door frame.

"Wait just a moment, Jamie." The door slowly opened. Below her, Jamie saw her favorite park and Mom, Dad and Bobby. And there was Grandma and Grandpa and Aunt Francis and Uncle Bert and her clos-est friends, Lily, Marabel, Julia, James and their parents! They were having a party to celebrate Jamie's life.

"Look at this, Mrs. T!"

"Jamie, I'm sure your family and friends will be happy to have you with them. They probably won't be able to see you, but I bet they will be able feel your spirit just fine. Hurry along now!"

"But … won't you come with me?"

"No, Jamie. This is *your* play. These are your family and friends. Just call to me when you're ready, and I will meet you at the door."

"But will I know how to find it again?" she asked in a worried voice.

"Call to me," said Mrs. Tipperwillow, who began fading until she had disappeared entirely.

Jamie found herself sitting next to her mother. "Hi, Mommy," Jamie tried. "I'm fine. I'm having fun."

Mother looked thoughtful. "Tom," she said, "I can feel Jamie here. Do you feel her, too?"

"You're better at that sort of thing, Anne, but I always think of her."

"Hi Dad," Jamie said loudly. There was no reaction. She tried again. "Hey, you!" she yelled. (This is what her father used to say to get Jamie's attention.)

Her father looked up and smiled.

"What is it, dear?"

"Oh, never mind. Just wishing, I guess."

Jamie shook her head. *He did hear me ... my stubborn, funny old daddy.* Jamie came around to give her father a hug and was surprised when her arms passed right through him. She tried several times. *This is so strange,* she thought.

Jamie drifted over to her little brother, Bobby. He was sitting on the ground digging up dirt with his plastic shovel and putting it into the back of his toy pick-up truck. He rolled the truck over to a small mound of dirt, and he dumped what he'd just collected on top. "Hi, little brother," Jamie said loudly. "What are you making?"

"I'm making a mountain. It's where Jamie lives."

Jamie's eyes grew wide. She leaned close. "You can *hear* me, Bobby?" This time he didn't answer. He just rolled his truck back to pick up more dirt.

The girl cocked her head to one side and stared at her brother for several long moments. When he didn't say anything more, Jamie went to sit with Grandma and Grandpa.

She watched as Grandma put her arm around her husband's shoulders and asked, "Henry dear, do you remember any of Jamie's wonderful stories?" Grandpa didn't say a word.

His Alzheimer's is worse, Jamie thought. She gave them both a kiss near their cheeks and kissed the air by her aunt's and uncle's cheek, too.

Then Jamie drifted over to be with her school friends. The scrapbook that she and Marabel had made was open on the picnic table. Julia and her dad were looking through the pages as Jamie's other good friends began to talk about all the sweet and funny things they remembered about her. Jamie's parents and grandmother joined in with their own stories. Grandma said that Jamie always seemed to light up a room just by walking into it. Jamie's heart felt warm and happy as she heard these words and felt all the love behind them.

All at once, an idea formed in her mind. Jamie imagined a huge ball of energy in the sky, and when she could see it clearly, she filled it to the top with all the love she felt for her family and friends. Immediately the sparkling ball turned pink as if a million rose petals were tucked inside. It floated it in the air a moment and slowly drifted down to cover everyone. Suddenly all was quiet, and there were smiles on every face.

"I did it, Mrs. Tipperwillow!" Jamie shouted. The Back door appeared in the air above her and shot open. A sort of cow with one gleaming antler smiled down.

"Ready, Jamie?"

"I sure am. Wait 'til you hear what I did!" She floated up to join her teacher.

"You have much magic in you, Jamie, and there are things you are beginning to remember. I felt your energy ball from the other side of the door. Now your family and friends will feel you with them every time they think of you.

"Let's go home now, and you can tell us all about what happened. I know the other children will want to hear your story."

"Okay!" Jamie said, stepping through the door. Back they flew and were soon floating above the beautiful striped tent in the grassy meadow. From the peak of the tent flew a bright new flag. The flag was sky blue. There was a golden sun in the middle of it, and the sun had a smiling face.

9

Telling Stories

Yoshi, Wallace, Lateesha, and Gino were playing tag in the meadow when Jamie and Mrs. Tipperwillow landed.

"You're it!" yelled Yoshi to Wallace, who with his long legs should have been able to get away from her easily. Wallace looked around to find Gino or Lateesha, and discovered them both hiding behind a tree.

"I see you," laughed Wallace.

"Children, Children!" called Mrs. T. "Jamie has just returned from her Life Celebration. Let's go inside so we can listen to her story, and you can each tell her what you discovered in your Life Books this time."

Because Mrs. Tipperwillow firmly felt that all good storytelling was best done at dusk, they chanted the sky to evening before opening the tent flap and going inside.

"Okay, Gino. You're on." Mrs. Tipperwillow looked expectantly from the boy to the empty fireplace and back. Gino's face turned red with concentration. Suddenly wood appeared, and then a blazing fire.

"I did it, Mrs. Tipperwillow!" he exclaimed.

"I never had any doubts," she replied.

Jamie told her story using lots of colorful words. Her new friends were excited that Jamie's brother and father had heard her voice. But they were most impressed by the energy ball she had created. Gino and Lateesha even wanted to go back *immediately* to the celebration of their lives and *do it again* so that they could try out the same thing.

"Not this evening, Children," said their teacher, firmly. "We are in the middle of our story time now." They settled down and took turns recalling what they each discovered during their last trip to the library.

As the evening moved on, and all the stories seemed to be told, there was sudden quiet. Gino said (and you know it's always Gino who starts these things) "What I didn't tell you is that in one lifetime I owned a cabin in Transylvania. That's where the vampires live, you know. And Count Dracula himself almost caught me and turned me into a vampire, too!"

"I bet Dracula really did get you Gino, and you just forgot," said Lateesha.

"Yeah," added Jamie. "And that's why you have such pointy little teeth." The other children laughed.

"I do not have pointy little teeth, Jamie, and besides, if I was a vampire I would live forever."

"But we *are* living forever," Yoshi reminded him.

"Well," said Wallace, not wanting to be outdone, "once long ago, I made friends with a real dragon, and she took me for rides on her back. Beat that!"

As the storytelling competition between the boys got more and more outrageous, Yoshi and Lateesha looked at each other, rolled their eyes, and with a nod, began rising in the air to their bunks. Jamie, who was still too excited from her day to rest, went outside to look for stars in the dusky light. She felt peaceful and happy listening to the laughter coming from inside the tent, and she soon saw one, and then two twinkling stars.

10

Soup and Circles

Mrs. Tipperwillow opened the tent flap and stepped outside. "Do you want to be alone, Jamie? Everyone needs some time to themselves now and then."

"No, Mrs. T. The boys are just too silly, and I wanted to look for stars."

The sort of cow plopped down beside her. "Here you go, Jamie ... stars it is!" The sky was suddenly covered with maybe a million bright stars.

"Beautiful," Jamie whispered. "Mrs. Tipperwillow?"

"Yes, Jamie?"

"I've been wondering about something. Why do we go to Earth in the first place?"

The small antler on Mrs. Tipperwillow's forehead began to glow and created a soft light all around her. She looked down at her front hooves and shined them on her flowered dress as she replied, "For longer than anyone can remember, it's been about soup and circles, Child."

"Soup and circles, Mrs. T.? That doesn't make any sense."

"Listen closely, Jamie. Suppose you had a big empty bowl, and then of course you would want to fill it with something. So you put in some broth. But every part of the broth was like every other ... a bit boring, don't you think? Let's say that Wallace is a carrot and Yoshi is a tomato. Lateesha is an onion and Gino is a green pepper...."

"Ugh, I don't like green peppers."

"But anyway, suppose all of the people in the world with all of their differences are going into this soup of life. Wouldn't that be tastier than plain golden broth, even if the broth was very good?"

"Well, yes, that would be lots better. But whose soup is it?"

"Well," said Mrs. Tipperwillow thoughtfully, "you could say God or you could say Goddess or you could say the one who loves us all just for who we are. Names are tricky here, Child, for no name is really big enough. You feel it though, don't you, Jamie, that wonderful love supporting you, everywhere around you and even inside of you, right now?"

The girl took a deep breath. "Yes, I do feel it, and it's connected to the golden light in the sky, isn't it?"

"That's right, Jamie, the light you're breathing in right now." Mrs. Tipperwillow looked thoughtful and patted Jamie's hand.

"Why do you say God *and* Goddess, Mrs. T.?"

"We are talking about All Love here, Jamie, which includes both the ways of woman and man, boy and girl. Every game you have played, every time you have laughed or cried or sang a song, All Love has done the same, has lived *through* you. Lives lived make the broth into a richer and richer soup."

Jamie thought about this new idea. "And what about circles, Mrs. T.?"

"Circles ... ah, yes, *circles*," said the sort of cow softly as she drew several loops of pencil-thin light in the air. "The circles tell everyone's stories, Jamie, of hurting others and being hurt and of loving others and being loved. It's trying things out and seeing where they lead. In the spirit world, these circles are sometimes called 'experience sets', but on Earth, 'karma' is the word most often used.

"Basically, what you do comes back to you. You experience one half of the circle, and then sometime later you experience the other half. This allows you to feel and understand both sides of every situation and, in this way, to bring balance to your spirit. This has been the way of life on Earth for longer than long.

"The hardest thing about these circles, though," she continued, "about this thing called 'karma,' is when the first half occurs in one lifetime and the second half comes in another. This is very confusing for folks on Earth."

"What do you mean?" asked Jamie, looking into her teacher's eyes.

"Well suppose, for instance, you broke into someone's house and stole something. You were poor and desperate, and well … these things happen. You felt the fear, the danger and the object you took in your hand, the getaway—all that. That is half the circle. But suppose that your life ended before the same thing happened to you. Then in your next lifetime your house is broken into, and something very precious to you is stolen. You don't remember ever doing this to someone else.

"People think themselves such victims, Jamie. They get angry because they can't remember that they started these circles in the first place. It's ever so much harder to forgive and move on, don't you see?"

"This sounds familiar, Mrs. Tipperwillow. I think I knew this."

"I think so, too. Now watch." Scarves of all colors began falling from the twilight sky: red, orange, green, blue and purple. Shiny and billowy in the evening breeze, they fell and landed on and around Jamie and her smiling teacher. A deep blue one landed on Jamie's head, covering her eyes. She blew the scarf out from her face.

"It is hard to see through the veils, Jamie. People on Earth forget that's it's a play they're in. They forget their own creation." Jamie took the blue scarf off her head and smoothed it between her fingers. "But watch this!"

Suddenly more scarves or veils fell from the sky, but these were thinner and easier to see through. Jamie picked up a thin, light scarf and looked through it at the evening sky. "I can totally see through this one."

"Yes, Jamie," Mrs. Tipperwillow said as she picked up the remaining scarves one by one and smoothed them on her lap. "This is part of the magic that has begun. The veils that separate you from knowledge of the Goddess and the God in all things are getting thinner. People are beginning to remember."

"Remember what, Mrs. Tipperwillow?"

"Everything, Jamie … simply everything." Jamie lay back and looked up at the stars.

11

Indigo, Crystal and Flowers

"And here is something not everyone knows," said Mrs. Tipperwillow, looking over at Jamie and clicking her hooves together in a merry little tune. "There are new types of children being born on Earth right now known as the Indigo Children and the Crystal Children. For some of these special ones, their old circles are completed. For others, it is their very first lifetime on Earth. And the veil which separates Earth and spirit is becoming *so* thin that they are remembering who they are.

"Some of these children can recall living other lives, and some can even picture these lifetimes clearly. Some carry talents from other lifetimes, and they surprise their parents by playing the piano perfectly at an early age or doing advanced math, for instance. Some can see or hear or feel spirits, too.

"Do you ever remember feeling different from other children, Jamie? As if you understood things that some of your friends didn't?"

The girl sat up. "Yes, but I was sick for a long time, too. I thought that's what made me feel different."

"Not entirely, Jamie. You and many children on Earth today carry a special wisdom. You carry a deeper feeling for the patterns of life and for who you really are.

Indigo Children have a big desire to create and to explore and a feeling of boredom for what is routine. These children come to shake up old patterns on Earth which don't work anymore. They carry a lovely deep indigo color in their aura, which is the energy field around their bodies.

"Crystal Children's energies may be either clear and twinkling or whitish, like a quartz crystal. These children are friendly and loving. They are the peace makers, and they bring a feeling of calm everywhere they go. Crystal Children can seem quiet and inward looking at times, for they are able to hear people's thoughts and see spirits quite easily. Because they sense so much, they need a calm home life and understanding parents. And, as you might guess, these special children have a great love of crystals.

"Both the Indigos and the Crystals are wise beyond their years, Jamie, and need to be treated honestly and fairly."

"I love crystals, Mrs. T. Am I a Crystal Child?" Jamie sat up and looked at her teacher.

"No, Jamie. You have lived too many lifetimes to be one of these children. But you have much in common with them, as you say, in your love of crystals and also in your happy and peaceful ways.

"You carry a fair amount of that deep indigo color in your aura, too, Jamie. I think of you as a kind of link between the two groups. And when you go back for another lifetime on Earth you will be so again.

"More and more of you wise ones are being born every year, and you are helping bring to Earth a new age and a new way ... the way of the flower."

Jamie gasped as a bouquet of multicolored rosebuds appeared in her hand. They began to open, one by one, until the whole bunch was blooming and glowing with a soft light.

"Now, all of these roses are different colors and types, like all the colors and types of people on Earth."

"Hey, I though we were vegetables!" Jamie laughed and Mrs. Tipperwillow laughed, too.

"But notice how beautiful these flowers are together, Jamie, even more beautiful than they would be separately. Notice how they bloom and bloom. Imagine a time when everyone feels that they are a part of each other and the Earth, and no one hurts anyone else anymore." A happy tear formed in the cow's eye.

"Imagine a time when everyone feels that great love, that God and Goddess in everyone else. Oh, the creativity! Oh, the fun! That is the day that you children are bringing in.

"Oh dear, I am quite beside myself," blurted Mrs. Tipperwillow, shaking her cow head with tears flowing freely down her face. She jumped up suddenly, clicked her hooves together, did a little jig, and pointed to the ground.

A huge, glowing copper kettle appeared on the grass. In it swirled a rich golden broth, twinkling with light. A basket of fresh vegetables appeared in Mrs. Tipperwillow's arms. She popped carrots and beans and broccoli and tomatoes and peppers into the soup. Jamie thought of Gino as a green pepper and laughed. Next a package of pasta circles was added. Then reaching down into a paper bag, Mrs. T. pulled out hoof-fulls of rose petals and threw them into the soup as well.

"Here you go, Jamie," said the sort of cow proudly, dipping a ladle into the swirling mass as a bowl appeared in mid-air. "Now, how would you like a nice *big* bowl of soup?"

Jamie stared at the rose petals just starting to sink onto the hard pasta circles and vegetables, and looked into the hopeful brown eyes.

"No thanks, Mrs. T. I'm not really hungry for soup right now. Let's leave this soup for God. But," and Jamie smiled her brightest smile, "I sure could use some more of that cotton candy."

With a whoop, Mrs. Tipperwillow jumped up and turned a circle in mid-air. Jamie laughed as she reached for the fuzzy, bright pink ball that came charging toward her waiting hands. And it tasted very good.

12

Snow Boat

The next day as they joined her in the meadow, the children couldn't help but notice that their teacher was dressed all in white. She wore a white hat, a white wool pantsuit, and a white feather boa slung around her neck over an unhappy snoode, who was squirming to peek out between the tickly feathers.

"How would you all like a trip to the snow?" Mrs. Tipperwillow chortled.

"Yes!" yelled the children, who were suddenly dressed in matching navy blue snowsuits with white racing stripes down the sides.

"Can I drive the boat?" Gino asked in an excited voice. A captain's hat appeared on his head.

"No!!" shouted Yoshi and Lateesha at the same instant.

Jamie shook her head and started to laugh and then laughed harder, thinking about all the crazy things that happened in Summerland … trains in the sky and now a boat to the snow. She jumped around in a circle unable to stop laughing. "We're taking a boat … a *boat* to the *snow!*"

"This is our usual means of transport up the mountain, Jamie," said a confused sort of cow, "and Gino, I think it is Yoshi's turn to be captain."

The hat flew from Gino's head to Yoshi's just as a large purple and white boat appeared, floating inches above the ground. Jamie was still chuckling as they got in.

Yoshi nervously took control for the first time. She gripped the big wheel tightly and formed her wish. The boat rose several inches above the ground. And they were off!

Over the fields they sped with wind blowing through their hair. They moved up into the hills which got steeper and steeper. Jamie spotted snow in the mountains.

"This is *boring*," Gino declared loudly.

"Jamie," Mrs. T. explained above the wind, "on Gino's last trip as captain, he decided to roll the boat over and over like some wild ride at the amusement park. Since none of us were strapped in, no one thought this was very funny."

Except Gino, thought Jamie.

"Yup," replied Mrs. Tipperwillow, reading her thoughts. "He loved it."

Suddenly thick snow was beneath them. The boat landed with a *whump*, and Yoshi let out a relieved sigh.

The children clambered out and rushed to grab handfuls of snow to make snowballs. Quickly, Gino formed a snowball and threw it at Wallace. While Gino was distracted, Leteesha lobbed a snowball at him, and it expanded to the size of a basketball before it hit. Instantly, the boy was covered with snow.

"I did it!" yelled Lateesha. "I thought it bigger and it *was*."

"Oh my," said Mrs. Tipperwillow as all the children's snowballs started getting bigger and bigger and bigger. Soon giant snowballs were flying this way and that. Then, just as quickly as the snowball fight had begun, it ended. All the children stood with snow up to their necks, unable to move.

"Ha-Ha!" laughed the magical sort of cow. "You five look quite a sight. Now let me see…. Should I leave you all this way?"

"No!" they yelled.

Then Melto Chango! The snow quickly became puddles around their feet. "Wasn't that just *fine?*" Mrs. Tipperwillow's cheeks were pink with excitement.

Together, the children rolled three snowballs of different sizes and stacked them to form a snowman. They found two stones for its eyes and smaller stones for its mouth. Yoshi discovered two twigs to use as arms. With his thought, Wallace created a top hat for the snowman's head. Satisfied, the children turn around to show their teacher. But Mrs. Tipperwillow had disappeared.

"Mrs. T.! Mrs. T.! Where are you?" Lateesha yelled.

What's this? Gino thought, as he spotted another snowman a short distance away. The children turned to look.

"Here, Children," said the snowman, which was slowly morphing into a snow cow sporting a floppy hat, a feather boa, and a pantsuit. The face of one *very* unhappy snoode was peeking out of the frozen feathers.

The children laughed, hurrying over to help their teacher brush off the layers of snow. "Good one, Mrs. T.!" Gino exclaimed.

Then Wallace lay down and began waving his arms up and down like wings, making an angel in the soft snow. Soon all five were doing it.

Yoshi jumped to her feet and grabbed Jamie's hand trying to pull her up. "Jamie, get up quick!"

The children stood. They moved out of the way quickly as twinkling lights appeared just where they had been lying. The sparkling lights spread outward and gradually filled in to become solid. They were taking human shape.

Shining like diamonds in the sun, the beings stood. They shook out wings of light and smiled warmly at the children. The brightness dimmed a bit so everyone could see them clearly.

"Angels," gasped Jamie. "… Real angels!"

"These are your guardian angels, Jamie. Don't you recognize one of them?"

There, standing in Jamie's imprint in the snow was the most beautiful angel that Jamie could have imagined. And she looked so familiar.

"I remember *you*," Jamie said in an excited voice. "You played with me when I was little. Mommy and Daddy called you my pretend playmate. And you were just my age!"

"You're right. I was."

"And you were with me all those times in the hospital. And when I could see you, you looked older just like you do now. You touched my hand and let me know everything would be okay. You sang me that song without words. Your name is Mela. I remember!"

"My full name is Milandra, Jamie, and I'm so glad that you remember me."

The children drifted apart, each speaking quietly to their own angels.

"Each lifetime on Earth, I have been with you, Jamie," the angel said in a musical voice. "You have known me time and time again. I have been at all of your births and followed you though all of your lifetimes. I have been at your passages back to the spirit world to make them easier for you. This time I stood at your bedside as you dreamed of birch trees. I was the red bird in the forest of birches."

Jamie's eyes glistened. "I remember! Oh, Mela, I am so happy to see you again." They hugged a long time.

"You and I are part of each other, Jamie, and I will always be watching over you."

There were more hugs and soft words all around until finally, one by one, the angels disappeared.

What a day, thought Jamie.

"Wasn't it just?" answered Mrs. Tipperwillow.

"I have a question, Mrs. T."

"Yes, Jamie?"

"Why do we take a boat to the snow? It seems like such a strange way to get here."

"Why, my dear, we've been traveling up our mountain this way almost forever. You see, once a long, long time ago, a small boy named Wesley came to live with me in Summerland. He must have been about five years old, and how that boy loved to sing! Over and over and over again he sang one line from the same song, as five year olds tend to do. The song went like this: 'I like to take you on a snow boat to China.' Well, I figured that a *snow* boat should go to the snow and not to some Earth place called China. So we've been boating here ever since."

Jamie laughed. "Oh, Mrs. Tipperwillow, I know that song. Grandpa used to have that old record, and it belonged to *his* mommy and daddy. I'm pretty sure the song goes like this: 'I'd love to get you on a slow boat to China.'"

"A *slow boat*," said Mrs. Tipperwillow in a quiet voice. All the children turned to look at the furiously blushing cow.

13

Dreaming

Jamie sat with Mrs. Tipperwillow on the blue and white plaid blanket, watching her friends at creation practice. Gino, Lateesha, Yoshi and Wallace were playing catch, and they were changing their balls into something else at the midway point as Mrs. Tipperwillow had shown them.

Wallace threw a brown ball to Yoshi. It became a soft Teddy bear by the time she caught it. She smiled at Wallace as she gave the bear a hug. Gino's red ball became a water balloon speeding toward Lateesha. Just as suddenly it changed direction and hit Gino's face with a loud splat.

Lateesha laughed. "What you do comes back to *you*, Gino!"

"Instant karma," he said, shaking out his wet hair. "Good one, Teesh!"

Jamie looked over at her teacher. "I finally know what I want to create for our tent, Mrs. T."

"What did you decide, Jamie?"

"I want to put a special rose bush right beside the entrance to our tent. All different types and colors of roses will grow on that one special bush. It will never need any water, and it will always remind us of how we're all connected to each other."

Mrs. Tipperwillow nodded her head thoughtfully. "That's a fine choice, my dear."

Jamie was happy. Everything seemed just right, even those things that had seemed sad and wrong not so very long ago.

Without warning, Jamie's inner sight opened and unfolded like the petals of a rose. She began seeing visions of her many lifetimes on Earth and the patterns that they formed. Soon she was filled with so many colors, feelings, and experiences that it almost brought tears to her eyes.

At last, the pictures faded. The eight-year-old shook her head in wonder and took a deep breath.

"Mrs. Tipperwillow?"

"Yes, Jamie."

"Will you ever be born again and live another lifetime on Earth?"

"I don't imagine I will, Jamie. You see, I like what I'm doing here. Helping you children to play again and to remember your creativity is my deepest passion and my deepest joy. I think it is always best to do the joyful thing and to do *everything* with joy. As a wise one on Earth once said, 'Do what you love and love what you do.' That's the happy way!"

"But wouldn't you like to teach the children on Earth like you are teaching us here?"

"But my dear child, I am, right now ... and *you*, Jamie, are in my story."

"Oh, Mrs. Tipperwillow, you're so *funny*."

"I certainly hope so!" said the beaming sort of cow.

A top hat appeared on Mrs. T's head, carefully balancing above her ears. The open top of the hat was filled with soil ... and three mushrooms! On the largest mushroom sat a tiny elf dressed all in green. The elf looked down at Jamie and winked. Jamie laughed.

"I know what I want to do in my next lifetime," Jamie said, looking again into Mrs. Tipperwillow's large brown eyes. "I'll be a writer, a stand-up comedian and a skydiver. Or maybe," and Jamie smiled at the lovable sort of cow, "I'll be a teacher like you ... and a skydiver! And I'll never be sick a day in my life."

Jamie lay back on the soft blanket. She sighed, looking up at the golden light of the sky and breathing it in. Then she closed her eyes and drifted into a dream of Earth.

Book Two
The Magic Mailbox

1

A New Day

Morning was quiet in Summerland. Just a few birds were singing as eight-year-old Jamie opened her eyes. Sitting up, she looked down from her cozy upper bunk to the empty stone fireplace. Running a hand through her curly brown hair, Jamie smiled, remembering the many evenings of storytelling and laughter around that fireplace.

No one else was awake, not Wallace, his long legs dangling from the top of the bunk next to hers, nor Yoshi, her small form sleeping quietly under the covers below Wallace, nor Lateesha, who was beginning to make stretching movements on the bunk below Jamie. Even "wild boy" Gino was abnormally quiet in his top bunk this morning. The empty bed below him was reserved for Mrs. Tipperwillow, who almost never used it.

Jamie imagined that while she and her friends slept, their beloved teacher, the magical sort of cow, traveled on colored winds to other worlds. Jamie pictured herself flying to planets with bug-eyed people who chirped instead of talked or worlds filled with tall, thin people with long arms and four eyes like diamonds who talked by burping and squeaking. A tiny laugh bubbled up through Jamie and broke loose, and though she was trying to be so quiet, all of her friends were suddenly awake.

"What's so funny, Jamie?" Gino asked, popping up. "You were so loud I thought elephants were stampeding the tent!"

Jamie sighed. "And I was trying to be so quiet."

Lateesha joined in. "Funny thing about that, Jamie! Unless we can learn to block our thoughts, when we get excited about an idea, it's like we're shouting."

"Yes," said Wallace stretching and sitting up. "In the spirit world, it's the strength of the picture that calls out. That's what *I* plan to study," the twelve-year-old said seriously. Jumping out of bed, Wallace pointed to the rug and drifted down to land in the fur-lined slippers he'd just created.

Gino noticed the slippers and rolled his eyes at the older boy, who now and then called himself the "King of Creation."

Wallace knew how much this upset the younger boy. *But sometimes,* he thought, *I just can't help it!*

Gino pointed dramatically to the fireplace and shouted *Alacazam*! A blazing fire appeared.

"Gino, you *are* the King of the Fire," Wallace said. "Now, let's go find Mrs. Tipperwillow."

Instantly, the five children were standing on the soft peach-colored rug. Lateesha twirled one of her tiny braids and moved toward the tent flap to open it.

2

Making Plans

"… Hellooo! Goody Morning!" sang the magical sort of cow, as she appeared out of a swirling golden mist by the fireplace. Today Mrs. Tipperwillow was wearing a pink jumpsuit with a red embroidered heart at the chest. "Gino, what a lovely morning fire you have made. Thank you."

Gino beamed and the other children did, too. They all loved Gino and wanted him to feel good about himself, even though he *was* sometimes over the top, like the time when he smeared *butter*flies on his friends, or the time when he rolled the snowboat over and over on their way up the mountain.

"What shall we do this fine morning?" Mrs. Tipperwillow asked as she looked from one child to another. "Do you have any grand ideas?" Jamie was still imagining wild looking aliens on far away planets. Everyone turned to look at her.

"Four diamond eyes!" exclaimed their teacher. "You have *quite* the imagination, Jamie!"

Gino stated loudly that he wanted to visit Playland again "Gino, dear, we've been there three times already. Aren't you getting a little tired of it by now?" Mrs. Tipperwillow asked hopefully.

"Well, *I* am," said Wallace, shaking his head. "First time, okay, new experiences and all that. And the log ride *is* excellent, especially with the colored bubbles all over the place. But I'm really getting tired of that kid stuff. Can't we do something more grown up, more meaningful, you know?"

"You mean like another trip to the Library of Lives?" Gino shook his head. "How many times do I have to look into my Life Book and see and feel myself as that boring bookkeeper who just stares at numbers all day long? And the lifetime when I was the butcher with the bald head and dirty apron is even worse. The smell and feel of cutting up that meat is *sickening*. Or what about the life when I was the rich society woman in Germany with her nasty smelling perfumes and her long, brown cigarettes? Ugh! Let's not even *go* there."

"But Gino," countered Jamie, "remember that lifetime you told us about when you were the African tribesman? You even did that dance for us!" Jamie repeated the steps that she remembered.

"Yeah, that *was* cool," he admitted, joining Jamie in a short dance.

Mrs. Tipperwillow twirled one hoof in the air. "I just thought of another choice which will suit us all, where we can play and learn at the same time. I think Jamie might have the idea."

"Aliens who chirp?" asked Lateesha.

"Tall ones with long arms!" laughed Yoshi.

"Can we see those, Mrs. T.?" asked Gino.

"I would love to learn about other planets," Wallace added, his eyes growing bright.

"Can we, Mrs. Tipperwillow?" asked Jamie. She could almost feel four diamond eyes staring at her.

"This will take me a moment," the sort of cow replied. Her little antler glowed as she planned furiously.

There was the sound of a bicycle bell out by the mailbox.

3

Mail

"Mail!" said Mrs. Tipperwillow breaking her concentration. "Jamie, I think it's for you, dear. Why don't you go see?"

"Okay!" Jamie opened the tent flap and stepped outside. A flowered sundress replaced her pajamas. Jamie was so used to this sort of thing happening that she hardly noticed. *I never got any mail here before,* she thought as she moved toward the mailbox. She looked around but there was no sign of anyone who might have rung the bell.

Moments later Jamie entered the tent with an open envelope in her hand and a confused expression on her face. Mrs. Tipperwillow's arms were open wide to cuddle the girl as she had already sensed what the letter contained.

"My grandpa is sick," Jamie told her teacher, snuggling against the red heart over Mrs. Tipperwillow's real heart. "He is very sick and will be here soon. This is an invitation to a party to welcome him back." Suddenly Jamie started crying, shuddering against Mrs. T. "Why am I crying?" the girl asked between her tears. "This is a happy thing, isn't it?"

"Of course it is, Jamie," replied the compassionate cow, in a soothing voice. "You are just thinking about how sad your family is feeling. They will miss your grandfather dearly. And their lives will change, especially your grandmother's life, with him gone. There, there, Jamie, cry as long as you like. The angels hear all sadness and wipe away all tears."

"Are you an angel, Mrs. T.?" Jamie asked, sniffling and snuggling even closer.

"I most certainly am—a cow sort of angel, you might say. And you, too, are an angel, Jamie—a human angel."

Jamie hugged Mrs. Tipperwillow for a long time. Meanwhile, large sheets of heavy paper and marker pens appeared on the carpet, and the other children sat down and began drawing pictures of wild looking aliens.

"Jamie, you are very special to your grandfather," said Mrs. Tipperwillow kindly. "And you have many stories to share with him about your adventures here in Summerland. Remember how you used to sit on his lap and tell him your stories?"

"You know that, Mrs. T.?" Jamie asked, sniffling.

"Yes, I do."

Jamie remembered how much Grandpa had loved what she made up in her head. "I have stories that are even better now," she said, smiling and wiping her nose on Mrs. Tipperwillow's jumpsuit.

"You do indeed, Jamie. Your grandfather will be very happy to see you at his grand homecoming."

"But ... what about our trip to space?" the girl asked in a small voice. "Will you go on without me?"

What do you say, Children? Mrs. Tipperwillow thought to the others, knowing that they had heard every word and every thought.

"We want to wait for Jamie," Gino replied, surprising everyone.

My wild boy with a tender heart, Mrs. Tipperwillow thought, and kept this thought strictly to herself. "Do you all agree?" she asked aloud.

The other children rose from the floor and joined Jamie and their teacher. "Later to space!" replied Wallace.

"Your grandfather needs you now," said Lateesha. "Of course we will wait for you."

"Yes," added Yoshi, looking up at Jamie, "because you're our new best friend."

Tears streamed down Jamie's cheeks again, happy tears this time. She smiled at Yoshi, Lateesha, Wallace, and Gino, and realized how like a real family they had all become.

"Come, let's have some fantastic chocolate chip cookies for breakfast, shall we?" asked the magical cow with a twinkle in her eye.

"With chocolate milk?" asked Jamie.

"I want whipped cream, too!" Gino turned in a circle with his arms in the air, doing a little Gino sort of dance.

Yoshi laughed. "And fresh peaches!"

"I want a cup of coffee!"

"Coffee, Wallace?" questioned Mrs. Tipperwillow. "My! My!"

The table appeared covered with the children's favorite treats. Wallace drank his coffee trying to look grown up. He made a face, but he tried to hide it behind a realistic cough.

As they were eating, Jamie's friends decided that while she visited Earth they would make a fort in the meadow. Mrs. Tipperwillow agreed to help create a variety of large and lightweight pieces so the children could make a truly fantastic building.

All of the children except Jamie emerged into the golden day to discover a most marvelous assortment of logs, blocks, triangles, and archway pieces in a variety of sizes, along with cans of colored paint and brushes. There was even a flag for the top of their fort. Gino, Lateesha, Wallace, and Yoshi rushed over to start their project.

4

Preparation

Meanwhile, at her open closet door, Jamie was trying to decide what to wear for Grandpa's party from her old collection of Earth clothing. Mrs. Tipperwillow asked, "How about this for a change?" The girl turned. A delicate robe, just Jamie's size, floated in the air between them. It was made of shiny yellow and sky blue silk, one color drifting into the other, like rainbow colors do. A bit of bright green showed where the two colors merged, and dark indigo lined the outer edge of the blue. A soft hood fell down the back of the robe.

"Oh, Mrs. Tipperwillow, this is just beautiful!" Jamie exclaimed, gently touching the soft fabric. "But do people wear robes like this at parties?"

"Yes, often we do wear special robes for celebrations." With the tips of her hooves, the sort of cow arranged the robe over Jamie's shoulders.

"I just love these colors, Mrs. T."

"I imagine you do. These are your main colors, Jamie, the colors of your energy. You may remember that we have spoken of this before. Each person living on Earth has an energy field surrounding them called an 'aura.' This energy shows their personality as well as their thoughts and feelings at each moment, and it remains part of who they are, even in the spirit world.

"Let's look at your colors, my dear. Your yellow says 'I am a happy spirit and I bring happiness to others.' Your blue says 'I love to create stories and poems and to talk to others about my feelings.' Your green says 'I love and I heal by loving,' and your indigo says 'I am a wise spirit who sees far.'"

"You can see all that from my energy, Mrs. T., from the colors in my aura?"

"That's right, Jamie. And one thing about these grand homecoming celebrations is that everyone wears their colors in whatever clothing they choose, whether its robes, dresses or suits. There are some rather unbelievable costumes, let me tell you! But you shall see for yourself soon enough."

"Now," said Mrs. Tipperwillow, slipping the robe off Jamie's shoulders, "before we get dressed up for the party, there is something else you can do. Can you guess what?"

"*Back?*" asked Jamie.

"Yes, dear, *back*. If you want, you can help your grandfather as he makes his change."

"I don't know how."

"Just beam that wonderful energy of yours. Send him your love, your happiness, the brightness that is Jamie Reed."

"Have the other children done this, too?"

"Only Wallace, but he's been here the longest."

"Is Wallace happy here, Mrs. T.? Lately, I'm not so sure. He tries to act so grown up, and he won't always play with us like he used to."

"I think our dear friend Wallace may be getting ready for a change himself," replied Mrs. Tipperwillow, patting Jamie's shoulder. "You know—that caterpillar to butterfly type thing."

Before Jamie could ask what Mrs. Tipperwillow meant, they were out of the tent and whizzing through the air so fast that all of Jamie's thoughts were blown away. Then just as quickly, they were standing in front of a huge wooden door.

5

Grandfather

"Back," announced the gold lettering running along the top of the door frame. Jamie remembered her first trip to Earth through the Back door to attend her life celebration and the beautiful energy ball that she had made, not even knowing how. She had helped all her family and friends that day, and now maybe she could help Grandpa, too.

The door opened near the ceiling of a hospital room. There was Jamie's grandfather on the bed … sort of. "Mrs. Tipperwillow, what's going on? He doesn't look right."

"That's because I'm right behind you, Jamie."

Jamie turned to see her grandfather, clear-eyed and younger look-ing. "Am I too late? You're here already?" Jamie laughed, only half believing that this was Grandpa. "You look so young and so *smart*!"

"No Alzheimer's anymore, Jamie." They hugged. "And no, I'm not totally here yet. I'm mostly here, and have been for a long time."

"How's that?"

"When the mind goes, Jamie, the spirit is set free to wander. So I've been in and out, like you, in and out of that Back door. Sometimes I've been watching from here, sometimes I've been out happily exploring different dimensions, and occasionally I've popped back into that part of me you see on the bed. Now, how about helping me with the final heave ho out of that tired old body?"

Jamie took Grandpa's arm, and together they flew down into the hospital room. Jamie looked from the younger, standing Grandpa, to the old, frail Grandpa in the bed. *This is really weird*, she thought.

"I know it is," replied Grandfather.

Jamie looked from Grandma's tired face to her mommy and daddy. They all look *so old*. "Hey, you!" she yelled at her father, who jerked suddenly and gave a tiny laugh of surprise.

"I heard that, too, Tom," whispered Jamie's mother to her husband. *We love you, Jamie. Thanks for coming.*

Jamie looked around for her brother. He was not in the room. Mother's voice came again into her mind. *Bobby is out in the waiting room with Uncle Bert and Aunty Fran.*

The girl thought fondly of her aunt and uncle. Then all at once it hit her, and Jamie smiled so big she thought she might burst. "Mom, you can *really* hear everything I'm thinking?"

I can now, Jamie. I've been changing, opening up in a whole new way. The painting I've been doing has helped my deeper senses to open. Now I'm able to hear messages from spirits, and sometimes I see images in my mind's eye, too. I think Bobby is discovering some of these same abilities, because of some of the things he's been saying. And by the way, Jamie, I like that flowered dress you're wearing today!

Jamie looked down, and her mouth opened in surprise. She was about to say something when the frail Grandpa let out a tiny sound. "It's time!" pronounced the standing Grandpa. "Jamie, make that energy ball I've been hearing about, and I'll do the same."

Smiling, Jamie gathered love at her heart, and with a wish sent it to the ceiling. A ball of pink light appeared floating overhead. It intersected with the ball of healing green light her grandfather created. The combined energies drifted down to cover everyone in the room.

There was a shift, a wiggle in the air, and a wisp of white light rose out of the top of old Grandpa's head and joined the standing Grandpa.

"That's all there is to it, Jamie," said Grandfather. "Blow kisses and let's go!"

Jamie raised a hand in the air and said, "Just a sec, Grandpa!" She popped through the closed door and quickly drifted to the waiting room. Jamie smiled as she spotted her favorite aunt and uncle in two of the chairs. But then she noticed the gangly twelve-year-old leaning into

Aunty Fran's side. It was Bobby! *It's been six whole years,* Jamie thought, shaking her head as she floated closer. *You've grown so big.* She reached out to try to touch her brother's cheek. *I love you, Bobby.*

Jamie disappeared from the waiting room to rejoin the rest of her family. So she missed the moment when her brother jerked upright and called her name out loud.

Jamie reappeared next to Grandpa and together they blew kisses all around the room. They rose into the air, and with a last look at their loved ones, they stepped through the Back door and into the golden light of the spirit world.

"I hear that there's to be a party in my honor," Grandpa said. "Will you be there, Jamie?"

"Sure! I even got a new robe to wear!" Henry Reed smiled at his granddaughter and began to fade until he'd disappeared entirely. "See you soon!" Jamie yelled to the empty space where he'd been floating.

Mrs. Tipperwillow was suddenly by her side. "Ready, Jamie?"

"Yeah, I'm ready now. That was amazing, Mrs. T.! My mommy could hear me, and my daddy could, too."

"Isn't it simply wonderful, Jamie?" The sort of cow sighed, and a happy tear ran down her cheek. "Even adults are starting to feel the changes. Earth is indeed coming into a new age. Now, let's go see what the others are up to, shall we?"

"Yes!" Jamie said, and hand in hoof, they flew toward home.

6

Costumes

Lateesha, Yoshi, Gino, and Wallace were nowhere to be seen as Jamie and Mrs. Tipperwillow flew in. But there was a huge fort, at least twice as tall as Jamie, in the middle of the meadow. A head popped out of the door. It was Wallace. "Darn! You're back already. We wanted to surprise you."

"I'm already surprised," Jamie replied. "But I'm only here to change clothes. Grandpa's homecoming celebration is about to start."

"Okay, see you!" Wallace disappeared inside the fort.

Jamie entered the tent house with Mrs. T., who helped her adjust the silk robe around her shoulders.

"At the party, you'll see people wearing clothing of many colors from many different lifetimes," Mrs. Tipperwillow said. "Watch also for the colorful patterns around them or over their heads. That's really something."

Jamie pulled the hood up to try it. "You look simply beautiful, my dear," Mrs. Tipperwillow said. She patted Jamie's cheek with her small hoof.

Outside by the mailbox, a cowbell clanged loudly as if to get the sort of cow's immediate attention. "Oh, dear ... so soon?" questioned Mrs. T., just as Lateesha entered the tent.

"It's for you, *Mrs. Daisy Tipperwillow*," the girl read and handed over a pale blue envelope.

"My, my," sighed Mrs. T., smiling softly and holding the envelope to her heart.

"Well, aren't you going to *open* it?" Lateesha asked.

"I'll open it a bit later, Teesha. Jamie and I have a celebration to attend."

"You look great, Jamie," her friend said. "What a pretty robe. But I think you need a feather in your hair ... doesn't she, Mrs. T.?"

"How well you know me, Teesha. I do *so* love feathers!" A sky blue feather floated down. Lateesha caught it and placed it behind Jamie's right ear.

"No, that's not right," she fussed, and tried it in several different places.

Jamie laughed and grabbed the feather. "I'll just carry it."

"Okay!" Lateesha replied and left quickly to return to the secret activities inside the fort.

Mrs. Tipperwillow twirled in a circle. When she stopped, she was wearing a long, rose-colored satin robe. It had green and gold banding around the sleeves and a deep red rosebud with a green leaf which rested over her heart.

"You look so pretty, Mrs. Tipperwillow. But where is *your* feather?"

"Here, Jamie!" responded the fashionable sort of cow. She turned. A long pink ostrich feather hung from the tip of her hood.

"That's a good idea, Mrs. T. Can I wear my feather like yours?"

"Of course you may." The blue feather drifted to the tip of Jamie's hood where it stuck. "Now it's time we are on our way. Come along, Jamie!"

7

Homecoming Celebration

Off they flew and were soon landing near a huge mansion that sat atop a green hill overlooking the ocean. The spicy, sweet smell of roses filled the air. People were strolling through a large rose garden looking at all the different varieties of the beautiful flowers.

"These roses are just like us," Jamie said, remembering Mrs. Tipperwillow's words, "different and beautiful and better together than apart from each other."

"You remember well, Jamie. Shall we go in?"

The huge double door opened all by itself. Jamie and her teacher moved, along with many other people, through the entrance, down a broad hallway, and into a large living room. Jamie notice colored lights bouncing off every wall. A second door opened. Mrs. Tipperwillow and Jamie found themselves in a large chamber with a circular stage at its center. As soon as everyone was inside, the door closed soundlessly.

"Who are all these people, Mrs. Tipperwillow?" Jamie asked, stepping up beside her teacher. "There must be at least two hundred."

"More like three hundred, Jamie. And these are all dear friends of your grandfather's from his different lifetimes."

"Wow!" was all Jamie could think to say as people in all colors and styles of costumes found their positions in the room. Everyone turned and looked back along the thick red carpet to the door. It opened once more, and in walked a handsome young man in a forest green suit.

The man noticed Jamie and waved. "Who's that, Mrs. T.?"

"Don't you recognize him, dear? That's your grandfather."

"But he's so young!"

"No reason to stay old around here unless you really want to," her teacher whispered. "People often choose to be the age they were when they felt strongest on Earth."

Jamie looked around at all of her grandfather's friends and noticed that the lights bouncing off the walls in the chamber were coming from the people themselves.

"Yes, Jamie. It is as I told you earlier. Everyone is wearing their glorious light patterns for your grandfather's celebration."

All was quiet as Jamie's grandfather climbed the stairs up to the small stage. A man in a gleaming white robe edged with gold braid joined him. The man began telling the story of Henry Reed, his adventures, his kindness, and his strength through the various challenges of his life. Then the white robed man looked around the room.

"I understand," he announced, "that Henry's granddaughter is here with us today. Jamie Reed, will you please join us on stage?"

"Oh, Mrs. Tipperwillow," Jamie whispered, embarrassed.

"Go along, Child, quickly now!"

Jamie threaded her way through the crowd to reach the stage and almost tripped in her nervousness. The man in white took her aside and handed her a big medal on a red velvet ribbon. "When I tell you, Jamie, I'd like you to put this over your grandfather's head, okay?"

"Okay," she whispered, holding the heavy medal carefully in both hands. She noticed that the medal was made of solid gold, and there was a wolf head engraved on the front of it. Turning it over, Jamie saw her grandpa's name and the dates of his birth and passing.

"Henry Reed was a man of many talents," the man continued, "but throughout his long life, what always mattered most was his family and friends. The strength of his love supported everyone he knew. Now his granddaughter, Jamie, will present him with his symbol—the wolf. For the wolf, the family, the clan, is everything."

Grandfather bent down, and Jamie put the medal over his head and kissed his cheek. "I love you, Grandpa. Welcome home."

"Thank you, Jamie," replied the handsome young man.

The formal part of the ceremony ended, and Jamie went with Grandpa to meet his parents and grandparents, who looked just as young as he did. *This is really confusing*, she thought. Then she met more of her grandfather's friends and family from different lives. He seemed to remember them all.

Finally the party was ending. Jamie had just charmed Grandfather with a long and colorful story about a certain trip to the snow, and he had turned to talk with yet another friend. Mrs. Tipperwillow gathered the girl into her arms. "Are you about ready to go, Jamie?"

"Yeah, I'm ready Mrs. T. I think Grandpa really liked his party, don't you?"

Henry Reed turned back to look at his granddaughter. "I can't imagine a finer celebration," he said, "especially with my beautiful Jamie as part of it."

She was sure that her heart was growing bigger as her grandfather kissed her cheek and said, "See you soon," just as he used to.

Jamie and Mrs. T. flew off hand in hoof and soon drifted down, landing in the green meadow next to the children's fort. "Now, Missy Jamie, let's see what all the fuss is about, shall we?"

8

The Fort

"We're back!" Jamie yelled. Four heads peeked out of the fort, two from the open doorway and two from the upper balcony. "Are you ready for us now?"

"Oh, yes," Wallace replied. "Enter, ladies!"

Mrs. Tipperwillow followed Jamie into the fort. The children had created quite a room. The inside of the building was painted bright red, and there was a blue table and two blue benches. A rose rested in a glass vase on the table near a lighted candle. There were stairs, fairly even ones at that, going up to the balcony, which was taller than Jamie herself.

"Gino really has a knack for making stairs," said Wallace seriously. "I helped him *just* a bit." Gino smiled proudly. "The girls did the painting." (Jamie had already figured this out as Lateesha and Yoshi were covered from head to foot with red and blue paint.) "Lateesha imagined the flower vase. I created the flower. Yoshi imagined the candle, and Gino lit it."

With a double blink of Mrs. Tipperwillow's eyes, the paint covering Lateesha and Yoshi dissolved. The children crowded onto the benches as the magical sort of cow imagined some striped ice cream sundaes for the occasion.

"Mrs. T," Lateesha asked as they finished their ice cream, "can we sleep out here tonight?"

"Surely you may!" exclaimed their teacher. "What a grand idea." Abruptly, the table and benches began wiggling to the door.

"Wait until we stand up, will you?!" Jamie exclaimed, and the five jumped up. Next, a pile of orange sleeping bags appeared. Each child took one and chose a place to sleep, either on the ground floor or on the balcony.

"Now, my friends," announced Mrs. Tipperwillow, "it has been a big day for all of us. Let's go outside to sing in the nighttime, and then say our blessings, shall we?"

Soon there was quiet chanting. "Softly, softly into night, softly, softly goes the light. Good night! Good night! Good night! Good night!" The sky quickly turned almost dark. "Now, children," Mrs. Tipperwillow prompted, and they joined together saying: "Blessings to all we've ever been and to all we'll ever be. Blessings to all we've ever loved, to the Earth, to spirit, and to dreams."

"All right, my friends, I will leave you here. Have a wonderful slumber party in your new fort."

"We will," Yoshi replied. "Thanks for the ice cream. It was yummy."

The children moved into the fort and wiggled into their sleeping bags. It was a long time before the talking stopped.

Mrs. Tipperwillow floated to her favorite resting spot under a spreading oak tree. "How I love what I do," she sighed, looking out over the nighttime meadow as a full moon rose in the sky.

9

Surprise

Morning arrived with an unusual fog in the air. It lifted slowly and lazily to reveal the golden day beneath. Daisy Tipperwillow, dressed in a blue bonnet and blue and white checkered dress, was in the meadow, gently talking with the wildflowers. Suddenly the morning stillness was broken by the impatient clang of a cowbell.

"Dearie Me!" exclaimed the startled sort of cow as all the flowers quickly closed their petals, folded their leaves, and pulled away.

Mrs. Tipperwillow hurried to the mailbox and pulled out another pale blue envelope. "Oh, I'm afraid that this just won't wait," she said. Sure enough, a moment later, she turned to see a young woman with red hair standing under the nearby tree, holding something in her arms.

"Annie! Just a minute, please!" yelled Mrs. T., as all the children tumbled out of their fort and gathered around.

"My friends, I have a big surprise for you ... well, actually a rather small surprise. It is waiting under that tree. Shall we go see?"

Gino scratched his head. "Is it a rocket ship to take us to space?" he asked.

Oh, dear, that's right, Mrs. Tipperwillow thought. *I did promise the children their trip today.*

"No, my friends, this is a bit of a different surprise, one that I have been expecting for some time."

"The blue envelope?" asked Lateesha.

"Yes, the blue envelope. Let's put an end to all this mystery, shall we?" The family hurried over to the tree, where their teacher introduced the children to Annie, who was holding something under a pale blue blanket. Yoshi waved a greeting to the young woman, who gave her a wink.

"And now, my friends, straight from our Summerland nursery, may I introduce to you ... Aaron Daniel Silverman."

The blanket was pulled back and there, awakening and blinking in the light, was a one-and-a-half-year-old boy with wavy blond hair and grey eyes. Seeing the children and the magical sort of cow, Aaron reached his hands toward them and laughed, revealing dimples on both cheeks.

"A baby, Mrs. T.?" asked Gino, wrinkling his nose.

"Yes Gino, a new member for our family," she replied, gathering the little one into her arms. Aaron wiggled in her grip. His small hands reached for the snoode, which quickly pulled up and wrapped itself turban-style around Mrs. T's head, balancing one foot against her antler to keep from falling. This looked so silly to the children that they all started to giggle ... even the usually serious Wallace.

"Aaron comes to us from Israel," said the sort of cow, trying to hold the wiggly little boy while keeping her head straight so the snoode wouldn't fall.

Mrs. Tipperwillow thanked Annie, who gave Yoshi a hug before flying away. Mrs. T. lowered Aaron to the soft grass, and the girls immediately sat down to play with him. The frightened snoode unwound from Mrs. Tipperwillow's head and gathered itself once again around her shoulders.

"Mrs. T.?"

"Yes, Wallace, what is it?"

"What about our trip to space?"

Mrs. Tipperwillow frowned (and it was very unusual for her ever to do *that*). "Well, as you can see, now we have a complication." The children looked at each other and then at Aaron.

"We can't go," Gino said in a flat voice.

"Sometimes," Mrs. Tipperwillow said, shaking her large head, "we must all learn to make sacrifices."

All of the children groaned … all, that is, except Aaron, who had no idea what was going on.

10

To Space

A baby backpack appeared on the lawn. "So my sacrifice," chuckled Mrs. T., her eyes twinkling, "is to carry this wiggly little creature on my back."

"To space?" asked Yoshi.

"To space!" exclaimed the magical sort of cow.

"Hooray!" all of the older children yelled, upsetting the little boy, who let out quite a little yell himself. A piece of silver fabric appeared on the lawn. Yoshi picked it up. It was a tiny jumpsuit with a hood, just Aaron's size.

"Can anyone tell me why this outfit is so appropriate for Aaron?" questioned their teacher, with a mischievous grin.

"I get it Mrs. T.," Jamie answered. "It's because this suit makes him what he already is … a *silver man.*"

"Aaron Silverman. That's funny!" said Lateesha, her dark eyes flashing.

Excited smiles creased the faces of the older children as they found themselves in padded silver spacesuits with clear round globes encasing their heads. Because she would be carrying a bulky backpack, Mrs. Tipperwillow created for herself the same simple jumpsuit that Aaron wore—but larger, of course.

She placed Snoody in a small pack at her waist. He curled around until only his head peeked out. Wallace helped arrange the toddler in the backpack and adjusted the straps over his teacher's shoulders. "To space, Children!" yelled the sort of cow. And they were off!

Aaron giggled as they raced along. *What a happy, easy child*, thought a grateful Mrs. Tipperwillow. Moments later they were floating in space high above the Earth. Wallace looked back just in time to see a door disappearing.

"Wow! This is amazing!" exclaimed Gino as they all stared at the beautiful blue ball of the Earth below them.

"On to the moon!" yelled Mrs. Tipperwillow, and the children flew, one after another, following their teacher. She looked back at her family. "Some people think," she stated in a serious voice, "that because of all its craters, the moon is made of Swiss cheese. Let's see if they're right."

Sure enough, when they landed on the surface of the moon, there were huge chunks of holey Swiss cheese everywhere.

"Hmmm," said Wallace, shaking his head.

"Lunch, anyone?" Their teacher chuckled and pulled a large loaf of French bread from a pocket that had just appeared on one side of her jumpsuit.

Gino laughed. "Oh Mrs. Tipperwillow, you're just crazy!" He picked up a block of cheese and threw it to Lateesha, who threw it to Yoshi, who threw it to Jamie. Taking the globe off his head, Gino nodded to his friends, and they removed theirs as well. Then they all settled in for a lunch of cheese and bread. After lunch, the older children played catch with more blocks of cheese as little Aaron sat with Mrs. Tipperwillow, watching the happy group and clapping his hands.

Heaving a last chunk of cheese to Gino, Wallace left the game and wandered over to his teacher. "Can we see how the moon *really* looks now, Mrs. T.? I was hoping to collect some moon rocks."

"Why, certainly we may, Wallace!" She called out to the others, "Everyone! Drop the cheese, please, and close your eyes!" Laughing, the children squeezed their eyes tight. When they peeked moments later, a very different moon showed itself.

"This moon is dull and rocky and dusty," said Gino in a disappointed voice. He made his "boring" face.

"No, it isn't," countered Wallace. Mrs. Tipperwillow blinked her eyes twice just as Wallace reached for the nearest rock. He picked it up. "This is how the moon really looks, and I think it's great."

No one except Wallace was impressed, however, and soon Gino started a chant of "To Mars! To Mars! To Mars!"

The girls joined in, and Aaron did, too. "Toe mas! Toe mas!" he yelled.

"Okay," said Wallace, giving up. "We can go now. I found some really good specimens here. Anyone want to see?" His friends shook their heads.

A shoulder bag appeared. The older boy placed the moon rocks into it and hefted it onto his shoulder. Mrs. Tipperwillow held out her arms, and Aaron floated up and into the carrier.

With a loud *whoosh*, the family was pulled off the moon and high into space. They sped along so fast that no one could see a thing until they glided down to land on the red planet.

"Mars really *is* red!" Lateesha exclaimed, looking at the reddish dust and silver and red rocks of the desert planet. "Here are more rocks for you," she called to Wallace, who was already on his knees, studying the surface of the planet.

"But where are the Martians?" asked Jamie, looking around.

"They lived here when there was water on the planet," explained Mrs. Tipperwillow, "but that was a long, long time ago."

"Oh," the girl replied in a disappointed voice.

"But how can time stop us travelers?" added the sort of cow, with a laugh. "The magic door can take us to any *time* we want!"

The familiar Back door appeared overhead and drifted down to land gently on the Martian soil. The children turned to see the door slowly opening. Mars on the other side looked just like Mars on this side. "Come along, Children," said Mrs. Tipperwillow, "through the door now, and quickly!"

Upon stepping through the portal, the Summerland tourists heard strange noises and turned to see three tall, pale-skinned women talking to each other in soft, whirring voices. The Martian women had long arms and legs, eyes that were deep set and dark, and long black hair. Their hair was wound in colorful ribbons that kept it neat in the stiff Martian wind. They were dressed in knee-length, belted robes in shades of red or deep blue with long, puffy pantaloons, and sandals for their feet.

The children spotted other Martians strolling beside a slow-moving reddish river. The men were taller than the women and wore similar clothing. They had long hair, too, which hung down over their narrow shoulders. The men's hair was oiled and held in sections by clips at the bottom of each strand.

Three children, who were dressed the same way as the adults, sat by the river's edge, wiggling their toes in the water. No one noticed the band of explorers.

"They can't see us … just like the people on Earth," Yoshi said to Mrs. Tipperwillow.

"We are in another dimension, Yoshi," replied Mrs. T., "and our energies are vibrating in a faster way." All the older children turned to listen.

"What do you mean?" asked the seven-year-old. Confusion showed in her almond-shaped eyes.

"Everything that exists is made up of energy, Yoshi," answered her teacher, "and whether you can sense it or not depends on how fast *your* energy is moving. If your energy is moving faster than the energy of another place and people, you may be able to sense what's there, but any people you encounter will not be able to see you."

"I don't get it." Yoshi turned to her friends. "Do you?"

They all shook their heads, except for Wallace. "I believe what Mrs. T. is talking about is called *frequency*," he stated in a serious voice. (Gino pulled the corners of his mouth out to form a frog face.) "And some people on Earth have found ways to raise their frequencies so they can actually sense us."

"Quite right, Wallace," Mrs. Tipperwillow agreed.

A loud tone sounded. All of the Martians turned and began to follow the sound. The space explorers followed.

Moving between two large boulders, they found themselves at the edge of a small village. Single-story buildings, some square and some rectangular, were lined up along narrow, dusty streets. Some buildings were the same red color as the soil and rocks. Some buildings were a lighter pink. Others were pale blue or brown.

Tall plants with spiky leaves and oddly shaped flowers were scattered here and there, and in one area there was what seemed to be a large vegetable garden. None of the "vegetables" looked familiar, though, except for some bluish "pumpkins."

Canals filled with murky water ran through the village, and there were foot bridges over the canals. In the center of the town stood a large building made of red stone blocks. Martians of all ages hurried along pathways and over bridges and began entering the building from all directions.

"Dear ones," Mrs. Tipperwillow said as the children gathered around her, "I think it is best that we leave them to their meeting. Have you seen enough?"

All agreed—except for Wallace. "I could study Mars for a month or two at least," he stated. (Gino puffed out his cheeks and popped them with his fingers.) "But I know that there are other planets for us to visit, so I'll come here by myself later on."

The Back door reappeared, and after taking a last look around, the family stepped across onto the deserted Martian landscape.

The rest of the day was spent flying between the other planets in Earth's solar system. The Summerland family floated above the hot planet, Mercury—the smallest planet in our solar system and the one closest to the sun, and Jupiter—by far, the largest of all the planets. All they could see of Jupiter was a swirl of gases, and around this, clouds with lightning flashing out of them.

They discovered that the beautiful rings around Saturn were made up largely of ice crystals of different sizes. And not only that—the rings made sounds!

Gino shook his head. "This is *so* weird," he said. "I've heard these sounds before, in a cartoon movie about outer space."

Lateesha nodded her head. "You're right, Gino. That's where I heard them, too."

After a few rounds of "Ooh-eee-ooh," the children and their teacher flew from the vicinity of Saturn's rings and sped once again toward Earth. Nearing their home planet, they came upon a meteor shower and carefully wove through the giant boulders that were hurtling through space.

"Children," Mrs. Tipperwillow commented, "if you were standing on Earth right now looking up at the night sky, these meteors would look like falling stars."

Leaving the last of the meteors behind, the Summerland family was once again floating high above the Earth.

"It's so beautiful," Jamie said with a sigh as she and her Summerland family looked down at the glowing ball of their home planet which was, from their current angle, half in day and half in night. Lights dotted the portion of Earth where it was nighttime, and Jamie realized that the largest splotches of light came from the biggest cities. She thought of all the people down below who had turned on their lights when it got dark and who were at that very moment eating dinner or reading or watching television.

Mrs. Tipperwillow gathered the children around her. "It's been quite a day, my friends, but now it's time to return to our own dimension. Close your eyes, and hold hands. We'll take the fast way home." The children did as their teacher requested, and a strong wind blew around them for a moment. "All right, you may open your eyes now."

The older children laughed as they dropped hands and found themselves standing beside their large striped tent in the meadow. It was already dusk, and soon all six explorers were warmly tucked into their beds and sound asleep, dreaming of their day in space.

11

A Secret

A small breeze blew across Jamie's face. "Jamie," whispered Mrs. Tipperwillow, "are you awake?"

"I am now," Jamie whispered back. "What's going on?"

"Will you meet me at the mailbox? I'll collect Lateesha."

"Okay, but...."

"*Now*, please ... and quietly!"

The girl nodded and floated down to the rug. She noticed that Yoshi was up already and playing with Aaron by the fireplace. "They look so cute together," Jamie thought, as she stepped out into the morning light.

In a moment, Lateesha and Mrs. T. joined her. "I need a little help from you two," their teacher requested.

"Sure," they both replied at once.

"What's the big secret?" asked Lateesha.

"Well, I know that you two would like to play with little Aaron, but I was hoping that you would give Yoshi lots of time to be with our new little one ... just leave the two of them alone for now."

"Why, Mrs. T.?" Lateesha asked, scratching her nose.

"I think Jamie might know."

"It has to do with Wallace, doesn't it?" Jamie guessed.

"Yes, Jamie, it does. As you know, our Wallace has been like a big brother to Yoshi, playing with her and helping her with her creations ... sort of looking out for her like a big brother would on Earth."

"Is Wallace leaving? Is he going back to Earth now?" asked Lateesha, sadly.

"He is about to do what you two might wish to do one day. He is about to grow up.*"

Lateesha laughed. "You mean, like being thirteen instead of twelve?"

"No, Teesh, I mean *really* grow up. He's going to instantly become twenty or perhaps twenty-five years old."

The girl raised her eyebrows. "You mean we can do that?"

"We can be any age we want in the spirit world," Jamie answered. "I saw it when my grandfather got younger."

Teesha thought about this and shook her braided head, which caused the many-colored stars to bounce around.

Jamie sighed. "So Wallace is really leaving us?"

"Yes, dear, he is, although I'm sure he'll visit now and again. Little Aaron comes here just in time to help Yoshi so she won't feel so sad. Now she can be like a big sister to our little one."

The girls thought about this. Lateesha asked, "Does Wallace know?"

"Yes, he knows, but he doesn't know exactly *when* he will get the call. It will be soon, so I wanted to prepare you girls. Yoshi will need lots of hugs and support from the two of you."

"We'll be happy to help, Mrs. Tipperwillow," replied Jamie. "But what about Gino? Does he know about this?"

"I'm going to tell him now."

"But Mrs. Tipperwillow...."

"Don't worry, girls. I'll put a little protective bubble around your thoughts so that they won't leak out. That will give Wallace a chance to talk to Yoshi."

"That's good," Lateesha said. "It's so hard not to think of secrets."

"You won't have to keep this one for long anyway." Mrs. Tipperwillow disappeared into the tent.

The two girls took a long walk in the meadow, and when they wandered back to the tent house, Gino was trying to get Wallace to play "throw the waffle" with him.

"Did we miss breakfast?" asked Lateesha, as she followed Jamie in.

"Here you go, Teesh, breakfast!" Gino grinned as a large waffle with whipped cream flew across the tent. Lateesha grabbed it out of mid-air, popping it into her mouth. "Delicious!" she mumbled around a mouthful.

"Hey, how about me?" asked Jamie, and a second waffle came flying. As she licked whipped cream off her fingers, Jamie noticed Yoshi feeding small pieces of waffle to Aaron as Wallace looked on, smiling.

12

The Magic Mailbox

"Today, Children, I thought I'd tell you more about our magic mailbox and how it works," said the fashionable sort of cow. This morning Mrs. Tipperwillow was wearing purple Capri pants and a pink mohair sweater. "Gino, will you please light us a cozy fire?"

Gino did a little dance, wiggling all over and turning in a circle. Pointing to the fireplace, he yelled *Alacazam!*

"Nicely done, Gino," said Mrs. Tipperwillow as they all sat down in front of the blazing fire. "Now, our mailbox is not quite like the mailboxes on Earth, although it looks the same," she began in her "teachery" voice. "Can anyone tell me a difference?"

"Well," replied Jamie, "there's the sound of a bell whenever we get mail, but nobody is ever there. The mailbox seems to just fill up all by itself."

"Yes. And what else?"

"There's no return address?" guessed Lateesha.

"That's true. What else? Wallace?"

"Mail can go out from here, too, and end up anywhere, even on Earth," stated the twelve-year old knowingly. Gino thought this was hilarious and started to laugh, but Mrs. Tipperwillow nodded.

"Wallace is right."

"You mean that I can send a letter home to Mom and Dad?" asked Jamie.

"Well, yes, but it will not appear in their mailbox. It will appear in their thoughts."

Jamie wrinkled her nose. "What? I don't get it."

"Wallace, will you please explain this to Jamie?" Mrs. Tipperwillow gave him a wink.

"It's called 'inspiration' or 'insight,' Jamie. We can send our ideas to Earth to help people. They suddenly understand something or get an idea to try something in a new way, and they have no clue where these ideas are coming from. They are coming from us in the spirit world!

"There are actual lines of energy that go out and make the connection," he continued. "I've seen them and the patterns they make. It's the most amazing light show you ever saw! And there are ways to send messages from here into this fantastic web of light that connects to places all over the world at once.

"Can we show them, Mrs. T.? Can we?" No one had ever seen Wallace quite *this* excited. "And one more thing," added the twelve-year-old not waiting for an answer, "I want to study how thought energy travels to Earth. I want be a part of a team that sends ideas to lots of people all at once."

"What kinds of ideas, Wallace?' asked Jamie.

Gino perked up. "Like where to put new amusement parks?"

"No, Gino, I want to help heal the Earth, to figure out ways to fix the dirty air and water and the messed up soil, so everyone can live on a clean planet again. The great thing," Wallace continued, "is that ideas can be sent to scientists and end up as major discoveries, or to producers and end up in the movies, or to authors and end up in books, or to people who write music and end up in songs, or to artists and show up in galleries."

Jamie heard the words "artist" and "galleries" and thought of her mother. "Mrs. Tipperwillow, remember when we went to the Library of Lives and I saw my mother in the future showing her paintings in galleries and teaching that class called 'Art as Healing?'"

"Yes, Jamie, I remember."

"Well, suppose that I sent a message to her in the magic mailbox with the idea of showing her paintings in galleries and teaching that class. I could help her create the future that I've already seen."

"Jeez, Jamie," Gino said, shaking his head. "You're too far out for me!"

"Maybe far out," said Wallace seriously, "but she's right."

All of the children were suddenly quiet as they thought about what this meant.

"Suppose we saw something we didn't want to happen," Yoshi said in a small voice, "like someone hurting somebody else."

"This does get complex." Mrs. Tipperwillow sighed. "We can't force, ever, but we can send ideas to create other possibilities.

"Now, my friends," said their teacher with a small smile playing on her large cow lips, "we have all been thinking so very hard that I feel quite certain something silly is about to happen."

At that very instant, confetti started raining from the ceiling of the tent, followed by balloons of every color. The older children began batting at the balloons and gathering armfuls of confetti to throw at each other as it billowed higher and higher on the peach colored rug. The fun was contagious, and soon Mrs. Tipperwillow joined in. Even Aaron was hitting at the balloons and laughing. But it was Wallace, who often seemed so serious, who was the happiest and freest of them all.

13

Changes

Jamie opened her eyes to see golden light streaming through the tent flap. There was a strong weight of sadness in the air, almost as if someone was pushing on her chest. She rolled over and looked down. Wallace was talking to Yoshi by the fireplace.

Jamie peeked over the edge of her bunk at Lateesha, who looked up at her and nodded. *Wallace is telling Yoshi he's leaving*, Jamie thought, and though she didn't *want* to eavesdrop, she really couldn't help herself.

"Yoshi, it's just that I have things I want to do now that I can't do as a child," Wallace said in a quiet voice. "Remember that lifetime when I was your mother, and you went to live and work in the city? You wanted so much to form your own life. I was sad because everything was changing. But that's how life is ... always full of change and growth. You know, don't you," Wallace continued, "that you will always be so important to me?"

"And you will always be so important to me, too," replied the seven-year-old in a hurt voice.

"And I'll come back to visit, Yoshi, after I'm settled and have started my studies. I promise."

"Okay," said the little girl, frowning.

"I have an idea!" Wallace reached out and took Yoshi's small hand in his own. "The next time we go to Earth let's be best friends just the same age."

"I wasn't sure I wanted to go back, but maybe if you were with me.... Will we be boys or girls?" she asked, sniffling.

"Let's decide that later, but we'll be the *best* friends ever, okay?"

Jamie noticed that Gino was awake and had been listening to every word and every thought. All at once, there was the sound of "la, la, la" coming from the bunk underneath Gino's. Aaron was awake, too. Yoshi turned, wiped her eyes with her forearm, and floated over to the toddler. She lifted him up out of bed and gave him a big hug.

Gino jumped out of his bunk and floated down to the carpet, trying to stick his hair down with his fingers. It popped up anyway.

Immediately, Mrs. Tipperwillow flew in through the tent flap. "What will it be today, Children?" she asked with a warm smile. Jamie and Lateesha joined the others, Jamie wiggling her toes in the soft carpet.

Lateesha stuck her hand in the air. "I have an idea, Mrs. T! Could we travel to different places on Earth to explore, like tourists do?"

"You have such a good idea, Teesha," the sort of cow replied, nodding her large head. "This will take a bit of thinking on your parts, Children." Pieces of paper floated down from the ceiling, and the older children grabbed them out of the air. Next, pencils appeared in their hands. "I'd like you each to write down all the places in the world you'd like to visit. Then we will compare notes and make our decisions."

Yoshi put Aaron down next to her with his own sheet of paper and handed him the blue marker pen she'd just created. As the older children began writing out their ideas, Aaron watched them for a moment and then made some marks of his own on his paper.

They were all so absorbed that they almost missed the sound of a bicycle bell at the mailbox. All except Wallace, that is! By the time his friends looked up, he was already out of the tent.

Wallace returned from the mailbox holding a bright red envelope and a red paper edged with gold. He had the biggest smile ever on his face.

"What does it say?" Gino asked. Wallace held out the paper, and the younger boy read:

You are hereby invited to grow up.
Meet me immediately at the round council chamber,
across from the Library of Lives.

Sincerely, Samos

"This is it!" said Wallace in an excited voice. "I will be back to visit, I promise. And when I do, I'll share what I've been learning. Or maybe Mrs. Tipperwillow will take you on a field trip to see that web of light I was telling you about, and I'll meet you there."

He turned toward Yoshi. "Remember what I told you … best friends forever, okay?" Wallace gave her a quick hug. "Thank you all for being such a good family. And thanks especially to you, Mrs. Tipperwillow, for *everything*."

"Do you know the way, dear?"

"I'll find it!" Wallace replied and was quite suddenly gone. Yoshi choked out a little sob, and Mrs. Tipperwillow scooped her up for a most tremendous hug. There was sudden silence and a feeling of loss.

14

Acting Out

"Well!" Gino said, finally breaking the silence, "I am *never* going to grow up!"

"You mean like Peter Pan?" said Jamie. "He never wanted to grow up either."

Righto! Gino said and flew up to the top of the tent, one arm out, pretending to be Peter Pan. Mrs. T. winked, and the boy was dressed in green tights and tunic and a pointy green hat with a red feather. "I am Peter Pan!" he yelled and circled the top of the tent several times. "I will fight Captain Hook and win!"

At this even Yoshi, peeking out from Mrs. Tipperwillow's warm arms, had to smile.

"Outside, Children! Our lists can wait!"

The group stepped through the tent flap and into the golden day. Some distance from the tent, a pirate ship floated above the meadow. Churning waves appeared underneath it and lapped against the sides of the large vessel.

"Wow, Mrs. Tipperwillow! This is your best creation ever!" Gino exclaimed as he approached the ship and flew up to look at the realistic masts and rigging. The others joined him on deck, with Mrs. Tipperwillow carrying the toddler.

"We have our Peter," stated their teacher with a wink at Gino, "and now we must assign the other parts for our play. Yoshi, how about it? Will you be Captain Hook? I think you'd be *perfect*."

"Okay … I guess," Yoshi answered, brushing away a last tear.

"For this scene," continued Mrs. Tipperwillow, "we need Tinkerbell to flit around above Peter Pan and urge him on. We need a Crocodile to gobble up Hook. And we need a crewman for the ship. I think Aaron will do nicely for our crewman. Lateesha and Jamie, it is your choice. Which parts do you wish to play?"

Jamie was just certain that Lateesha wanted to play Tinkerbell, so she answered quickly. "I'll be the Croc. It will be fun to gobble up Captain Hook."

"Don't gobble me too hard, Jamie!" Yoshi demanded.

"I won't!"

"All right, everyone! Places!" ordered Director Tipperwillow.

Jamie was instantly dressed in a crocodile suit. She started swimming in the water, which floated several feet deep over the grass. A short, bright pink fairy dress with small transparent wings appeared on Lateesha, and she began flitting here and there in the air around Gino.

Yoshi was outfitted in a black captain's hat with a feather and a black moustache that curled up at the ends. She wore black leggings, a black velvet vest over a white, billowy shirt, and a broad black belt. A gold watch hung on a chain from the belt.

From Mrs. Tipperwillow's lap, crewman Aaron took off his pirate's bandana and pulled at it with his tiny fingers.

Two long rubbery swords appeared, floating in mid-air. Hook and Pan each grabbed one.

"All right, *Action!*" yelled the director, and a fine sword play ensued. Yoshi really got into it, slashing away and looking very determined, even angry. Gino, who was kept busy bouncing back Yoshi's sword, looked briefly over at Mrs. Tipperwillow with a question in his eyes.

In thought and just to Gino, she replied, *Yoshi is very hurt and even angry that Wallace is gone. This swordplay gives her a chance to release her anger in a way that doesn't hurt anybody. So don't win too quickly.*

Gino nodded, and the thrusts and counter thrusts continued. Finally, Yoshi appeared to be tiring.

"Now," ordered the director, "Peter Pan makes the final thrust with his sword, and Captain Hook falls over the railing to the water below."

Yoshi did a most excellent "Arrggh ... you got me!" as she fell over the railing and performed a perfect double somersault on the way down.

Jamie the crocodile jumped on Hook saying, "Gobble-gobble." Hook laughed hysterically. Then a watch ticked loudly.

"All right, actors, *cut*!"

15

Alice

"Oh, wasn't that just fine!" exclaimed Mrs. Tipperwillow. The children were excited and jabbering all at once. "How about another since we're on a roll?" suggested their teacher.

Lateesha raised her hand. "Could we do a part of *Alice's Adventures in Wonderland*?"

"Yes!" exclaimed Jamie, remembering how she used to pretend that she was Alice when her mother read the stories to her in the hospital.

"Well, we could do one scene," Mrs. T. replied. "Why don't we create 'Down the Rabbit Hole' with the tea party?"

"Yes!!" all of the older children yelled.

"Jamie, why don't you play Alice?" Lateesha suggested. "I think you'd be perfect."

Thank you, Jamie thought to her friend.

The other parts were chosen. Lateesha would play the Mad Hatter. Yoshi would be the White Rabbit, and Gino would take the part of the Dormouse. Aaron and Mrs. Tipperwillow would be other guests at the party.

"Close your eyes," said Mrs. Tipperwillow, "and don't open them until I say." Some moments later.... "All right, you may open your eyes now." The children blinked a few times to take in the changes. They were no longer standing in the meadow. Earthen walls surrounded them, and in some places tree roots broke through the rounded walls. A tunnel entrance was visible on one side of the large chamber.

The children grinned, looking first at each other and then down at their own costumes. Jamie noticed that she was dressed in the simple blue pinafore with white blouse and shiny black shoes that she remembered Alice wearing in the stories. Lateesha reached up to steady the teetering top hat on her head. She wore a matching dress jacket with long pants. Her entire costume was made of brightly colored patches of shiny satin.

Mrs. Tipperwillow twirled around to model her frilly, pale pink party dress. A pink satin ribbon was tied around the base of her antler and formed a floppy bow. It was obvious to the children that she thought she looked simply marvelous.

Gino stifled a laugh as he looked quickly from the bow at her forehead to her thin cow legs peeking out from under two layers of ruffles.

Lateesha pointed at Gino and chuckled. "You look really good in your mouse suit, Gino!" He broke his gaze from Mrs. T. to study his bright red jacket and to pat his furry haunches. Then he reached around to run a finger down his long tail.

Yoshi hopped around the room to get the feel of her white rabbit costume. She wore white gloves and a splendid blue velvet vest. A gold watch (the same watch she wore as Captain Hook) hung on a chain from her pocket.

Aaron looked down at his dark purple jacket and matching shorts and immediately pulled off the lavender bow tie from around his neck.

A long table appeared in the center of the rabbit warren with chairs, six tea cups, and a large tea pot of steaming tea. Mrs. Tipperwillow settled Aaron on her lap as the older children took their places.

Lateesha poured everyone cups of tea and began making up dialogue. "I am sometimes called the Mad Hatter, but I'm not really sure why that is," she said, taking a sip from her cup and delicately putting it down again. "I am certainly *not* angry, but I do wear a very fine hat. As you can see," she said grinning, "I'm perfectly perfect in every way. There's nothing at all wrong with me!" She stuck out her tongue, rolled her eyes, and wiggled her fingers at everyone.

All eyes turned toward Jamie. "My name is Alice, and I've had lots of adventures here in Wonderland. I met the Red Queen, and she said 'Off with her head!' and I said 'Forget it!' No … that's not right. I said 'Nonsense!' Yes, that was it, in a very loud voice, so she left me alone. And there was this huge chessboard, and I had to walk backward to get to where I wanted to go. I drank from a little bottle that said *Drink Me*, and I got smaller and smaller until I was the size of a mouse. Then I ate a little cake with the words *Eat Me* spelled on top, and I got really huge. But somehow I got small again, and I almost drowned in my own tears. Lots more happened, but those are my favorite parts," Jamie finished.

"I was late! I was late! But now I'm here, so I didn't miss my party after all," Yoshi said in a voice she hoped sounded like the White Rabbit. "Welcome, everyone, to my wonderful rabbit house. Please have some tea!" She twitched her nose in a rabbity sort of way and took a sip from her cup as her friends did the same.

"Eep Eep! I'm the dormouse. I guard the door," piped Gino, not knowing what else to say. Yoshi looked at him and shrugged. Not the response he was looking for. Confusion filled Gino's face. "Tutt tutt, it looks like rain," he tried. Laughter erupted around the table. Better!

Lateesha rolled her eyes. "Where's your umbrella, Mouse?"

Wrong story, Gino! Jamie choked and laughed until she was crying.

In the excitement, the youngest guest spilled his tea, then the Dormouse spilled his, and the White Rabbit spilled hers and Alice and the Mad Hatter spilled theirs with rounds of "Excuse me!"

"No, excuse me!"

"No! No! Excuse me!!"

"Home for hot cocoa and cookies in the tent," Mrs. Tipperwillow chortled, and five satisfied children and one magical sort of cow skipped through the tunnel, which angled upward and opened into the meadow near their tent.

They quickly chanted daylight to dusk. As they stepped through the tent flap, the children's costumes were replaced by white pajamas, and Mrs. Tipperwillow's frilly dress became a black velour pantsuit.

A table appeared at the center of the tent, set with two lighted candles, a large plate of peanut butter cookies, and six cups of hot chocolate with a big marshmallow floating in each. Benches appeared next, and the Summerland family sat down, talking and joking as they grabbed for the cookies. Finally, when the last of the cocoa was finished and only crumbs were left on the plate, night was called in and sleepy blessings were said.

After the children were tucked into their beds and fast asleep, Mrs. Tipperwillow floated out to her favorite spot in the meadow, near the spreading oak tree. She looked up, and suddenly the sky was covered with stars. The stars began moving around to create the figures of the six children that formed her family. Then the tallest star figure flew off. The magical sort of cow lay down in the soft green grass. "Yoshi will be just fine," she said to herself.

16

Her Mushroom Hat

The girls were out in the meadow with Aaron, showing him the wild flowers. "Isn't this a pretty flower?" asked Yoshi. "Can you say *flower?*"

"Fower!" repeated the toddler. Lateesha and Jamie looked on, smiling. Yoshi was doing so well. Concentrating on little Aaron was helping to ease her loneliness, and the girls were staying close for listening and hugs. Gino flew down from the pirate ship, still launched in the meadow, just as Mrs. Tipperwillow flew in from somewhere.

"Mrs. T?" he asked.

"Yes, Gino, dear, what is it?"

"Will Aaron ever grow up so he can play with me?"

"Oh, I do expect so," she replied. "He will be a toddler for a while, and then I expect that he will grow up rather suddenly from watching the four of you.

"Now, my young friends," she continued, "I have just received word from Wallace." Yoshi looked up, smiling more brightly than she had in a long while.

"Wallace says that his growing-up ceremony went well, and he wants to show us all that web of light he was telling us about and how messages are sent from here to Earth and back. So how would you all like a field trip?"

"Yea!" the older children yelled.

"Yea!" said little Aaron, copying them.

"We need to wait for a bit until Wallace is ready for us. He said he would contact us through our magic mailbox. Until then, I thought we could have a little family conference."

Gino made his "boring" face.

"Now, children, as you know...."

Gino interrupted. "Mrs. Tipperwillow, what about our field trip to Earth, to all of the places we've been planning?"

"Ah, yes, Gino, this is one of the things I wish to speak to you about. Your lists are so long, and you have so many wonderful ideas, and I, my dears, may have an idea or two of my own. Therefore, I think we should wait...."

"Again?" Gino groaned.

"Until the next book," finished Mrs. Tipperwillow.

"What?" Gino, Lateesha and Yoshi asked at the same instant.

Jamie chuckled. "Mrs. Tipperwillow told me once that I was in her story." She shook her head. "And then I told her she was funny," the girl continued, looking at the ground as she remembered, "and then there was this hat...."

"*That* hat?" asked Lateesha, pointing to Mrs. T's head.

Jamie looked up. Yes! The same hat was teetering on Mrs. Tipperwillow's head. Three mushrooms grew out of its open top, and the very same green clad elf sat cross-legged on the largest mushroom. The elf winked at Jamie and stood up, leapt down, and bounced off the sleeping snoode who let out a tremendous sneeze. Without a backward glace, the elf streaked into the tall grass and disappeared.

Mrs. Tipperwillow smiled mildly. "Now, Children, when we get to the Light Web I want each of you to watch and listen very closely. There will be much more going on than you might imagine at first. And I don't want anyone going off into the web by himself. Gino, this message is especially for you." Gino made a face.

17

Light Web Junction

A bicycle bell rang loudly, and the older children raced to the magic mailbox. Mrs. T. scooped up Aaron and joined them. Gino reached into the box first, but Jamie put a hand on his arm.

"Yeah, you're right," he said. "Yoshi, why don't you do it?" The seven-year-old eagerly reached in and grabbed out a rainbow-colored envelope. She opened it to find a bright yellow paper inside. It read....

> *Take the train to where it leads you.*
> *Your Friend Forever, Wallace*

"Excellent!" exclaimed Mrs. Tipperwillow. "We'll go in style today, Children!" With a wave of their teacher's hand the entire group was dressed in matching rainbow-colored robes. Everyone was delighted ... well, *almost* everyone.

"Couldn't I wear something a little less *girly?*" Gino asked, making a face. With a casual wave of his teacher's hoof, the boy was dressed in a wizard's blue robe and a pointed hat covered with stars. "Much better!" he exclaimed, just as the sky darkened.

The fountain of light pushed up through the ground and turned the night sky bright with many colors. The Sky Train appeared overhead.

"All aboard for Light Web Junction!" yelled the conductor.

The children and Mrs. Tipperwillow rose into the air and floated through the open door of the train, choosing seats as it began to move. The magical rainbow made its way through the train car, bright green passing through the children first this time. Breathing in the green light, they felt love and healing, as if all the sadness that ever was and ever could be had disappeared. They passed through the yellow light of happiness and then the bright orange of excitement. Gino yelled "Yes!" as the orange light passed through him. Next, the strength of red filled the children. Shifting into purple, they felt quiet and peaceful.

The train passed out of the rainbow and moved into a darkened sky. On and on it rolled, the darkness getting deeper and deeper. In the distance, the children saw a spark of light and then another. Suddenly, as if they had come over an invisible hill, the sky before them lit up with millions of twinkling lights. Lines of light between the twinkles formed into a huge, really huge, web.

"Where's the spider?" Gino asked and made wiggly spider fingers at Lateesha, who batted his hands away as she studied the gigantic web of light.

Yoshi was holding Aaron on her lap as he reached out toward the lights with chubby fingers. "Wow!" exclaimed Jamie. "Look at this!" The train pulled to a stop at a platform, which floated in the brightened sky.

"Light Web Junction!" yelled the conductor. The family stepped off the train. Gino began making spider fingers at Jamie, who paid him no attention. She was watching how thicker areas of light were moving through the lines of the web and disappearing in the distance.

"Mrs. Tipperwillow," Jamie said, "those bulges look like frogs being swallowed by boa constrictors!"

Mrs. T. laughed. "Snakes eating frogs? You have *quite* the imagination, Jamie." She turned quickly to gaze in the distance behind her. "Look everyone! Here comes Wallace!"

The children sensed Wallace before they saw him. Even though they knew that he had grown up, they were still surprised by the tall man who joined them. But they immediately recognized his blue eyes and knowing smile.

Wallace picked up Yoshi. "You're all grown up now," she said, touching the rough beginnings of the beard on his chin. "You've gotten so big."

"I know," Wallace replied in a deep voice, "but I'm still me. Well, what do you think?" he asked, looking from the children to the Light Web that was stretching across the sky.

"It's pretty cool," Gino said, "but what are those bulgy things moving through the strings of light?"

"Ah, yes," responded the young man, putting Yoshi down. "This is what I've been studying. Let's fly closer and I'll show you something." The children and Mrs. Tipperwillow lifted off the platform and, following Wallace, they floated down near the outer edge of the web.

"Gino, you first," Wallace prompted, looking from Gino to a nearby strand of light with a bulge slowly moving through it.

"What do I do?" asked the boy.

"Okay, carefully reach out your hand to the light strand. No!! Gino! Don't touch it or it will get thrown off course!" Wallace shook his head to clear it. *Whew … that was close. I should have said that first.*

The young man smiled nervously. "Now, very gently, put your hand *near* the line of energy and tell me what you sense."

All the children were excited, but Gino was the most excited of all at being given the honor of going first. Mrs. Tipperwillow held Aaron close against her body and moved back a bit from the light strings so those chubby fingers couldn't touch part of the web.

Gino reached out again, slowly this time. "Its music, I think," he said, cocking his head to one side. "I get the idea of music, the feeling of the ups and downs, you know?"

"You're right!" Wallace responded. "Now put your hand near that bundle of energy moving through."

"Now I hear music." Gino hummed a bit.

"Can we try?" asked Lateesha.

"Sure. One at a time though," Wallace said seriously, "because if you're all doing it at once, you will just start to feel each other instead of the music."

Gino moved back out of the way so that his friends could take their turns. First Lateesha, then Yoshi and then Jamie took turns at feeling and then hearing the music.

Lateesha looked up at the twenty-year-old. "Wallace, there seems to be energy moving in both directions inside the lines of light."

"That's absolutely right, Teesha," he replied. "You're paying good attention. The music is going to Earth while the energy of the wish for the music is coming from someone *on* Earth."

"But who is sending it from here?" asked Jamie in an excited voice.

"All right, let's follow it back and find out, shall we?" said Tour Guide Wallace.

"Wait a minute!" exclaimed Mrs. Tipperwillow, whose full attention had been on keeping Aaron's hands away from the lights.

"Where's Gino??!"

18

Caught!

"Oh no," said Wallace. "He's out in the web!"

"Jumpin' junebugs!" exclaimed Mrs. Tipperwillow. "Tell that boy not to go somewhere and that's *just* where he heads."

"Do you see him, Mrs. T.?" asked Lateesha, a worried frown forming on her face.

"I think so. He's somehow gotten himself right into the middle of the web of light."

"Will he get hurt?" asked Yoshi.

"It's hard to tell what will happen," Mrs. Tipperwillow replied. "But Wallace and I had better get out there, pronto!" She turned to the young man. "Do you know the way in?"

"I've never been all the way to the center," Wallace said, shaking his head. "I'm frankly surprised that he made it that far."

"Well," said a very concerned sort of cow, "we'd best stay together and watch out for each other so we don't trip a line."

"This is dangerous," Wallace said, and he blew out his breath. "Everything is moving in a type of balance. Disturb one line, and everything moving in that area will be affected, and worse, Gino may actually be thrown all the way to Earth, to the person the energy is going to!"

"Oh, My Gosh!" he continued. "I just realized … if Gino touches one of the bundles that are going to many places at once.…"

"Oh, my *dear*!" exclaimed Mrs. Tipperwillow. "Yoshi, will you please take Aaron?" She handed over the squirming toddler. "Children, please, all of you move quickly and carefully back to the platform and wait for us there. And Yoshi, please make sure Aaron's hands don't touch any light strands on your way out."

She turned back to look at the web. "Stay still, and don't touch anything," she thought to Gino. "We're coming!"

19

Waiting

The girls and Aaron floated quickly up to the platform. Lateesha imagined some soft pillows for them to sit on, but they were too upset to use them. "I'm worried about Wallace," Yoshi said. "He hasn't been here very long, and he said he didn't know the way in."

"Do you see them?" Lateesha asked Jamie.

"Oh yes! See? Follow my finger ... there!"

"Dare!" repeated the toddler, pointing his finger, too, as he tried to pull out from Yoshi's arms.

They stood and waited as the figures of Mrs. Tipperwillow and Wallace got smaller and smaller in the distance.

"Oh, this waiting is awful," remarked Jamie, staring at the web. "And worrying is not going to help anything. When I was worried about being sick, Daddy would always play a game with me. Do you know how to create any games?" she asked, turning to look at her friends.

"Well," answered Yoshi, "I can make simple things like balls and teddy bears and blocks for Aaron, but I've never tried a game."

"I have, once," said Lateesha, taking her eyes off the web to look at Jamie. "I think I can do checkers."

First the checkered board appeared and then the red and the black pieces.

"You did it, Teesh. Good job!" said Yoshi. She imagined some blocks to keep Aaron busy and then teamed up with Jamie to play against Lateesha.

"Hey, I've got an idea," Jamie remarked. "How about we create a leash for Aaron so he doesn't fall or float off the platform?"

Instead of a leash, Lateesha imagined a long strip of cloth. She tied one end to Yoshi's wrist and the other end around the toddler's waist.

Jamie laughed. "We should have done this with Gino."

"But with handcuffs," added Lateesha, shaking her head. The three friends suddenly were quiet, imagining what could be happening out in the web, not only to Gino, but to Wallace and to Mrs. Tipperwillow as well.

The girls played a game while Aaron stacked and restacked his blocks. Finally sensing something, they all looked up.

"Here they come," yelled Yoshi, "all of them!"

"Look at Gino's face, will you?" Jamie said. "He looks so frightened and ashamed."

Wallace and Mrs. Tipperwillow landed on the platform first, with an unusually quiet Gino coming in behind. "Well, I'm glad we got that settled," said the sort of cow, clicking her hooves together. "Gino here was in quite a pickle."

"I wish I had been in a *pickle*," Gino said in a small voice. "That would have been safe."

"Gino was right next to a major transfer point," explained Wallace, still shaking from the experience. "Remember what I was telling you about? If he had touched that big bulge, he might be in a million pieces by now!"

"Well, we don't know *that*," said Mrs. Tipperwillow, taking a crying Gino into her arms. "We simply don't know what might have happened."

Gino cried harder. "I'm so sorry ... so, so sorry," he sobbed.

"I expect, dear boy, that you shall always remember this day. We are all just very grateful that everything turned out okay this time."

"There won't be another time," replied Gino weakly.

"That's good," Mrs. T. replied, "because we love you, Gino. We couldn't stand it if you had gone missing."

The other children joined Gino and Mrs. Tipperwillow for a group hug, with the long arms of Wallace surrounding them all.

20

Going Home

Wallace rode back to Summerland with his old family, glad for the soft, soothing chugging of the train. On the way, he shared with everyone what he hadn't had time to show them.

"Groups of five to fifty people will work on ideas that are put into those energy blobs and sent to Earth. I am part of a group of forty, and we work in several parts of the web thinking up ideas and forming the energy packets. I work with people who were scientists and great thinkers on Earth in different times. I am one of those, if you can believe it." The children nodded.

"There is one energy ball that I especially wanted to show you. I was so excited when I ran across it, and I think you will all find it *quite* interesting."

"Not one you made?" asked Yoshi.

"No, Yoshi. Not one I made, but I was a bit *involved*, you might say."

"Well, what is it Wallace?" asked Jamie, bursting with curiosity. "What did you find?"

"I'd rather wait until I can show you," he replied, smiling slightly and keeping his thoughts carefully guarded.

Just then, the train passed through the healing rainbow. A sleepy sigh went through the entire group as soothing blue light streamed over them. Blue was followed by healing green and warm and happy yellow. Orange brought smiles to their faces, and as they passed through red, they felt strong and safe. They were filled with the peacefulness of purple, and by the time they found themselves standing beside the big striped tent, all of them, even Gino, were feeling much better.

Wallace picked up Yoshi for a goodbye hug. "What a day," Mrs. Tipperwillow sighed, looking at her family. "Thank you for riding back with us, Wallace. We'll look forward to our next trip to see you."

"Let's have a less exciting adventure next time, shall we?" replied the young man, as he looked over Yoshi's shoulder at Gino.

"Okay," said Gino in a very small voice.

21

Creations

Days rolled into weeks or maybe even months or a year. It's so hard to tell in Summerland, where there are no clocks and night comes only when night is created.

After his fateful trip into the web of light, Gino was not quite so wild anymore. Instead of thinking of ten other things and wiggling his fingers in the faces of the other children, the boy actually listened when Mrs. Tipperwillow spoke. Every morning, he created a fire in the fireplace without being asked, and because he was paying closer attention, he was learning to create lots of other things as well.

One morning Gino had given himself a real challenge—making a toy truck for Aaron. "Dang it!" he cursed. The front part of his truck had disappeared just as the back part had shown up.

"Mrs. T., what am I doing wrong?"

"Oh, Child, you have given yourself such a challenge this time. Remember the fires that you make so well. You picture all that a fire is. Try thinking of the whole truck, not just the parts. Think of how a truck moves, the sound a truck makes on the road, how it feels to ride in a truck."

There was a moment of silence. "Oh, my!" exclaimed Mrs. Tipperwillow, as she blushed bright pink. "I meant to say a *smallish* sort of truck."

"Wow! I did it ... a *real* truck!" Gino stared at the massive double cab vehicle pushing out the canvas of the tent. He was doubled over laughing when the girls stepped through the tent flap, Lateesha carrying Aaron this time.

"Where did *that* come from?" Jamie asked.

"It came from my mind," answered Gino with that great Gino smile that no one had seen since the Light Web incident.

"Wow, that's really something!" Lateesha exclaimed. "Can we sit inside?"

"Surely you may," replied Mrs. Tipperwillow. "But before you do, what do you think I should tell you, Gino?"

"Don't turn on the truck and drive it through the side of the tent?" he suggested, wrinkling his nose in that Gino sort of way.

"My thoughts exactly," she agreed. The children piled into the truck and took turns at the wheel. Thankfully, the truck stayed in one place. Then Jamie created the realistic sound of a moving truck.

"Cool, Jamie," said Gino. "You really know how a truck sounds."

Jamie nodded. "Before he got sick, my grandpa had an old banged up truck, and sometimes he took Bobby and me for rides in the country."

Finally, the children jumped down from the truck, and Mrs. Tipperwillow showed Gino how to make it smaller by imagining it sitting in his hand.

"I did it!" he said proudly, staring at the miniature truck in his open hand.

His teacher winked. "You are becoming *quite* the creator, Gino."

Everyone was so glad to see Gino happy again. The girls looked on as Gino showed Aaron his new toy. Then they went outside to finish the project they'd been working on in the meadow.

"I've never seen a beetle that looks like that," Yoshi said to Lateesha and Jamie, who were sitting on the ground by a bright blue sort of beetle they had created.

"It's a Summerland sort of beetle," replied Lateesha as she concentrated. The energy on the beetle's back shivered.

"No, no ... like this!" Jamie said. One long wing showed up on the top of the insect.

Lateesha laughed. "That wing's too long for a beetle ... how about these?" Two perfectly matched shiny blue wings appeared.

"Yes!" all three girls said at once, as the beetle, which was tired of being messed with, wandered off into the tall grass.

"Did you hear something?" asked Lateesha.

"I don't ... yes! It's the mail!" exclaimed Yoshi.

All three girls were up in a flash and running toward the mailbox. Gino hurried from the tent, carrying the toddler.

"What do we have here?" asked Mrs. Tipperwillow as she joined them.

Jamie gave the envelope to her teacher who opened it and read....

If you're ready to try again
Meet me at Light Web Junction

Your Friend Always, Wallace

22

Discovery in the Web

Gino pulled back and pretended to play with the toddler in his arms.

"Gino, dear," said Mrs. Tipperwillow, "it is all right, really. We know that you won't make the same choice this time."

"I just don't know if I can go there," Gino replied, looking at Aaron.

In a kindly voice, Mrs. T. said, "You know what the folks on Earth say. They say that if you fall off a horse the best thing to do is get right back on it. Everything will be fine, Gino. And you have your whole family supporting you. Isn't that right girls?"

"Right!" the three girls said in unison.

"Right!" repeated the little boy in Gino's arms.

"I sense that we should go immediately," continued their teacher. "Do you wish to wear robes or what you have on?"

"These clothes are fine," said Jamie, looking down at her blue jeans and T-shirt. The other children agreed. Almost before they knew it, the family was standing once again on the floating platform, staring at the magnificent field of light that was the Light Web. There was a brilliant flash of blue light, and Wallace appeared. "Is everyone ready?" he asked.

"Yes," answered Gino bravely, and they flew down.

They stopped close to two energy bundles running through the outer portion of the web and took turns sensing what each one contained and what the lines of light they were moving through contained as well. The first had something to do with computers. It was a new idea that someone on Earth would be receiving. It all looked very confusing to the children, and they shook their heads and looked at Wallace with raised eyebrows.

"I don't have any idea what that one means," he said, "but it will make perfect sense to the person on Earth who receives it."

The second light bundle seemed to be about jewelry designs. "Wow, these are really great," said Lateesha, who could see the jewelry the clearest of anybody, "especially that first necklace. I'd sure like to have one like it."

Suddenly it was around her neck. Mrs. Tipperwillow winked. "No harm in that."

"Uh … Mrs. Tipperwillow.…"

"Yes, Wallace?"

"We're really not supposed to take anything from the web … sorry."

"Oh, of course! I had forgotten."

Lateesha sighed. "It's all right." The necklace disappeared.

"Now," said the young man, rubbing a hand across his small beard, "let's find what I wanted to show you. It's part way to the center and looks to be big, because it contains lots and lots of pictures."

Oh no, thought Gino.

"It's all right, dear boy," said Mrs. T., feeling his worry. "We'll stay together for this one. Won't we, Children?" They nodded. Even little Aaron said "Yes" in a serious voice, looking up into Mrs. Tipperwillow's eyes. Snoody, in case you were wondering, was sound asleep around Mrs. Tipperwillow's neck. Once, not long before, Aaron was scratched when he grabbed at the little creature's foot, and since then he wisely had been leaving the snoode alone.

Gino stayed close to his teacher as the family moved cautiously out into the web of light following Wallace. They stopped at a large energy bundle. The children felt a little odd here, as if.…

"Okay," said the young man, breaking into their thoughts, "one by one, put your fingers near this line of energy. Yes … there!" He motioned to Yoshi, who was first this time.

"What? This feels really familiar somehow … Summerland?" she gasped. All of the children took a turn at feeling the energies and agreed.

"Somehow, this is about … *us?*" Jamie asked, shaking her head.

Mrs. Tipperwillow chortled, "Oh, Wallace, how very clever of you to find it."

"Now," he said, "one by one, put your fingers near the big energy ball. Let's wait until you have all tried it, and then you can each tell me what you saw. Okay?"

"Okay," they repeated.

Jamie was the first to speak. "I saw birch trees and the red bird, my first meeting with Mrs. Tipperwillow, cotton candy, and then meeting all of you."

Wallace asked, "How about you Gino?"

"I saw the snowboat and our trip to the snow that day Mrs. T. became a snow cow and we met with our guardian angels!"

Yoshi said, "I saw Aaron showing up and our trip to space."

"And I got a feeling of those things, but something else, too," added Lateesha. "I got a name."

"A name, child?" asked Mrs. Tipperwillow, as if she knew something.

"The name is … *Crystal?*"

"Almost, dear … *Krista* is what you mean, I think."

"And I see the ocean, Mrs. T., and surfers in the water." Lateesha shook her head in confusion. "What does *that* mean?"

"My goodness, Teesha … you have looked so far that I feel you would make a very fine web worker one day if you choose to do so." Wallace looked intently at the girl and nodded.

"You do all remember when I told you about being in a story, don't you?" asked the magical sort of cow, as she looked from one child to another.

Gino asked, "You mean we really *are?*"

"…. Of course! Why would I make that up? And Krista is the name of the woman on Earth who is writing down this story right now, even as we speak."

"Ooh!" they all said at once. The children floated in silence as they thought about this.

"What about the ocean?" Lateesha asked finally.

"Oh, my very perceptive child, this one is easy. As this woman writes, she occasionally looks up and out her window and sees … guess what?"

Lateesha laughed. "She sees the ocean and surfers in the water."

"Yes, indeed, she does. And you know the funniest thing of all?" asked their teacher, chuckling. "Here! Feel this!" One by one the children put their hands where Mrs. Tipperwillow showed them.

"Hah!" Gino laughed. "I know what it is. The funniest thing is that this Krista person thinks we are made up. She doesn't think we are *real.*"

All the children hooted with laughter at this idea … even little Aaron. Then Gino (it's *always* Gino) began poking Lateesha. "Are you real?" he asked playfully.

"Are *you*?" And Lateesha poked him right back. Then Yoshi poked Jamie and Jamie….

"For goodness sakes, Children!" exclaimed Mrs. Tipperwillow. "Not here!!"

Book Three
From Here to Earth
And Back Again

1

Choices

It was a warm, Spring-like day in the spirit world. A light breeze blew through the golden sky and across the green meadow and carried with it a score of yellow and blue butterflies. At the center of the meadow stood a large red and white striped tent, which was home to Mrs. Daisy Tipperwillow, a magical sort of cow, and her family of children. The tent was empty.

But on a rounded hill overlooking the meadow, a large blue and white plaid blanket had been spread. On the blanket sat Lateesha, who had been nine when she had first arrived in Summerland, Gino and Jamie, who had been eight, and Yoshi, who had just turned seven. Aaron, a happy toddler who had passed to spirit when he was only one-and-a-half, sat close to Mrs. Tipperwillow. The sort of cow reached up and absently touched the snoode, that white furry creature the children called Snoody, which was curled around her shoulders and half-asleep.

Frustration showed clearly in the faces of the older children. Masses of crumpled papers billowed around them like lumpy clouds. These papers contained the discarded ideas of places to visit during their tour of Earth. They had been working on their lists for what seemed like hours and were getting nowhere. Aaron copied what they were doing, shuffling and crumpling his own papers with a serious expression on his round face.

"Ha!" Gino exclaimed, with a glint coming into his eye. "Watch this!" Quickly folding one of his papers into an airplane, he threw it skyward and watched it soar. Laughing, Lateesha followed suit. Then Yoshi and Jamie joined in. Soon half a dozen planes were whirling through the air. But unlike the short flights of paper planes on Earth, these did fancy dips and spirals, all guided by the children's thoughts. Aaron clapped his hands, enjoying the show.

"Well, look at you!" exclaimed Mrs. Tipperwillow. "What fun you are having! Perhaps we should postpone our trip to Earth and just fly airplanes all day. What do you think?" All of the planes except one drifted down into the children's waiting hands. Gino's plane continued to loop in the golden sky above.

Lateesha gave a frustrated sigh as she smoothed out her paper plane. "There are just so many places we want to visit, Mrs. T. We don't know how to choose."

Jumping into the air, Gino rose ten feet over the heads of the others, grabbing wildly at his plane as it spiraled around him. With a triumphant shout, he captured it and floated down to join his friends. No one seemed to notice.

"Let's try out a new way," suggested Mrs. Tipperwillow. "Lateesha, give me a color."

"Pink!" blurted the girl, and the colored stars bounced around her braided head. "I like bright pink!"

"The color of love," mused Mrs. Tipperwillow.

Lateesha's dark brown eyes darted to Gino as their teacher asked, "How about you, Gino?"

The boy popped both arms in the air. "I pick orange!"

"You and your bright energy, Gino ... of course it would be orange."

"And you, Yoshi?"

"I'll take green," the seven-year-old replied quietly.

"That's a very healing color, Yoshi. And what color would you like, Miss Jamie? Will your choice be, perhaps, storyteller blue?"

"You know me pretty well, Mrs. T. I was just going to say that."

"Now let's see. We have pink, orange, green, and blue. Aaron dear, you get a choice, too." Colored cards suddenly appeared between her hooves, and she held them up. "Which color do you want?"

"Popal!" the toddler said, as he grabbed for the purple card.

"Very good," Mrs. T. replied. "Who has been teaching Aaron his colors?"

"I have," Yoshi answered proudly. "He knows nine colors already."

Mrs. Tipperwillow smiled warmly at the girl, who had taken on the role of big sister to Aaron after her best friend Wallace had left them in order to grow up.

"Aaron, you have chosen the color of peace," the sort of cow continued. "Now let's see, we have orange, purple, green, pink and blue."

With a wave of her hoof, five colored squares of paper appeared in the sky overhead. The children watched as the papers began twisting down like a dizzy kaleidoscope and formed a circle as they landed in the nearby grass. As one, the papers rose off the ground and started spinning until one colored square popped out. It floated down to land at Yoshi's feet. The rest continued to spin overhead.

"Our first color is green," said Mrs. Tipperwillow cheerfully, "so the very first country we will visit is ... Japan!"

Yoshi looked down at the green square of paper, where *Japan* was printed in large letters. She looked up into her teacher's large eyes. "That was just one of my places. How did you choose it?"

"Oh, no, my dear, *you* chose it. The answer was in your heart all along. So often the mind confuses things, you see."

The sky blue paper twisted down and landed next to Jamie.

"Well, Miss Reed, please *read* us what your paper says."

Jamie ran a hand through her curly brown hair. "It says London, England. I wanted to see Buckingham Palace and the changing of the guards, just like my grandpa told me about. He said the guards never smile."

"I bet I can make them smile!" piped Gino, making wiggly spider fingers.

Mrs. Tipperwillow chuckled. "We'll see about *that*, Gino!"

Next the orange paper spiraled down and landed next to Gino, whose eyebrows shot up as he read *Venice, Italy*. In his mind, he saw the faded picture of his Italian grandpa, the one he had never met.

The bright pink paper landed beside Lateesha. It read *Ghana*. "That's a country in West Africa, on the coast," she explained. "It's where my mom's family came from, and that's why I have such lovely dark skin."

For a moment the girl got a faraway look in her eyes, remembering her mother's words as she would tuck her into bed each night. "I'm the chocolate syrup and Daddy's the milk. And that makes you our sweet cocoa … dee-licious!" Then Mom would kiss her cheek and turn out the light.

Lateesha broke out of her memories as the final square of paper floated to the ground. "And now just one more, and it is your purple paper, Aaron," said the magical sort of cow. "It says *Jerusalem*. That is the city in Israel where you lived for one and a half years before coming to Summerland." Aaron nodded as if he understood.

"As you can see, Children, all of your choices are about visiting where either you or your parents, your grandparents, or even, in the case of Lateesha, where your great-great grandparents came from."

"But Mrs. T-e-e-e," Gino began in a whiny voice, "what I *really* meant to say is that I want to visit one of those big theme parks with all the cool rides."

Mrs. Tipperwillow chuckled. "Perhaps, Gino, we can fit in just such a place for you at the end of our great adventures, as a final *hoorah*, you might say. You other children wouldn't want to spend a day at a *boring* theme park, would you?"

The three girls answered in unison, "We do want to go, too!"

"So," Mrs. T. said, circling her small hoof in mid-air, "now we have our list. First we explore Japan, then on to London, England, then to Venice, Italy, to the country of Ghana in West Africa, and finally to Jerusalem, Israel. Then if you are not *too* tired," Mrs. Tipperwillow teased, "we will visit one of the grand amusement parks somewhere in the U.S. of A."

A baby backpack appeared on the lawn. Gently removing Snoody from her shoulders, Mrs. T. secured him in the small pack at her waist. Only his furry head remained visible. She blinked her eyes twice.

The entire group, including Mrs. Tipperwillow, was dressed in blue jeans, pale blue sweatshirts, and running shoes. Of course there were no running shoes for Mrs. T., since she still had her hooves. On the front of each sweatshirt there was an image of a white crane taking flight. The bird flew from the lower left hem of each sweatshirt diagonally to the neckline and disappeared, reappearing at the bottom to fly up again. Mrs. T. chuckled at her clever creation.

Yoshi looked around at her friends' shirts and then down at her own. "In Japan these birds are s'posed to mean good luck," she said in her small voice. "But they're just making me *dizzy*."

Mrs. Tipperwillow clapped her hooves, and the birds stopped moving. "There! That's a bit less confusing," she said cheerfully. "Come, Aaron!" The toddler floated smoothly into the child carrier, which floated up and fastened itself over Mrs. T's shoulders. "Now, ready! Set! *Go!*"

The Summerland family rose into the air as one and then felt the pull of an invisible force which sped them through the sky. Moments later they found themselves hovering next to a familiar portal. It was a heavy wooden door with the word "Back" in gold lettering on its frame. Its golden knob turned by itself, and the door swung slowly open.

2

Passing Through

Mrs. Tipperwillow and Aaron, followed by Yoshi, Gino, Jamie, and Lateesha, stepped through the open door to find themselves standing on a sidewalk in a busy, noisy city. It was nighttime, and brightly colored lights were flashing from buildings on both sides of the street and reflecting off wet pavement. People were hurrying in all directions.

"This is *Japan*, Mrs. T?" Yoshi asked, shaking her head. "This doesn't look like what Mommy told me about … no, not at all."

"This is Tokyo, the biggest city in Japan, Yoshi, and the city where you were born. I thought we would take a look here first."

The group was standing on a street corner and looking around just as the traffic light changed. A crowd of people began crossing the street toward them … and passed right *through* them.

"Woo, that was weird!" Jamie sighed, as the last of the pedestrians went in and out of her.

"Wasn't it just, Jamie?" Mrs. Tipperwillow agreed. "Now tell me, what did you all feel when that happened?"

"Nothing, Mrs. T." answered Gino casually.

Lateesha looked at Gino and raised her eyebrows. "Well, I felt something."

"Me, too," added Jamie.

"So how about you, Yoshi … did you feel anything?" Mrs. Tipperwillow asked. The girl was looking around herself in confusion. Tears were forming in her eyes.

Oh dear, I forgot. Children, let's move to some place quiet where we can share our impressions, shall we?"

146

Mrs. T. snatched up Yoshi just as she began to cry. High into the air they flew until the city was just specks of light beneath them. "Now into the new day!" proclaimed the sort of cow, and they streaked toward the horizon. Pink light began to show in the sky. The sun rose. It was mid-morning when they stopped several minutes later.

"Are we still in Japan?" Yoshi asked in a small voice.

"Why, yes, I do believe we are," Mrs. Tipperwillow answered. "Remember, everyone, that we in spirit are not bound by the rules of time as people are here on Earth, just as we are light as a feather and can fly. I thought it might be fun to pass from night to day. Did you like it?"

"Yes, that's...."

"Cool," replied Jamie and Lateesha at the same time, turning to look at Gino just as the word escaped his lips.

Mrs. Tipperwillow laughed. "Now, let's find a quiet place to land, shall we?" They drifted toward the ground and touched down in a grassy field below a tall snow covered mountain.

"I've seen that mountain in pictures," said Jamie.

"Yes," added Lateesha, "that's...."

"Mount Fuji!" finished Yoshi.

"Fuji," repeated Aaron, reaching toward the mountain with his small hands.

The blue and white blanket appeared overhead and floated to the grass where it settled. "Let's sit and talk a bit," Mrs. T. suggested. She landed and put Yoshi and then the snoode down next to her. "Then we'll explore some more."

Aaron floated out of the backpack and to the center of the blanket as the others got settled. The snoode climbed into Lateesha's lap and squeaked to be petted.

"Can we explore the mountain?" piped Gino, already tired of sitting.

"Yes, we may, Gino." He jumped up. "But let's talk awhile first." Gino quickly sat back down, took off his shoes, and began playing with his toes.

"Okay, Jamie. You're first. What did you feel when the people on the Tokyo street passed through you?"

Jamie looked at over at Yoshi, who was leaning into Mrs. Tipperwillow's side, and then at her teacher. "It was like a cool breeze," she answered, "like a breeze that passed right through me. It didn't *hurt*." She looked again at Yoshi with a question in her eyes.

"Lateesha, what were your impressions?"

The girl scratched behind the ears of the little creature as she replied, "It was like I could almost see a difference in the air. I could feel the pattern of it."

"Could you draw it for me, please?"

"Sure, I think so." A piece of paper and pen appeared floating in front of her and she grabbed them. She drew a wavy pattern on the paper and turned it around to show her friends.

"Hmmm," said Mrs. Tipperwillow. "That is very interesting, indeed!"

"You saw *that*?" Gino teased.

"Not really, Gino. I *felt* that," Teesha replied, looking at him hard.

"Gino dear, I bet if you think about it, you did feel something," coaxed Mrs. Tipperwillow.

"Yeah, that air-type feeling, I guess. Can we go now, Mrs. T.?" He wiggled his legs.

"My dear, you have grasshopper legs today." She pointed to a spot a few feet away. "Why don't you go over there and bounce up and down for a minute or two while we finish sharing."

"Okay!" Quick as anything the boy was twenty feet away and bouncing. He bounced higher and higher.

"Yoshi, did you feel the people pass through you?"

"Yes, I did," the seven-year-old replied with a frown. "I felt that air thing like Jamie said, but I also felt the hurry. Somebody was late and upset about it. And somebody else was thinking bad thoughts about a...." Yoshi's voice trailed off, and she shook her head.

"Do you feel like talking about it, Yoshi?" Mrs. T. asked.

"I don't want to," replied the girl stubbornly.

"Very well. We all respect your choice ... don't we, Children?"

"It's all right," Jamie said, looking at her younger friend. "You don't have to talk about anything you don't want to."

"We're just sorry something hurt you ... that's all," added Lateesha.

"Thank you," Yoshi whispered, climbing into Mrs. Tipperwillow's lap.

"Now everyone.... Oh, no! Not again! Gino ... where *are* you?!"

3

Mt. Fuji

"I'm up here!" Gino shouted clear as day in everyone's head at once.

"Look! Up there!" exclaimed Jamie, pointing, "… that speck on Mt. Fuji. See, he's waving!"

"Gino," said Mrs. Tipperwillow firmly, "will you please join us immediately."

Like a bird with wings spread wide, Gino swooped down in zigzags and landed beside them.

Mrs. Tipperwillow shook her head. "I believe I said *bounce*, Gino."

"Uh, yeah, you did for sure, Mrs. T., and I was, but one bounce got me really high. Then a big wind came out of nowhere and blew me right into the side of that mountain. Maybe it was a *typhoon*."

"A typhoon, is it? The sky is awfully blue for one of those. Gino, it would be best if we all stayed together now."

"I'll stay close, Mrs. T. I just love to explore, that's all."

"I know you do, dear boy, but sometimes there are very good reasons for not going off on your own."

"But what could happen here?" asked Lateesha, scratching Snoody behind his ears. "We can fly. We can hear each other's thoughts. And the people on Earth can't even see us."

"Let's just leave this for now. There is the possibility of danger but not if we all stay together," replied Mrs. Tipperwillow mysteriously. With a click of her hooves, the snoode rose into the air and floated over to rest around her shoulders.

The children were very curious, and questions began to fly from their mouths, but their teacher would have none of it. She smiled at her wild child. "Gino, I would like to give *you* the honor of carrying Aaron this time," she stated, leaving no room for argument.

The girls giggled as the toddler floated into the pack and onto Gino's shoulders. "What are you laughing at?" Gino asked, tightening the straps.

"Better than a leash," Lateesha whispered to Jamie as the group lifted off, heading toward the mountain.

Moments later they were at the base of Mt. Fuji. "Do any of you know why this mountain is so perfectly shaped?" asked Mrs. T. in her "teachery" voice.

"I know! I know!" said Yoshi, very much her happy self again. "It's a cone volcano. Daddy told me that once lava pushed really hard from the middle of the Earth and pushed up the land to become a mountain." She put the palms of her hands together and raised them above her head to demonstrate. "When the volcano blew, lava flowed down the sides real fast to make it that shape!" She wiggled her fingers as she lowered her arms to her sides.

"Mommy said this mountain is *magic*," Yoshi continued in a hushed voice. "She said that people come here to meditate, and they have *visions*. That means they see things that other people can't see."

"It does feel different here," commented Lateesha, "almost like bees buzzing." Gino rolled his eyes but stopped as he noticed Jamie, Yoshi, and Mrs. Tipperwillow nod in agreement.

The family floated along in the warm spring air until they came to a wide waterfall, which fell like a shimmering curtain over the cliff beneath it. "This is beautiful!" whispered Yoshi. Gino wanted to fly through the water, but carrying little Aaron stopped him cold.

They drifted above a narrow trail and came upon several groups of hikers making their way slowly up the mountain. Rounding a bend, the children spotted an old man with white hair sitting on a small mat. The man was wearing a dark red robe, and his eyes were half-closed.

"Oh, ho!" said you know who and floated right over. Gino put one hand to the man's ear and said in a deep voice, "I am the gho-o-ost of Christmas pa-a-st."

The old man's head jerked. His eyes opened. He took a deep breath and closed them again.

"That was very funny, Gino," said Mrs. T., who was not smiling at all. "But you are missing something important here." Mrs. Tipperwillow drew the children to her. "This special man has something to show us. I would like you each to shift your attention *now!*" With the tip of her hoof, she reached over and touched Gino in the middle of his forehead.

"Wow!" exclaimed the boy. "What's *that?*"

As their teacher touched each child's forehead in turn, the man and the air around him were transformed into colored lights. Rose, green, blue, purple, and gold light spun around his meditating form like a cocoon. Sparks of white light encircled the colors and began spinning up into the sky like a whirlwind.

Jamie whispered, "Mrs. T., is this the aura you were telling me about when my grandpa came home?"

"Indeed, Jamie … indeed," replied Mrs. Tipperwillow, so completely taken by the sight herself that she could hardly speak.

The children watched as more and more white entered the old man's energy, spinning faster and faster.

"What … what's that, Mrs. T.?" Gino asked, edging closer to his teacher, his eyes wide.

Oh, there you are, spoke a voice in Gino's head. *Christmas past, is it?*

Gino sensed a smile. "Who's that?" he asked, looking at the man whose lips had not moved.

Who do you think it is?

"What is it, Gino?" asked Jamie.

"Don't you hear the voice?" His friends shook their heads.

I believe we have a field trip here, if I'm not mistaken, stated the loud voice in all the children's heads at once and in Mrs. Tipperwillow's, too.

"My apologies for interrupting your meditations, Master Matsuyama," replied Mrs. Tipperwillow, blushing.

No need to trouble yourself, Madam. This gives me needed practice switching dimensions. I am preparing to pass to the spirit world. This will occur tomorrow afternoon at four o'clock exactly.

"You can choose when you're going to die?" Yoshi asked.

I have decided to choose, young one. I have learned the way and have been practicing.

The children stared wide-eyed as a torpedo of white light totally surrounded the man. *What you see now is my beginning course. From here, my spirit will pull free of the body, and rainbows of light will form around what's left. Some have called this the rainbow body.*

"Wow!" exclaimed Gino. "That's so totally cool!"

Yes, replied the voice, *and you, Madam, have your hands full with this one.*

Now it was Gino's turn to blush. Mrs. Tipperwillow tenderly put a hoof on top of the boy's hand. "Gino has a lovely heart, for which I am always grateful."

I can well sense that, the old man replied. *I must go now, but perhaps we will meet again on the other side.*

"We'd like that, wouldn't we, Children?" asked the children's teacher, as the energy surrounding the man changed. His aura showed more colors and moved into a range of soft blues and purples.

The family flew from the mountain. Soon they were relaxing on their blanket beneath a grove of blossoming cherry trees. Aaron was asleep next to Gino, who was unusually quiet as he lay on his back looking up at the pink flowers and at the blue sky beyond.

4

Festivals

As the children rested, Mrs. Tipperwillow looked over at Yoshi. A tiny tear appeared in the corner of her eye. She wiped it with the tip of one hoof. She said softly, "One thing that all Japanese children anticipate with excitement is the many festivals that occur here throughout the year."

Yoshi turned her head to look at her teacher. "Yes! Mommy said that when she was growing up, she loved the festival days best of all."

"We are blessed," continued Mrs. Tipperwillow, "because time is not an obstacle to us. Just as we passed from night to day in moments, so can we pass from fall to winter to spring to summer in whatever order we wish and visit as many festivals as we desire."

The older children sat up. "You mean," began Lateesha, "that we can go from a summer festival to a winter festival, just like that?"

"Just like that!" said the magical sort of cow. Without any notice, the backpack was resting on Gino's shoulders with Aaron tucked inside. And a moment later, the Summerland family was standing in softly falling snow. Warmly dressed children wearing parkas, snow pants, and boots were running through the drifts of whiteness. Others walked with parents along paths through a large park.

Mrs. Tipperwillow chuckled. "Welcome, my friends, to the Sapporo Snow Festival!" With a click of her hooves, the children were dressed in matching red snowsuits with tall black boots and red and purple-striped stocking caps. "I don't think you'll get lost too easily in these," chortled Mrs. Tipperwillow, who was now wearing a fashionable long, red wool coat and hat.

Through the thick flakes of falling snow, large white shapes were barely visible.

"Look! Snow sculptures!" exclaimed Lateesha.

Jamie pointed. "Look over there. It's a castle!"

"And look at that one!" Gino yelled. "It's a giant robot!"

"Animals!" said Yoshi. "See ... a bear, a tiger, and a wolf!"

"I'll call you back in a while, Children," said Mrs. T., adjusting her hat to fit over her ears. "Thank you for carrying Aaron, Gino."

"It's okay!" he yelled as he rushed toward the robot.

The colors of sunset were glistening on the snow when Mrs. Tipperwillow finally called the children back from their exploring. And together they flew into summer.

The family landed and found themselves in a huge grassy field that was crowded with people. Their winter outfits disappeared and were instantly replaced by clothes of shiny silk.

The girls and their teacher wore matching red and yellow flowered jackets with long red pants. In contrast, the boys' pants and jackets were black, with a red, fire-breathing dragon wrapping around from the front to the back of each jacket. The children looked down at their new clothes and ran their hands over the silky material.

"These traditional jackets are called *hapi* coats," said the fashionable sort of cow, "and we are now visiting the Tokoshima Dance Festival!"

Music began over loudspeakers. Sixty women walked into a large open area and stopped in a circle. The Summerland children laughed as they noted that the women were wearing the very same outfit that Mrs. Tipperwillow and the girls wore. Mrs. Tipperwillow chuckled.

A sort of dance began as the women moved slowly around the circle, matching their movements to one another's.

Yoshi clapped her hands with excitement. "My mom told me all about this festival. It was one of her favorites of the whole year! This is the Harvest Dance, and Mommy even taught me the steps. See how they pretend to till the field and plant the seeds?"

Yoshi began copying the dancers' movements, and soon the other children and their teacher joined in. Gino followed along for a bit but quickly shifted to his own pantomime of stomping grapes and eating corn on the cob.

All of the children except Yoshi began copying Gino, who had moved on to scrubbing himself in the shower.

Yoshi stopped at "harvesting the wheat" and stared at her friends, who were now pretending to throw soap at each other. "You guys aren't taking this very seriously," she said.

Mrs. Tipperwillow patted Yoshi's hand. "My dear, it's up to us to finish the dance without these sillies." And they did.

Lateesha took a turn carrying Aaron as the Summerland family flew into August to greet a brilliant pink and orange sunset. They landed at the edge of a large lake and waited for nightfall with the many people who had gathered. Finally darkness came. Hundreds of tiny lanterns, which each held a candle, were launched from the shore and floated out onto the lake until it glittered like stars.

"I remember what this is called!" Yoshi said in an excited voice. "This is the Lantern Festival. Those lanterns are carrying dreams and blessings to the ancestors," she said, remembering her mother's words.

"Right you are, Yoshi," Mrs. Tipperwillow said, as she gazed out over the rippling water. The group watched silently until the last light had flickered out.

Returning to daylight, the Summerland tourists visited an ancient Shinto temple, which was decorated in bright patterns. The open-sided temple was located at the center of a large garden. There were meandering gravel paths, carefully trimmed evergreen trees, rock formations, and even a little waterfall pouring into a large reflecting pool.

While the girls were quite impressed with the beauty of this place, Gino, being Gino, began to fidget.

5

Sumo

"Japan is pretty and all, I guess," Gino said, "and this temple and garden are okay. But isn't there something a boy like me would be interested in?"

"Like what, Gino?" Mrs. Tipperwillow cocked her cowish head, one ear twitching.

"Well, I'd like to see sumo wrestlers. They're from Japan, aren't they?"

"Oh, my, yes, they most certainly are. They represent a long and venerable tradition here in Japan."

"Could we see a sumo wrestler, Mrs. T.? Could we see one of those?"

Jamie and Lateesha raised their eyebrows and turned to look at Mrs. Tipperwillow to gauge her reaction. Only Jamie noticed the tiny glint come into her teacher's eyes.

"My boy, I think that would be a *fine* idea." The magical sort of cow clicked her hooves. There was a wiggle in the air.

Gino's head remained the same. But his body! From the shoulders down Gino *became* a sumo wrestler, complete with large muscled arms and legs, a huge round belly, and a black loin cloth with a wide band under his middle.

The boy looked down at himself and patted his belly as if it might explode any second. Then the girls and Mrs. Tipperwillow did explode … in laughter!

"I knew you were up to something," Jamie said, when she finally caught her breath enough to speak.

"Mrs. T-e-e-e-e!" Gino wailed, poking at one beefy arm with a chubby forefinger.

"My dear boy," snuffed Mrs. Tipperwillow, wiping a tear of laughter from the corner of her eye, "I thought you might like to explore what it feels like to *be* a sumo wrestler. Tell me, do you feel strong?"

Gino shook his head. "I don't know. Will you change me back now?"

A huge barbell appeared on the ground. On the bar was written "100 Pounds."

"Why don't you just try to lift this weight," suggested the sort of cow, with a winning smile.

The laughter died out as the girls looked from the barbell to Gino and back.

"I don't know if I can, Mrs. T." Gino checked out the muscles in his arms. They seemed solid enough. "Okay, I'll try." He tested the weight with one hand. "It feels heavy."

"Sumo wrestlers work long and hard to develop their size and strength, so take it slowly," Mrs. Tipperwillow advised. "Remember also that the center of your power is in your belly. Concentrate your strength there."

Gino squatted with his legs wide apart as he had seen weight lifters do on television and put his hands under the barbell. With a jerk, he began lifting, his legs and arms straining.

"You can do it Gino!" encouraged Lateesha.

The boy Sumo concentrated on his belly as his muscles did the work. Finally with his face bright red, he managed to raise the barbell over his head.

"Good job, Gino!" Lateesha said, as Gino carefully lowered the barbell to the ground.

"Incredible!" exclaimed Jamie with a laugh.

"Wow!" Yoshi added. "You're *so* strong."

"That was very nicely done," Mrs. Tipperwillow said, clapping her hooves.

Gino smiled proudly. A moment later he was his own right size and shape. "I like being me-e-e-e!" he shouted, leaping into the air.

6

Rice

The Summerland tourists floated through the park until they came to a broad expanse of lawn. Their blanket appeared overhead and drifted to the ground.

"How would you all like some dinner?" Mrs. Tipperwillow asked as they landed. She pointed to the center of the blanket, and a feast of Japanese foods wiggled into existence.

There were plates of something Mrs. T. called *gyoza*, which were noodle wrappers filled with ground pork and cabbage. There was puffy fried shrimp and vegetable tempura, chicken teriyaki with its sweet smelling brown sauce, and lots and lots of rice.

"No beef?" asked Gino, with a little smirk.

"Not even sort of beef today!" replied Mrs. T. with a wink.

Chopsticks and blue plates with scalloped edges appeared before each child, and the food was passed around. Lateesha and Yoshi already knew how to use chopsticks, so they showed Jamie and Gino how to hold them.

"This stuff is slippery!" Gino complained moments later, as the teriyaki fell back on his plate for the third time. Deciding that the chopsticks were better for poking than eating, he jabbed Jamie, who jabbed him right back. Soon they were having a brilliant sword fight. Finally they both gave up on chopsticks altogether and joined Aaron, who was eating with his fingers.

"This food is delicious," mumbled Gino around a mouthful, "but there's *way* too much rice." He began making a rice ball with his hands, and soon his friends were doing the same thing.

"Hmmm," said Mrs. Tipperwillow.

Gino yelled "Catch!" And the play was on. The girls and Gino were off the blanket in a flash. Rice balls were flying everywhere. Soon all the children had rice stuck in their hair and on their clothes ... everyone except Aaron and Mrs. Tipperwillow, that is.

Mrs. T. chuckled. "You children are beginning to look like rice balls yourselves." With a clap of her hooves, Gino, Yoshi, Jamie, and Lateesha were instantly covered from head to foot in rice with just their faces sticking out. "Now," said Mrs. Tipperwillow, as giant chopsticks appeared between her hooves (and holding them was quite a challenge in itself), "which one of you delicious rice balls am I going to eat up first?" She clicked her chopsticks together and headed toward Jamie.

"We'll protect you, Jamie!" yelled Lateesha, and she and the other two rice balls jumped their teacher. Soon they were all rolling on the ground, smearing rice everywhere. Of course, Mrs. Tipperwillow was just as messy and laughing just as hard as the children.

Aaron was so intent on making his rice ball that he hardly noticed the pandemonium taking place a few feet away. And the snoode was curled up by Aaron's side, sound asleep as usual.

Finally, shaking rice from her clothing and picking more from her antler, Mrs. Tipperwillow asked, "How about it, Children? Are you all ready for a bit of rest at home before our next adventure?"

The children quickly agreed, and almost before they knew it, they were floating down to land in the flower-speckled meadow beside their own striped tent.

A gentle fire was burning in the fireplace as the children, who were all cleaned up and in brightly patterned pajamas, clambered into their bunk beds, sunk into their soft pillows, and fell fast asleep.

"Nighty-night, and sleep sweet!" Mrs. Tipperwillow whispered as she floated out of the tent. "So far, so good," she thought to herself, as she rose and drifted away into the nighttime sky.

7

Changeling

Morning dawned in Summerland. All but one of the children still slept. Feeling very odd upon awakening, the eight-year-old boy got out of bed and stood by the empty fireplace.

Alacazam, he thought. Nothing happened. He turned and moved silently toward the bunk beds.

"Yoshi," he whispered. "Wake up, will you?"

"Huh, what is it?" mumbled the girl, who was still half dreaming. She turned over to look. "What ... *who*?" Yoshi got out of bed quickly as she kept her eye on the boy. "Mrs. Tipperwillow, come quick!"

In a flash, the magical cow was standing next to Yoshi. The other children awakened, wiped their sleepy morning eyes, and floated out of their beds to the floor.

"Well, hello, Aaron," Mrs. Tipperwillow said. "Welcome to middle childhood."

Yoshi's mouth dropped open. "Aaron ... is that really you?"

"Of course it is. Don't you recognize me, Yoshi?"

"You're so big ... and your hair got so dark. But ... but ... how did this happen?" Yoshi stammered.

"All I remember is wishing I could grow up so I could play with all of you better. It's hard being so little. Then I woke up like *this*!" Aaron patted his chest.

Yoshi choked out a sob and rushed into her teacher's arms. "Oh, Mrs. Tipperwillow!" she wailed.

Hugging the sobbing girl, the sort of cow looked fondly over her head at Aaron. *Yoshi is just surprised, that's all. She has been through a lot of changes recently, and now has to get used to another one. Don't worry. She'll be just fine.*

"Aaron," said their teacher aloud, "why don't you go outside with the other children and try out those new long legs. I bet they run fast!"

The new eight-year-old looked at the girl who had been his big sister. "Okay, but … Yoshi, please don't be sad."

Yoshi cried even harder. Shaking his head Aaron headed outside with the others. Their pajamas were replaced by play clothes as they stepped through the tent flap.

Gino was beside himself with excitement. "Another boy, just my age … yes!" he yelled and challenged Aaron and the girls to a game of running, flying tag.

Because Aaron was just getting used to his long legs and because he'd never flown before on his own, the new eight-year-old was "it" until his friends began moving more slowly so that he could catch them.

Finally leaving the game behind, Aaron lifted higher above the meadow to get his first clear look at Summerland. Jamie floated up to join him. "Pretty, isn't it?" she asked.

The boy looked down at their red and white striped tent, at the yellow flowers surrounding it, and at the multicolored rose bush by the entrance. His gaze moved to the striped green fields leading up into the hills and on to the snow covered mountains, which glistened in the golden morning light. Turning in the other direction, he spied other hills leading to a long white sand beach with an aqua ocean beyond.

"It's beautiful," he agreed.

As Lateesha and Gino continued to chase around in the sky below, Jamie told Aaron about their trip to the seashore and about everything that had happened on that magical day … about riding on the dolphins and all the rest.

"I hope I get to go there," Aaron said.

"Well, of course you will," Jamie assured him, just as Teesha and Gino rose up to join them.

"Mrs. T. wants us back at the tent now," Gino said, scratching his nose.

Yoshi, red-eyed, still sniffling a bit, but with a smile on her face, greeted Aaron as he entered the tent. "I'm sorry if I scared you," she said softly. "I was having so much fun being your big sister, and it's not so long ago that Wallace left us. But I'm okay now. Did you have fun flying?"

"Yeah, it was fun," replied the boy, reaching out to take Yoshi's hand in his own. "I love being able to move better and to say what I'm feeling. Now I can say thank you for taking such good care of me, Yoshi. You were a good big sister."

Tears formed in Yoshi's eyes again. "You're even taller than me now."

"Just a little bit," Aaron said. "I want to thank the rest of you, too. Gino, I love the truck you made for me. When I woke up this morning, it was still on my pillow from yesterday when I was a baby."

"I can show you how to create your own things," said Gino proudly. "It isn't hard, really."

"Okay!" The new eight-year-old was grinning from ear to ear.

"There is much we can do today," said Mrs. Tipperwillow. "It's up to you, Aaron. We can continue our journeys to Earth, or we can stay around here a little longer so you can get used to your new size. Before you decide, how about a breakfast of hot pancakes and syrup?"

The table was already set with a bouquet of yellow daisies at the center and platters with two large stacks of pancakes at either end. There was a slab of butter on a little tray, and there were small pitchers of different flavored syrups; blackberry, strawberry, coconut, and maple. A cow-shaped pitcher contained milk.

Aaron enjoyed himself so much, laughing and talking with the others as they ate, that Yoshi's sadness just dissolved itself in his happiness.

8

Detour

As the children finished their breakfast and pushed back their chairs, Mrs. Tipperwillow asked, "Aaron dear, have you decided what you would like to do today? Would you prefer to explore Summerland first, or would you rather continue our journeys to Earth? I believe London, England is our next stop."

The boy ran a hand through his wavy, dark brown hair.

"I like to explore new places. I even remember our trip to outer space when I first came to live with you. I'd love to see London."

"Yes!" Gino exclaimed, raising his arms high. All of the children laughed as the plates, syrups, and empty pitcher dissolved. And they jumped up quickly as the table and chairs disappeared as well.

"You didn't get us this time," Yoshi said, remembering another meal when their chairs disappeared so fast that they all ended up sitting on the floor.

"You five are just past fooling, I guess," replied the sort of cow, with a wink of her large brown eye.

Instantly, the group was dressed in private school uniforms like the ones many British children wear. The girls and Mrs. Tipperwillow wore dark blue and green plaid skirts with white blouses and forest green jackets. The boys were dressed similarly in plaid slacks, white shirts, and jackets like the girls' and Mrs. Tipperwillow's. Each uniform had a circular insignia at the chest, with a smiling sun at the center and the word "Summerland" scrolling around the outside.

The snoode awakened on Mrs. Tipperwillow's shoulders, scratching and sniffing the unfamiliar fabric that had appeared under him.

"Shall we be on our way, Lovies?" asked Mrs. Tipperwillow in her best English accent.

"It would be simply gr-ah-nd to accompany you," answered Jamie, sounding very British, indeed.

"Righto," said Lateesha.

"Let's *go* already!" This was Gino, of course, who was very happy not to be carrying a wiggly baby on his back this time.

Mrs. T. took the lead as they rose into the sky and whizzed along so fast that the scenery was just a green blur beneath them. The children and Mrs. Tipperwillow came abruptly to the Back door, almost smashing into each other as they stopped. They were surprised to find the door already open.

"My goodness … who?" Mrs. Tipperwillow looked down. "Oh my!" she exclaimed. "Dear ones, gather quickly now! We may be able to help down there!"

Smoke and dust were rising in the air from the impact of two long passenger trains that had just collided. A fire had started at one end of the mangled mass.

"Where are we?" asked Lateesha, as she looked from the train to the dry landscape and the hills in the distance.

"No idea yet," replied Mrs. T., "but we'll know soon enough. Follow me, Children!"

"What do you want us to do?" asked Jamie, as the Summerland family hovered over the broken trains.

"There! Do you see?" Thin ribbons of white light were beginning to swirl up out of the wreckage. Jamie remembered when her grandfather's spirit rose out of his body in the hospital. It looked just like this.

"Go to the passengers as they form up. Introduce yourselves and tell them someone will be here for them soon."

The first passenger appeared out of a swirling whiteness. It was a boy about thirteen years old. "What happened?" he said, to no one in particular.

Jamie flew over. "Hi! I'm Jamie."

"My name is Manuel Villegas," said the boy. "What's going on?"

"You don't remember what happened?"

"I was asleep, and there was this loud noise. Is this a dream?"

"No, it isn't. There was a big accident down there, see?" The boy looked down. "You're in your spirit body now. But everything is all right, and someone will be here for you soon."

"You mean I'm *dead*?"

"Only the outside part of you," Jamie replied. "Touch yourself. Is *that* dead?"

"No, but I feel different. I'm floating, aren't I?"

"Yes, you are, and here comes someone for you, Manuel!"

A bearded, long-haired man shivered into sight. He wore a pure white robe that gleamed with gold and yellow highlights. The man took Manuel's hands in his own, and not taking his brown eyes off the boy, he said in a kindly voice, "Thank you, Jamie. Sorry I was late. There was a bit of confusion out on the Light Web as to the timing here."

"It's okay," Jamie said as she turned away. *I know him from somewhere.* She shook her head in confusion as she flew off to greet another passenger, an older woman wearing a colorful woven skirt and shawl.

The children and Mrs. Tipperwillow were quite busy for a few minutes, introducing themselves and reassuring the confused passengers. One by one, glowing figures appeared and then disappeared with those they came for.

Mrs. T. called her family to her.

"I think I know where we are," said an excited Lateesha. "I think we're in Mexico!"

"I figured that might be the case," said Mrs. Tipperwillow, "after Manuel, Maria, Rosita, Pedro, Juan, and Javier showed up."

"Well, I just *asked* someone," Gino said. "One train left from Mexico City this morning and was heading to some place called Guadalajara."

"But Mrs. Tipperwillow," Yoshi asked, "why was the door opened here?"

"I don't really know, but I did see an angel below us flying in and out of the train windows. Perhaps in her excitement she left the Back door open. It has to be closed to reset the destination, you see."

"How do you do that?" asked the newest eight-year-old.

"Like everything else in Summerland, Aaron, with a *wish*. But the real mystery, Children, is why someone wasn't here sooner. These accidents are usually planned well in advance, and angels are at the ready."

Yoshi shook her head. "But Mrs. Tipperwillow, does that mean that accidents aren't really accidents at all? And," she added, not waiting for an answer, "who plans when we are going to pass into the spirit world? Does God and Goddess decide?"

"Accidents in which people are badly injured and pass away *are* planned, Yoshi. You are right about that. You make these plans, the part of you that knows all of your lifetimes and patterns. We call this part your higher self or soul. The soul plans, but these plans are usually hidden from the part of you that is living on Earth."

Tears formed in Yoshi's eyes and began running down her cheeks. "And what about the way we come here … and … and people who do bad things?" she whispered. Mrs. Tipperwillow nodded. "But … but why?" she stammered.

Taking the girl into her arms and holding her close, Mrs. Tipperwillow responded. "Life is all about experience and growth, Children. Each person is born on Earth to try out different ways of living with others. By sometimes being the *good guy* and sometimes being the *bad guy*, the spirit living on Earth discovers what works and what doesn't work. That person who was your worst enemy in one lifetime may become your best friend in another. Over time, people learn to understand and forgive themselves and each other. And the soul gains from this, too.

"You see, Children, each soul's biggest wish is to become in every way its *very* highest self, which is All Love."

Lateesha eyes widened. "You mean us as ... *God?*"

".... Yes."

The children were quiet as they took this in. Jamie shook her head as another thought came to her. *I do remember him!*

"Mrs. Tipperwillow, the spirit who came for Manuel, was that ... Jesus?"

The sort of cow nodded. "That's who Manuel's heart wanted most to see."

"I *knew* he seemed familiar," Jamie said, a smile coming to her face. "I remember now! One night when I was feeling afraid of dying, he came to me in a dream. He put his arms around me, and I felt all warm and peaceful and happy. By the time I woke up, the dream was fading like dreams do, except after that I wasn't afraid anymore." She shook her head in wonder.

"Anyway, Jesus said that there was some sort of confusion on the Light Web about the timing of this crash."

"I see," said Mrs. Tipperwillow, looking down at the smoking wreckage. "Perhaps someone touched something they weren't supposed to."

"Well ... *it wasn't me!*" Gino said loudly. "Can we go to England now?"

"That we may," said Mrs. T. "And thank you all so much for your help. I was very proud of you out there."

Sirens were blaring in the distance, and dust rose from police cars as they raced to the scene. The Summerland family flew to the Back door which was still hovering where they had left it, and they stepped across the threshold. The door closed behind them and reopened on an entirely different scene.

9

London, England

The children, followed by Mrs. Tipperwillow, stepped through the Back door once again. They found themselves standing inside the gates of Buckingham Palace. Out on the street, car horns were honking loudly. Sun was peeking through puffy clouds and quickly drying the dampened pavement. The children looked at the ornate black and gold palace gates and then back toward the building itself.

"Wow!" exclaimed Jamie. "This is even neater than the pictures Grandpa showed me."

Gino had already located two of the palace guards. They were standing totally still, one on each side of a large doorway. The guards wore tall, fuzzy black hats with chin straps, red-belted uniforms, and black boots. Each young man held a long lance under one arm and wore a serious expression. The rest of the family floated up to join Gino just as he lifted off the ground to look one of the men straight in the face.

"Hello there, guard man!" Gino said as he reached his hand straight through the man's chest. The merest shiver went through the guard, but there was no change in his expression. Again and again the boy tried, moving his hand faster and then more slowly, through one man and then the other and getting the same results each time. Even wiggling his fingers didn't cause a reaction.

Gino frowned. Mrs. Tipperwillow touched his arm with the tip of her hoof. "They feel you, Gino. They really do. Because they are standing so quietly, they can feel what I call the 'spirit shivers.' But they don't understand what they are feeling and probably just think they are getting sick."

Gino shrugged. "How could anyone stand such a boring job?" He turned to fly through the closed palace door. His head popped back out. "Well, are you guys coming?"

"Oh, yes, we are!" replied Mrs. Tipperwillow with a laugh. By the time his friends were all inside, Gino was already swooping up and down an ornate staircase. The children and their teacher went their separate ways. They skimmed the red carpeted hallways, checked out the gold framed paintings on the walls and visited the huge dining room, the sitting rooms, and the bedrooms, some with canopies hung over the beds. A few people were hurrying down the halls, but there was no sign of the queen.

After a few minutes, Gino stopped in front of his teacher. "Okay, I'm done! Where are we going next, Mrs. T.?"

"What's the hurry, Gino?" she asked. "The girls and Aaron are still exploring."

At the word "exploring" the rest of the family appeared. They floated through the closed outer door to find a crowd gathered.

"It's the changing of the guard!" Jamie exclaimed. "We're just in time."

The family watched the ceremony closely. Gino made wiggly fingers only once as the new guards marched in time to take their places.

"My grandfather used to come here with his parents when he was a boy," Jamie explained. "He said it was one of his clearest memories of living in London. I'm so glad I get to see it, too."

They flew across the street to St. James Park. As they drifted over the curving paths of the large park, Jamie told her friends about her grandfather's childhood.

"Grandpa's mom and dad had a shop in the center of London," Jamie began. "They owned a dry goods store."

"Instead of a *wet* goods store?" quipped Gino. A laugh popped from Lateesha's mouth. She quickly covered her mouth with one hand, but laughter filled her eyes.

"It's always good to respect other people's stories, Gino," Mrs. Tipperwillow said in a serious tone.

The boy frowned and angrily kicked at the dirt beneath his feet. "Well, *I* thought it was funny," he grumbled.

Jamie shook her head. "You don't always get to be the center of attention, Gino. It's my turn now." Gino stared at the ground.

"*Anyway*," Jamie continued, "the three of them lived in a little apartment over the store. By the time he was our age, my grandfather was up early every morning putting canned goods and packages of stuff on the shelves. He liked to line things up neatly, but his favorite part was greeting the 'regulars—that's what he called them. They were the people who came in every week to buy their groceries. By the time he was six, my grandpa knew them all by name. Then when he was ten," Jamie continued, "his family left England for America, and they settled in Portland, Oregon. That's where he lived the rest of his life. We moved there to be close to Grandma and Grandpa after Bobby was born."

"Does your grandpa have an English accent?" asked Yoshi. "My best friend Lizzie said that my mommy and daddy have Japanese accents, but they always sounded just like Mommy and Daddy to me." She shrugged.

"Grandpa told me he wanted to sound American so he changed his voice," Jamie answered. "Sometimes, though, we would play 'English'—that's what he called it. We'd have 'high tea' together and speak just like real English people. It was fun!"

"Can we see the store where your grandfather's family worked?" Lateesha asked.

"No, we can't do that. It was torn down a long time before I was born. Grandpa told me there's a big skyscraper there now."

Mrs. Tipperwillow raised her cow brow and smiled a funny little smile. "I think a side trip might be in order!" she chortled, as a familiar door landed with a thump beside them on the path.

"Where are we going?" Aaron asked.

"Not where so much as *when*," replied the magical sort of cow. The door opened. Mrs. Tipperwillow's eyes were gleaming as she said, "After you, Jamie!" The girl stepped across the threshold followed by Gino, Aaron, Lateesha, Yoshi, and finally, Mrs. T.

They found themselves inside an old-fashioned grocery store with a dark wooden interior. Shelves lined the walls on all sides, and they were stacked almost to the ceiling with boxes and cans. A man and a woman were standing behind the counter. The woman was working at the cash register, and the man was putting cans on one of the shelves.

Jamie's eyes opened wide. "Those are my great grandparents," she said in a hushed voice. "I met them at Grandpa's coming home party and they looked just like they do here."

"Henry!" the man called. "Bring out that box I showed you, and stack the contents over here, if you please." A boy with wavy brown hair and freckles walked out from the storeroom carrying a heavy looking box.

"That's my grandfather when he was my age," Jamie whispered. The child put down the box where his father had pointed and began stacking the contents neatly on an empty shelf.

Jamie floated over and reached out to touch him. Her hand went right through. "Hi, Grandpa," she tried. "I'm from the future … well, from Summerland, actually. You become my grandpa when you grow up."

"Jamie, dear," said Mrs. Tipperwillow, "he can't hear you, of course."

"I know. I just wanted to try."

After watching the scene a bit longer, Jamie nodded, and the time travelers stepped through the closed wooden door and out onto the sidewalk.

If she had stayed just one moment longer, Jamie might have seen young Henry pause in his stacking, shake his head, and whisper "Grandpa?"

◆   ◆   ◆

"What year is this, anyway?" Gino asked, looking up and down the narrow street.

"Judging from the look of it, I'd guess the year to be about 1930," Mrs. Tipperwillow replied.

"Will you look at all these old-fashioned cars?" Gino said. "This is super!"

They drifted down the sidewalk, watching people hurrying by in their long winter coats and hats and gazing at the displays in all the store windows.

At last, with a loud thump, the magic door reappeared. The Summerland family stepped across into the future and back into the park that they had left only minutes before.

Weeping willow trees swept their leafy branches over the little lake behind them as the children and Mrs. Tipperwillow sat in the shade, enjoying the traditional British treat of tea with blueberry scones, which were spread thick with clotted cream.

Gino and Jamie were both licking cream off their fingers when they looked up and into each other's eyes. Gino cleared his throat.

"Jay, I'm sorry I interrupted your story. I don't know why I did that. I remember when my brothers did the same thing to me. I *hated* it."

"It's hard to stop a thought from coming out sometimes," Jamie replied. "I forgive you."

"Just like that, Jamie … you sure?"

"Sure. I figured that out after I got sick. Staying mad just made me feel terrible, and I knew I didn't want to waste the time I had left." There was silence.

Finally Yoshi said, "I was never allowed to interrupt like you did, Gino. Mommy and Daddy said children in Japan are taught to be polite, and it wouldn't be any different for me just because we lived in America."

"How did they make *that* stick?" Gino asked, draining the last of his tea.

"Huh? Oh, I get it. They didn't spank me or anything. They just gave me this look." Yoshi demonstrated.

Gino laughed. "That's a good one!" He tried *the look*, and then Lateesha and Aaron and Jamie did, too. It became quite a contest in seriousness. But when Mrs. Tipperwillow did her own stare ... that was it.

The laughter didn't stop until two white pelicans wandered over and stopped at the edge of the blue and white blanket. The large birds stared straight at Mrs. Tipperwillow and bobbed their heads up and down.

"Can they see you, Mrs. T.?" Lateesha asked. "They seem to be looking straight at you."

"Why yes, I do believe they can," answered their teacher, as one of the birds shook its head at her. "Yes!" said the magical sort of cow.

"Yes, what?" asked Aaron.

"They are sensing us, Aaron, and questioning in the way birds do."

"Can they talk?"

"Well, not exactly. There is a thought impression and a feeling, almost like a musical note, coming from them. Can any of you feel it?"

Lateesha laughed. "I can, Mrs. T!"

"Are you gonna draw those wavy lines again?" Gino asked, frowning.

"No, I am *not!*" The girl stared him down.

"Perhaps we should take a look at feelings here for a moment," said Mrs. Tipperwillow, kindly. "Gino, dear, why does Lateesha's ability to sense vibrations bother you so much?"

Gino looked at his feet and then into the large, caring eyes of his teacher. A tiny tear appeared in the corner of his eye. He angrily brushed it away with the back of his hand.

"We've always had so much fun playing together," he said, looking down at his feet. "But now she's different. She's doing things I can't do. And well, I kind of wish I could see those wiggly lines, too."

"I'm proud of you, Gino, for saying your feelings so honestly. Lateesha, how do you feel?"

"Hurt ... I feel *hurt*." She looked at the boy. He would not meet her eyes. "We've always been best buddies, but I'm beginning to think you don't like me anymore because of the way I see things."

Gino looked up at Lateesha and brushed one last tear from his eye. He glanced over at Jamie and took a deep breath. "I'm sorry, Teesh. I wasn't being fair. You can't help the way you see things, and the stuff you see is really great. I just wish I could do that, too."

"But Gino, you do lots of great things. For one thing, you're just about the bravest person I know."

"I am?"

"Yes, you are. You remind me of what my dad said he was like when he was our age. Now, what was the word he used? 'Irrepressible.' Yes! That was it."

"I hope that's something *good*," Gino said, cheering up a bit.

"Sure it is!" Lateesha replied. "It means that you're a go-for-it kind of boy."

"You're also really good at creating things," added Yoshi. "Remember the great big truck you created in our tent?"

Gino smiled at the memory. "Well, yeah, I guess I *am* pretty terrific." A faraway look came to his eyes. "I just wish I could show my brothers how I can create stuff now ... like the fires in our fireplace. They'd really be impressed with *that*.

"Okay," he said suddenly, "I'm ready for more exploring. Where to next, Mrs. T?"

"Could we hug?" Lateesha asked. "I think I need it."

"Yeah, that would help ... I guess." Blushing wildly, Gino gave Lateesha a quick hug.

"Excellent work, Children," congratulated Mrs. Tipperwillow. "I'm proud of you both."

10

Big Ben and Beyond

The Summerland family flew high over London, following the river Thames until they reached the British Houses of Parliament and the tall clock tower called Big Ben. "I remember this clock from the movie *Peter Pan*!" Gino shouted. Taking off his jacket and holding it behind him like a cape, Gino circled the top of the clock tower three and then four times. The other children joined him, and finally Mrs. Tipperwillow did, too. The snoode held tightly to her neck as they flew faster and faster around the clock tower.

"What are we doing?" asked their teacher as they sped along. "Trying to make time fly?"

Gino clutched his sides as he slowed down to laugh. "Ooh, Mrs. T.! That one hurts!"

Soon the group was hovering over the Tower of London, which was once an infamous prison. Drifting down to land in the large courtyard, the children and their teacher spotted a tour guide wearing a red plaid kilt. "Gino ... *don't you dare*!" warned Mrs. Tipperwillow.

The man was explaining the history of the prison to a group of tourists. "Let's just listen awhile, Children," she suggested. But it was already too late. Gino had located the door to the dungeon.

"It's this way!" He motioned for his friends to follow as he stepped inside.

Before the others were even through the door, Gino bumped into them coming back out. "Uh ... maybe you don't really want to go in there," he said. "There's torture stuff and ... it's ... not good."

This made his friends really curious. "We'll just be a minute," Lateesha said, as Aaron, Yoshi, and Jamie followed her though the small door and then down the dimly lit corridor to the dungeon. "Right," she said exiting the door only a moment later with the others blinking behind her. "Terrible things happened in there. That energy felt *awful.*"

The family sat down on the lawn to collect themselves. Three shiny black ravens wandered over, and the children watched as Mrs. Tipperwillow seemed to have a silent conversation with the large birds. She turned to the children. "They're curious about us the same way the pelicans were. They were challenging me a bit, too, sending me the feeling that this is *their* place and wondering what *we* are doing here."

"But Mrs. Tipperwillow," Jamie asked, "why can birds see us at all?"

"Can other animals see us, too?" asked Gino.

"Like cats and dogs?" added Lateesha.

"Or fish?" asked Yoshi, thinking of the gold fish she had won at the fair.

Mrs. T. smiled at her children, and then looked over at the nearest raven which was preening its feathers with its large black beak. "Animals aren't bothered with things such as thoughts and plans, Children, so their other senses are stronger. I daresay, if people stopped thinking so much about the past and future and if they just watched and listened and felt what was around them at each moment, they would sense us, too."

Mrs. Tipperwillow stood and stretched and slowly rose into the blue sky. Her family followed. They drifted over streets crowded with cars and buses and eventually landed on a sidewalk near steps leading down. Flying through a crowd of people down two levels of steep stairs, the Summerland tourists found themselves deep underground in the tunnels of the London subway system called (as you may have guessed) The Underground. They entered a subway car and took seats as the train began to move.

"Children, I told you earlier that there might be a place or two that I especially wanted to visit on Earth. So I beg your indulgence for our next stop." She smiled at Gino.

"Is it someplace especially *boring?*" he asked, scratching his nose.

"Not to *me*, it isn't. This is our stop. Follow me!" Mrs. Tipperwillow dashed off the subway car and up the stairs to street level. The children followed quickly on her hooves and found themselves by the entrance to the Victoria and Albert Museum.

Following a group of tourists inside, they entered a large room lined with costumed store mannequins in different poses. "I should have guessed," said Gino, with a smile spreading across his face, "*clothes!*"

"Aha!" exclaimed Mrs. Tipperwillow, clapping her hooves together in a merry way. "Look at all the fashions from the different ages of Earth, Children!" The girls followed their entranced teacher through the exhibit, studying the satin and lace dresses with stiff underskirts popular during the time of the French revolution, the slinky silk dresses worn during the nineteen twenties and thirties, and the hippie wear of the sixties, to name a few styles. Aaron and Gino trailed behind, whispering and joking.

After moo-ving slowly through the display for a second time, the sort of cow turned to the children. Her cheeks were flushed with excitement. "I have an idea! Let's have a fashion show when we get home. We can recreate these costumes and perhaps create something of our own design!" The girls and Mrs. Tipperwillow spoke in excited voices.

Aaron practiced rolling his eyes and making faces with Gino. "Can we go *yet?*" he asked.

Gino applauded. "Good job, Aaron!"

◆   ◆   ◆

The sun was sinking toward the horizon as the family once again floated high above London, England. They watched as puffy clouds turned pink, throwing reflections on the river Thames and on the windows of the buildings beneath them.

A familiar door appeared, floating in mid-air, and opened. Taking one last look at the birth place of her grandfather, Jamie followed her friends and their teacher through the Back door.

The Summerland family found themselves standing in the tall grass right beside their own striped tent. They quickly chanted the daylight to evening and joined hands and hooves to say: "Blessings to all we've ever been and to all we'll ever be. Blessings to all we've ever loved, to the Earth, to spirit, and to dreams." They called in the nighttime chanting: "Softly, softly into night, softly, softly goes the light. Good night! Good night! Good night! Good night!" The sky dimmed to almost dark.

As she tucked the children in one by one, Mrs. Tipperwillow touched each forehead lovingly and whispered, "Sweet dreams!"

Aaron was the last one to go to sleep. "I love being bigger," he thought to himself and wrapped a hand around his toy truck before nodding off.

11

About Gino

"Are you *sure* we shouldn't visit the theme park first?" Gino asked the next day, as the family, who were still dressed in pajamas, shared a light breakfast of cinnamon buns and apple juice.

"It was your heart's call Gino, so let's follow *that*. Would you like another bun?"

"No, thanks, Mrs. T." The boy stood and the energy around him shimmered.

Gino was wearing an Italian gondolier's outfit: slim black pants, shiny black shoes, a red and white striped t-shirt, and a woven straw hat with chin strap. A red ribbon circled the hat brim, its ends falling down his back. Gino looked down at the outfit. Then he took off the hat and twirled it around in his hand before replacing it on his head.

"I have it on good authority," Mrs. Tipperwillow said, "that the Italian grandfather for whom you are named was a gondolier. He carried passengers in his long boat through the canals of Venice and serenaded them with song!"

"Yeah," replied Gino. "Mom tried to get me to join the school chorus because she thought I would have his good voice. But I wouldn't go. My brothers made rude noises when I sang in the shower, and I figured *that* was enough. This outfit's kind of cool, though."

Aaron was immediately dressed in the same outfit. "How many brothers did you have?" Aaron asked, looking down at his new clothes and then over at his friend. "I didn't have any brothers."

"I had four."

"That must have been fun!"

"Nah ... I was the youngest, and they usually didn't have time to play with me. They were all too busy with *their* friends. My oldest brother was already in high school when I came to Summerland. Oh, but *this* is cool," Gino said, looking at Aaron. "I bet you didn't know that my dad works in a factory making luxury cars. He is a welder and uses this big blow torch. And fire comes out the end!" Gino pictured his dad at work, while Aaron and the girls shared the picture in their minds.

"Wow!" exclaimed Aaron. "That is so totally cool!"

"What does your mommy do?" asked Yoshi.

"She might have another job now, but when I was there she stayed home and took care of all of us. My brothers were really a handful."

Yoshi and Lateesha giggled. Jamie was trying to keep from smiling as she said, "And *you* weren't, Gino?"

"Not so much."

The girls burst out laughing.

Gino looked at the girls hard. "What??"

Mrs. Tipperwillow gave a dramatic wink of her eye, and the girls were dressed in red pleated skirts with white sweaters. The word *Venezia* was printed across the front. "That means 'Venice' in Italian," Mrs. T. said cheerfully. Shiny red patent leather shoes completed their outfits. Mrs. Tipperwillow spun around and was wearing her own skirt and sweater with a fashionable red hat and feather ... but no shoes, of course. The feather was so long it dipped down and brushed the sleeping snoode, who awakened and batted the feather with his front paws.

"Ready to visit Italy?" asked Mrs. T.

"We are!" exclaimed Lateesha.

12

Trouble on the Web

A warm wind swept the family from the tent and pulled them high into the Summerland sky. Faster than fast, they were once again at the Back door, ready to see Venice. The door was closed this time, but there was a small folded paper stuck at its center. "What's this?" asked Mrs. Tipperwillow. She removed the paper and read:

> *Trouble on the web, Mrs. T.*
> *Will you and the children come quick?*
> *Wallace*

"How peculiar," Mrs. Tipperwillow said. "Children, this is a note from Wallace. How he found us here...." She shook her head. "Oh yes! How silly of me. He looked at our *web messages*. That was very clever of him."

"What do you mean?" asked Jamie, as she smoothed her skirt from the quick flight.

"Where we go is in the Light Web even before we get there, Jamie. Remember the energy bundle that is our story?" The children pictured in their minds the day they discovered the big ball of energy in the center of the Light Web that contained their adventures and even the name of the woman on Earth who was writing them down. "Wallace must have read about where we were going next and sent this note here ahead of us!"

Gino shook his head. "More craziness, Mrs. T.!"

"But why does Wallace want us?" Yoshi asked, wrapping a finger around a strand of her black hair.

"I have no idea, dear, but we'd best get moving. He said it was *urgent!*"

"Is it a long way?" questioned Yoshi.

"Not by train, it isn't!" And without any notice whatsoever, a familiar train appeared in the sky above them, white smoke puffing out of the smokestack.

"Light Web Junction!" yelled the conductor. "All aboard!"

The family barely had time to get to their seats before the train sped off. They passed through the feeling rainbow so quickly that all they sensed was a blur of color and emotion before they moved into total darkness. Moments later, a twinkle of light appeared and then another. And quicker than you could say "abracadabra," the sky was lit up by thousands of tiny lights.

"Light Web Junction!" yelled the conductor. "Off you go!"

The six found themselves on the familiar platform floating in the sky. The girls looked at each other, thinking of a time not so very long ago when they waited on this very platform for Wallace and Mrs. Tipperwillow to rescue Gino when he was caught in the web. Gino heard the girl's thoughts and frowned as he carefully examined his shiny Italian shoes.

A swirl of soft blue light zoomed toward them, and Wallace materialized sporting a small blond beard and mustache. He appeared rather frazzled.

"Thank you all for coming," he said, picking up Yoshi for a hug. His eyes widened as he noticed the new eight-year-old. "Well, Aaron, I see you've grown up. Congratulations." Wallace turned to his old teacher. "We have a bit of a situation here."

"Did the situation make you grow a beard?" Yoshi asked. "You look different."

"I decided to be a bit older. But here's why I called you. All of the web workers have been over and over the Light Web, but we simply can't figure it out."

"Figure *what* out, Wallace?" questioned Lateesha.

"Is this connected to the train wreck we discovered in Mexico?" Jamie asked.

"I heard about that, Jamie. That train wreck is only one example of what's been going on. Somehow our time link to Earth is confused. Accidents and natural disasters are occurring *before* they are scheduled. This is happening with increasing frequency. We've narrowed the problem to strands labeled 'group homecomings,' but try as we might, we simply can't figure out what's wrong with our system."

"You don't talk like a kid anymore," Gino said, scratching his head.

"I know, Gino."

"But why call us?" Yoshi asked from Wallace's arms. "We're only children."

".... Exactly! All of the thousands of adults working on the Light Web have gotten nowhere. I thought we could use a fresh perspective."

"What's a *perspective*?" asked Aaron.

"It means a way of looking at things," Wallace replied, putting Yoshi down. "We need a new way of looking at things. Perhaps one of you will see something we've forgotten."

Gino practically shouted, "Well, *I didn't do it!*"

"Of course you didn't, Gino," replied Mrs. T. in a concerned voice. "No one said that you did." Gino looked at his shoes. "Guilt only serves to remind us that we can choose differently when the same type situation comes up. Otherwise, feeling guilty is entirely useless. Why would you want to hurt yourself so?"

The boy looked up, and a single tear trickled down his cheek. "Do you think sweet Goddess/God/All Love would want that for you, Gino, or for anyone else for that matter?" Mrs. Tipperwillow asked.

"No," he answered, sniffling. "I guess not."

Without warning, complete silence surrounded Gino, and he felt as if he were inside of a bubble looking out. Into the quiet dropped the words, *Don't hurt yourself so over what you cannot change.*

".... Who?" he whispered and felt a smile.

I am the deepest part of you—the heart of your heart, said the voice, which seemed to be neither a man's voice nor a woman's voice but somehow both.

Be healed of this, Gino. I love you just for who you are.

The words thrummed through Gino's body, and he smiled through his tears.

"You still love me even when I mess up?"

Just for who you are, the voice repeated as golden energy filled Gino's heart and spread outward.

"What is it, Gino?" asked a worried Jamie. "Who were you talking to?"

"Don't you know, Jamie? Can't you see it?" Lateesha asked in an excited voice.

"You mean that glow around Gino's body? Yes, I do see it!"

"It was All Love. It was God and Goddess," Gino said in a soft voice. He smiled and a single tear rolled down his cheek. "And it was coming from inside of *me!*"

"Yes, dear boy," Mrs. Tipperwillow said kindly, "the energy of the God and Goddess lives inside of you and inside of me and inside of everyone, everywhere. And we are all so very loved. There are no exceptions."

Yoshi shook her head. "Even people who…." she began.

"Yes, Yoshi, even people *who.* Now, let's see how we can help Wallace."

13

Visions

"Boys, let's rid you of your hats for now. We don't want those long ribbons touching any part of the web." Mrs. Tipperwillow raised a hoof, and the straw hats disappeared in little puffs of smoke. "Very well.... Single file, Children! You follow Wallace, and I will pick up the rear."

"This way," motioned Wallace, "and be careful, everyone!" Off they went, Lateesha first, then Gino, Yoshi, Aaron, and Jamie, followed by Mrs. Tipperwillow. The family flew, weaving like a ribbon through the strands and bundles of light. They came to a stop behind Wallace.

"This is it!" Wallace turned to look at them. "This is the center of the information segment that controls group homecomings. We've been over it many times ... nothing. I hope you will sense something that we missed."

"What do you want us to do?" Yoshi asked.

"Just send out your feelings and see what comes.... One at a time, okay? Yoshi, will you go first?"

"I guess," she said and closed her eyes. Everyone was quiet. Even Gino was not doing his usual fidgeting. He waited silently and stared at Yoshi. Finally she opened her eyes.

"Did you sense anything, Yoshi?" Wallace asked.

"I didn't at first, but maybe I started to dream. I don't know. I heard a noise like a clock ticking. Then I saw a clock. It was ticking away. Then the little hand stopped moving, and the clock was quiet. But in a moment, it started up again."

"Hmmm.... That's a good start, Yoshi. Thank you."

"Jamie, it's your turn." The girl closed her eyes and held out her hands to feel the energies. She was quiet for what seemed like a long time. Jamie opened her eyes again. "I had the most peculiar feeling," she said. "I don't think the problem is here *at all*. You've been looking and looking, and I don't think it's here."

"Where is it, then?" Wallace asked.

"Earth!" blurted Gino. "Something is different on Earth!"

"Where on Earth, though?"

"Everywhere!" exclaimed Lateesha. "Something happened on Earth that *changed time*!"

"Now we're getting someplace," Wallace said in an excited voice. "Hold on while I find a few friends." He disappeared.

While they waited, Aaron closed his eyes. Wallace and three others appeared just as Aaron began to speak. "I saw something, Mrs. T. I saw the ground shaking. And there was this big crack that opened up in the land underneath the water. It kept on going and going and going. And then there was this huge wave."

"Really!" exclaimed Mrs. Tipperwillow.

Then Gino added, "I saw the Earth spinning in space, and then it … jiggled."

The adults stood stock still with their mouths open. There was complete silence as they shared Aaron's and Gino's visions. Finally, Wallace broke the silence. "You've done it. You've all really done it!"

"Good work, Children!" Mrs. Tipperwillow chortled.

Gino raised his hands in the air and turned around, doing a Gino sort of dance.

"We would really like to stay longer to visit with you," Wallace said. "You haven't been introduced to my friends. This is Jan, Marla, and Fogarty." The three nodded their heads in turn. "But there is so much to do. We must call in others who work directly with Earth changes to help us revise our system. I can't thank you all enough for solving this mystery. You are excellent imaginers. Once things get settled, I think a party would be in order. What do you say?"

"We'd like that, wouldn't we, Children?" asked Mrs. T. as she smiled at her family.

"Here, I'll show you the way out while my friends begin calling in others to tell them of your visions." The other three adults disappeared, and Wallace quickly and carefully led the family out of the Light Web. Then he disappeared as well.

"My goodness, *that* was remarkable," commented Mrs. Tipperwillow, as the family once again boarded the sky train. "I hope you all know just how appreciated you are."

All at once the children felt a warm and loving energy touch their hearts. "Did you do that?" asked Aaron, looking back at his teacher.

"No, dear, it wasn't *me*," said Mrs. Tipperwillow, mildly.

14

Venice, Italy

Gino decided in the first minutes out that Venice was a bore. The Summerland family drifted overhead, watching as a gondolier poled his long, narrow boat through a canal lined with houses. The man, who was dressed in the same outfit as the boys, was at the moment singing love songs to a kissing couple. This was almost more than Gino could take. The girls thought it was sweet, but *not* Gino. Aaron joined Gino in making *smoochy-smoochy* faces.

"I really *did* say a theme park," Gino complained. "Can we go now?"

"There is a lot more to Venice than love songs, Gino," replied Mrs. Tipperwillow.

The boy, who was embarrassed that his grandfather would ever *do* such a thing for a living, sulked. "Would you *pa-leeze* take this outfit off me!"

"Me, too!" added Aaron with his hands on his hips and his scowl a close imitation of his friend's.

"Certainly, Children," said Mrs. Tipperwillow. Instantly the boys were dressed in blue jeans and sweatshirts. "All Boy" was stamped in bright red letters across the front of each sweatshirt.

"Mrs. T-e-e-e-e...." whined Gino, not sure whether this was a good thing.

"What is it, Gino?" asked the sort of cow, most pleasantly.

Gino and Aaron looked at each other and then down at their shirts. Gino made a decision. "Cool," he replied, patting his chest. "Cool," repeated Aaron, and he patted his chest, too.

Off the family flew into the misty morning light of Venice. They looked from the multi-colored houses that lined the waterways to the large canopy-covered boats that carried passengers along the canals. The children and their teacher swooped back and forth over and under the many bridges. "That bridge is called the Rialto," Mrs. Tipperwillow explained, and she pointed a hoof at the fine arched bridge with its walkway for pedestrians. "It is very famous on Earth."

"My mom showed me pictures of this!" said Gino, who was happy once more.

Next, on foot and hoof, they explored some of the narrow, cobblestone alleyways of Venice. Doors along the alleys were painted bright colors; green, red, yellow, or blue, and there were buckets with bright sunflowers by some of the doors.

The children followed Mrs. Tipperwillow through the entrance to an art museum. "Welcome to the art of Salvador Dali," she said, sweeping out her right hoof. "I think you will find it *most* interesting. You can spread out here, and I will call you back later."

The children hardly heard their teacher. "Wow, this is different," Gino whispered. In the paintings that covered every wall, strange, tall people moved in even stranger landscapes. Clocks dripped over tables. A red rose floated in mid-air. Moving from painting to painting, the children felt as if they had stepped into another world.

Tourists from many countries wandered through the different rooms, and Jamie stopped to listen to their whispered comments about the art. "Wait a minute!" she said suddenly. "Mrs. Tipperwillow!"

The sort of cow appeared next to her. "Yes, Jamie, what is it?"

"How can I understand them, Mrs. T.? They can't all be speaking English. I understood the Japanese man who was meditating on Mt. Fuji and the people in Mexico, too. How can that be?"

"I was wondering who would notice first. You get the prize, Jamie! What you are doing is picking up the thought impressions of the people. Then you translate them into your own language. This happens quite naturally. If any of these people had the ability to pick up your thoughts, it would be the same for them, as it was for Master Matsuyama in Japan. More and more people on Earth are developing this ability. It just takes imagination, trust, and a certain letting go."

"Could I do that after I'm born on Earth again? Could I even hear you, Mrs. Tipperwillow?"

"It's entirely possible, Jamie."

"What's up?" Gino asked, as all the Summerland family gathered around.

"I'll explain during lunch," said Mrs. Tipperwillow. "Who wants pizza?"

15

Lunch and Afterwards

The Summerland family entered a dimly-lit restaurant. They chose a table near the back where only a few customers were sitting. A waiter walked through the swinging kitchen door balancing two large pizzas in his arms. He approached the table where Mrs. Tipperwillow and the children were sitting, put the pizzas down, and walked away. Without thinking, the children each grabbed a piece.

Lateesha stopped on her second bite. "Hey, wait a minute! That waiter.... How? Mrs. Tipperwillow?"

The magical sort of cow chuckled. "He's my creation, Teesha. How do you like him?" The waiter came through the kitchen door again and walked straight to their table. He winked at Lateesha. All of the children were paying attention now.

"You *made* him?" asked Jamie.

"And the *pizzas!*" said Mrs. T, proudly.

"He's almost as good as the pirate ship," mumbled Gino around a mouthful.

"Vood you like zumzing to drink?" asked the waiter in an Italian accent.

The children gave their orders and soon were slurping their sodas through different colored straws.

"Children," Mrs. Tipperwillow began, "Jamie noticed something interesting in the art museum that we just visited. She could understand visitors from all over the world, and she realized that they must be speaking different languages."

"Yeah, that's right!" Gino exclaimed, "I could understand everybody, too!" His friends nodded their heads in agreement.

"You have learned that in the spirit world we can hear each other's thoughts and feel each other's emotions," the sort of cow said. "And today you are discovering that we can do the same thing with people here. But something quite interesting is beginning to happen with people living on Earth. And this is something that you might want to be aware of before you are born again for another lifetime, because it will affect you." Mrs. Tipperwillow looked around at her family.

"The energies of Earth and its people are moving to a higher vibration, Children. As part of this change, more and more people are beginning to sense at deeper levels than they could before."

Jamie chimed in. "Like my family, Mrs. T.! Remember when they could hear me? And my mom even saw the dress I was wearing!"

Mrs. Tipperwillow smiled across the table at the girl. "Then you know *exactly* where I am heading, Jamie. Just as Jamie discovered with her own family, more and more people are seeing visions and hearing spirits' voices. And everyone's inner knowing is growing, too.

"These abilities have names," Mrs. T. continued. You have probably heard of clairvoyance.

Clairvoyance is seeing beyond what is seen with the physical eyes, such as when someone sees a spirit."

"Or when she sees something happening in another place," Jamie suggested, "or maybe even the *future?*"

"Right you are, Jamie! And clairaudience is hearing beyond what is heard by physical ears. This type of hearing is done mostly in the throat and sometimes in the center of the head."

"You mean people hear in their *throats?*" asked Yoshi, scratching her head.

Mrs. Tipperwillow nodded. "I know it seems strange, but yes. Last of all, there is clairsentience. This is the ability to pick up the emotions of people or feel energy changes in the air or sense that something is about to happen without seeing it or hearing it. Most people on our home planet have *this* ability. It is also called intuition.

"One wonderful thing about the 'clairs' is that they can bring people on Earth closer to us in the spirit world." The children thought about this.

Gino piped up. "Next time I go to Earth I want to be clairvoyant. I want to see accidents happening across town and fly off to save people like Superman!"

Jamie said, "First you have to learn to fly in a heavy Earth body."

"Then you need super strength," added Lateesha.

"And proper clothing!" chortled Mrs. Tipperwillow. Gino looked down. He was dressed in a Superman costume, complete with tights, a cape, and soft shoes.

"Neato!" said Gino, floating out of his seat. He raised one arm in the air and flew around the top of the restaurant several times before landing with a thud in his chair, which promptly fell over backward with Gino still in it. Everyone laughed. But Jamie noticed something strange. At a nearby table, an old man with white hair was staring straight at Gino, and *he* was laughing, too.

"Look!" said Jamie, pointing. They turned toward the man, who raised his arm, wiggling his fingers in a friendly greeting.

"Is this what we've been talking about, Mrs. T?" Yoshi asked in an excited voice. Is that man clairvoyant?"

"Indeed, it does seem so."

Gino was off the floor in a flash and standing next to the man. "Hello," he tried. "I'm Gino. Can you hear me?" Gino reached out, and the old man watched as Gino's hand disappeared into his own, but he didn't answer. "Guess he isn't clairaudient," Gino said, drifting back to pick up his chair. The man waved again and the children waved back. By now, several people in the restaurant were staring at the old man, shaking their heads and whispering. "They think he's crazy," Gino said, shaking his head, "when they're the ones who can't see."

"It won't always be this way, Children," replied Mrs. Tipperwillow. "Someday most people on Earth will have developed their extra senses. Now if you're done eating, who's ready for more exploring?"

All the children raised their hands and waved goodbye to the old man. They emerged into the sunny day and looked back toward the restaurant door to see if the man would follow them out. But the door remained closed.

Gino was still dressed up in his Superman costume as the family flew to their next destination. After the brief flight, they landed in front of a large cathedral at one end of an enormous courtyard.

Mrs. Tipperwillow was now wearing a tour guide's gray uniform and cap. She looked from the children to the church and flourished her arm dramatically.

"Before us, we see the famous marble cathedral in the Byzantine style, built to hold the stolen bones of St. Mark. It is aptly named the Cathedral of San Marcos. Notice the fine paintings called 'frescoes' in the archways, there … and there." She pointed, and the children followed her hoof with their eyes.

"Look!" exclaimed Jamie. "See the angels up there?" The family floated up to take a closer look.

"Our guardian angels are *far* more wonderful," Yoshi said, putting her hand through one golden wing, "and besides, real angels don't have feathers."

They drifted down to the entrance of the large church. "Shall we go inside for a peek?" Mrs. T. asked. They entered through the closed door and into the central area of the cathedral, which Mrs. Tipperwillow called the "basilica."

"Gold!' exclaimed Gino. He rubbed his hands together greedily as he looked at the rounded walls covered entirely in gold that curved up to form the ceiling. On every surface there were paintings depicting scenes from the Bible.

Jamie sighed. "This is beautiful."

Lateesha sighed, too. "It's the most beautiful church I've ever seen."

They lifted into the air and followed the curve of the walls to study each picture. "Look at all the angels!" exclaimed Aaron.

"But not *our* angels," said Yoshi, as she studied each face.

Minutes later, the tourists from the spirit world were standing in the warm sunshine of the huge courtyard that fronted the cathedral. They looked around at the many shops and outdoor cafes surrounding them and at the many people and pigeons walking every which way.

Lateesha noticed that, while the people walked right through them, the pigeons moved to avoid the Summerland group just as they did the other tourists. Gino noticed, too. "Clairvoyant pigeons!" he exclaimed.

The family's next stop was the island of Murano, the glassmaking center of Italy. They entered a large workshop, and they sat down on benches to watch a demonstration of glass blowing.

First, a man wearing a heavy apron and gloves pulled a long metal tube out of a glowing brick oven where a low fire was burning. There was a glowing blob of something at the end of the tube. The man's face grew red as he blew through the tube and turned the rod over and over. The blob of liquid glass expanded quickly, like a bubble. An assistant touched part of the spinning glass with a smaller rod, and it became narrower toward one end. In a few moments, as if by magic, the glass became an elegant vase with a bright blue stripe running around it. The vase was cut from the tube and set aside to dry. The process began again. But this time as the glassblower and his assistant worked together, the swirling glass became a perfect prancing horse with a flying mane.

"Woo!" exclaimed Aaron.

"And double woo!" said Gino. "That's what I really want to do when I grow up next time."

"So now you've decided to grow up?" Jamie asked, raising her eyebrows.

"Well, yeah … someday, probably. But only if I can have *fun*," Gino added.

"Well, of course!" laughed Lateesha. "What good is living if you can't have any fun?"

"Some people don't," said Yoshi, frowning. "Some people just pretend."

Mrs. Tipperwillow smiled knowingly. "Are you all about ready to go? Have you seen enough of Venice?"

"I'm ready for a nice warm fire in our fireplace," Jamie replied.

"And some hot chocolate," said Yoshi.

"With oatmeal cookies this time," added Lateesha.

Gino raised both hands in the air. "I'll make the fire!"

"Can I help?" Aaron asked.

"Why, sure you can, Aaron. We'll make it together."

The children and Mrs. Tipperwillow wandered out of the glass-blowing studio into daylight. A large red boat appeared in the air above them. A bell on the bow clanged. "All aboard for Summerland!" said Mrs. T.

They lifted up quickly to find places to sit. Lateesha was first to notice what was written on the side of the boat, and she poked Gino to show him. "*High Spirits!*" Gino said with a laugh. "That's a real good name!"

Moments later, the Summerland tourists were skimming through the blue sky leaving Venice far below. The boat flew through a large Back door, and almost before they knew it, the family was sitting on their peach-colored rug, sipping cocoa and eating cookies before a blazing fire.

Yoshi finished her warm drink and climbed onto Mrs. Tipperwillow's lap. Listening to the sounds of the crackling fire and feeling the happiness of the day's adventures, Yoshi soon was fast asleep against her teacher's soft belly.

Very quietly, the sort of cow rose into the air carrying the sleeping girl and gently tucked her into bed. Returning to the fireplace, Mrs. T. settled in beside the remaining children and stared into the dancing flames.

16

Yoshi's Story

"What happened to Yoshi, Mrs. T.?" Jamie asked. "Sometimes she seems so sad and even angry, and she won't ever talk about it."

"She said that she came here after a car accident, but there's more to it, isn't there?" Lateesha asked.

"Somebody was really mean to her, I bet," added Gino.

"Yes, there *is* more to her story," replied their teacher. "Just a moment, please...."

A glazed look came to Mrs. Tipperwillow's eyes. She sat very still several moments, as if listening to something the children couldn't hear. Finally, she roused herself. "Very well, I have just received permission from Yoshi's higher self to tell you what I know. I will tell Yoshi of our talk in the morning. Now, where to start ... at the beginning, I suspect.

"Yoshi's parents, as you may know, came from Japan to live in New York City when Yoshi was just a baby," said Mrs. Tipperwillow in her story telling voice. "Yoshi's father works in a bank, just as he did in Tokyo, and Yoshi's mother works part-time as an interpreter for Japanese tourists.

"Now, Yoshi's father has a much older brother who has lived for many years in the city of Kyoto, Japan, with his wife and son. The two brothers were never close. It had been a long time since they had seen each other, and Hiromi, the shy little boy Yoshi's father remembered, was now a grown man.

"One fateful day, Yoshi's uncle called to ask if Hiromi could stay with them while he looked for work in the city. Yoshi's father pushed away his feelings of uneasiness, and because he felt a family obligation, he said yes.

"Soon after his twenty-first birthday, Hiromi's plane landed in New York City. From the very first moment she met him, Yoshi didn't trust her cousin. She felt he was just *pretending* to be nice. She had some clairsentience, you see, and she felt that something about her cousin was really wrong.

"One afternoon while Hiromi was out job hunting, Yoshi tried to explain this to her mother. But her mother was busy and said they'd talk later. They never did.

"At any rate," Mrs. Tipperwillow continued, "one grey autumn morning, Hiromi agreed to drive Yoshi to the zoo while her parents were both working. Normally, Yoshi would have been at the neighbor's playing with her best friend, but on that day there was a mix-up, and Lizzie and her mother were not at home.

At the zoo, Yoshi was feeling worse and worse. Her cousin kept looking at her strangely, and he was sweating, even though it was a cold and cloudy day."

"Oh, I don't like this story," interrupted Lateesha.

"Nor do I," Mrs. Tipperwillow replied, "but the story has a good ending.

"Hiromi bought them both hot dogs, and they went to the nearby park to eat them. Because of the chill in the air, the park was nearly empty. They had finished lunch and were cutting diagonally through the trees to where they had parked when Hiromi stuck out a foot and Yoshi tripped over it, falling to the ground with a startled yelp. At that very instant, big drops of rain began falling. Cursing under his breath, Hiromi pulled Yoshi smoothly to her feet and brushed her off. 'I'm *so* sorry,' he said in a silky voice. 'I must have tripped. Are you all right?'

"Now, Yoshi *knew* that Hiromi had done it on purpose. But being a smart girl and just wanting to get home safely, she nodded her head. 'Accidents happen sometimes,' she said and tried to smile as if she believed him. There was no one around as they ran through the rain toward the car, and Yoshi was thinking about what she'd tell her mother. 'You just wait, Hiromi!' she said to herself.

"They got into the automobile. Hiromi locked the doors. He took off driving but in the *opposite* direction of their apartment. Yoshi looked straight ahead. She looked out the side window. She looked everywhere but at her cousin. But she could feel him staring at her and finally looked over. She knew in that instant that he had no intention of taking her home. Yoshi pulled as far away from him as she could and stared at him with frightened eyes.

"The rain was coming down hard now and batting the windows and the hood of the car. Hiromi was looking at Yoshi instead of the rain-slicked street, when their car struck an oily patch of pavement and veered into oncoming traffic. A huge truck struck them head-on. Neither of their bodies survived the accident."

"But ... but ... what is the good ending?" stammered Lateesha, wiping away tears.

"Why, Yoshi coming here to Summerland, of course ... first to the nursery, where she was soothed and cared for so lovingly by Annie and the rest. And then she joined us here." Mrs. Tipperwillow motioned Lateesha over for a hug.

Jamie asked, "Mrs. T., did Yoshi go to the nursery first because she was so scared right before she died?"

"You're exactly right, Jamie. People who leave their physical bodies when they are afraid often need special time for healing, which includes lots of rest and gentleness. Babies will normally be in the nursery for awhile as well, because sleeping is what they did most on Earth."

Lateesha sniffled and asked in a small voice, "Mrs. Tipperwillow, why do people do mean things?"

"Maybe someone was mean to them," Aaron suggested. "Where I came from, lots of people were afraid and angry all the time. I was only little, but I could feel it. I would cry sometimes, and Mommy wouldn't know why. She would check my diapers and feed me, but that wasn't it."

"Just like Yoshi, you could feel something was wrong," said Lateesha from her teacher's lap. "You were clair ... what is it?"

Clairsentient, answered Gino, proudly.

"Yeah ... clairsentient."

Mrs. Tipperwillow nodded. "When people are hurt they get angry, and when they are angry they often hurt someone else. That is a great sadness on Earth, but it is a pattern that *can* change with understanding."

"But what happened to Hiromi after he died?" Gino asked. "Did he go to" ... Gino swallowed hard ... "that *other* place?"

Mrs. Tipperwillow shook her head sadly. "People who have harmed others generally get caught up in their own guilty and painful memories, Gino. They see and feel not only what they did but also the pain and emotions of anyone they hurt and anyone who had *ever* hurt them.

"This can run over and over like a movie they can't escape, until finally they understand enough of the pattern to find a measure of forgiveness for themselves and for those who hurt them. At this point, the pictures around them dissolve, and guides are finally able to get through to help."

"Mrs. T.," Gino began, "about a week before I came here, my brothers were around the breakfast table talking about a kid from high school who killed himself. Does the same thing happen in a suicide?"

"Yes, Gino, except when a person has a terminal illness and has chosen to end their suffering. There is no harm in that, for family and friends must surely understand, so there are no heavy feelings or guilt to carry over.

"In most cases, though, people who commit suicide are angry and depressed. They believe they will somehow make things easier by ending their lives and assume that they will go into some long sleep and never have to face what they have done. This couldn't be further from the truth. And their energies on leaving Earth will draw to them the same type of situation in their next lifetime. It is likely that someone they love will kill themselves, and they'll have to deal with that."

"That's karma, huh?" concluded Gino.

"Indeed, Gino, indeed. But I want you all to understand that karma is not some kind of punishment. It is an automatic energy thing. It is as if during your last moments of life you pack an energy suitcase and, when you awaken on this side, your suitcase opens to what you were carrying with you in life and sometimes even what you were picturing in those last few moments.

"Think about your own experiences. Jamie, just before you switched dimensions, you were thinking about the three trees in your grandma's backyard, so when you arrived in Summerland...."

"I saw birch trees," Jamie said, "a whole forest of them."

"And I saw daffodils," Lateesha chimed in, "but lots more than I'd imagined."

Gino laughed. "And I was playing, so I found myself at the entrance to *Play* Land. How cool is that?"

"But you see," said Mrs. Tipperwillow seriously, "it would not have been so *cool* if your last thoughts had been angry, depressed, guilty, or destructive. Those thoughts and pictures would have become bigger, too. They would have become your whole world." The children were quiet, taking this in.

"But," Aaron began, "what about me and Yoshi?" How did we end up in the nursery?"

"Your guardian angels saw to that, Aaron. The guardians help the young and the frightened across and take them to that most special place for rest and healing.

"Before we finish, there's something else I'd like you all to consider. Earth is entering an exciting new era unlike any that has come before. We here in spirit don't even know how it will all turn out. But we do know that much will be changing and quickly. It may be that by becoming kinder and wiser, the people of Earth will decide to let go of judgment and fear and guilt and outgrow karma altogether."

Mrs. Tipperwillow stood, and the children got to their feet, also. "Now, it's been a long day with many challenging things to think about. Perhaps tonight, dear friends, *these* might be in order."

The children followed their teacher's gaze to the top of the tent, where four Teddy bears were floating. One was dark brown. One was light brown. One was black, and one was snowy white. The bears drifted down, and each child took one.

Then, hugging their new bears tightly, the children said their blessings. They added an extra blessing for Yoshi and for all the sad and scared people in the world before calling in the nighttime and crawling into their warm bunks. A light pink bear appeared between Mrs. Tipperwillow's hooves, and she tucked it gently beside Yoshi's sleeping form.

17

Healing Lake

When Yoshi awakened the next morning, she was surprised to discover that she was hugging a soft pink bear. Taking the bear with her, she rolled out of her bottom bunk onto the rug. Fuzzy blue slippers appeared, and she slid into them.

"Thank you, Mrs. Tipperwillow," she said softly so as not to awaken her friends.

"You're quite welcome, Yoshi. May we talk a minute?"

Mrs. Tipperwillow pointed her hoof at the rug near the fireplace and motioned for the seven-year-old to sit with her. "Sure, what is it?" Yoshi asked, hugging her new bear tightly as she lowered herself to sit on the soft carpet.

Mrs. T. gently patted Yoshi's small hand with her hoof. "My dear Yoshi, last night I first asked the permission of your higher self, and then I explained to your friends how you came to be here in Summerland. I hope you don't mind. I thought it might be easier for you this way."

Confusion filled Yoshi's eyes for a moment. Then a smile crept to her face. "Thank you, Mrs. Tipperwillow. I'm glad you did that. I wanted to tell, but sometimes it still hurts to think about it, and I didn't know the right words to say."

Soon, a little shyly, the rest of the children joined Yoshi and their teacher by the fireplace.

"Are you okay?" Jamie asked, sitting down and taking her friend's small hand in her own. Yoshi nodded.

"Children, before we continue our travels, there is a very special place I'd like to take you all. It is a beautiful lake with healing waters. I suspect that Yoshi isn't the only one with a few Earth memories which still might need some healing. Am I right?" Mrs. Tipperwillow asked, tipping her large head to one side.

The children nodded their heads. Laughter erupted as swimsuits of pink, green, orange, blue, and purple appeared *over* their pajamas. "Oops!" said the blushing sort of cow. The nightclothes dissolved.

"Let's be on our way," said Mrs. T. who, with a wink of her eye, was wearing a sky blue swimsuit with puffy white clouds moving slowly across the fabric. The family rose as one, drifted through the tent flap, and lifted into the golden sky.

Over hills and fields they flew. Soon small cottages dotted an evergreen forest beneath them.

"Wait for me a moment," said Mrs. Tipperwillow and swooped down toward one of the cottages. The children watched as she climbed the steps to the porch and knocked on the door. In a moment she was back. "One of my very favorite spirits named Tobias lives there. I hoped to say a quick hello, but he was not at home."

"Maybe he was hiding behind the door," Gino suggested.

"Oh, you!" said Mrs. T.

◆   ◆   ◆

As the group approached the edge of the forest, a large emerald green lake appeared. Lights twinkled off its surface.

"Here we are!" said the sort of cow cheerfully, as the six landed on a sandy shore beside the sparkling lake. Colorful birds were singing in the nearby trees as Mrs. T. removed Snoody from around her neck and gently put him down on their blue and white blanket.

"Last one in is a rotten egg!" she yelled and took a flying leap into the lake. The children rushed to join her, and really, it was so very hard to tell who was last, that no rotten egg was chosen.

They splashed around at first, but soon all of the children, even Gino, were floating and drifting lazily through the waters. It felt as if every sad or hurtful memory was being lifted out, as if they were being washed clean.

All at once, a feeling of such joy came over the children that they began swimming fast underwater, rolling over and over like dolphins, turning somersaults, and singing happy underwater songs. On and on they swam, further and further from shore. What was this?

"Mrs. T.!" Aaron called. "There's someone else here!"

"There *is*?" All of the Summerland family converged on the lone swimmer.

Aaron ... is that you? I asked, looking at the eight-year-old boy with the dark, wavy hair, *and Lateesha, Gino, Yoshi ... and Jamie!*

"You know us?" Jamie asked, looking me over.

"Well, well, this is quite a surprise!" said Mrs. Tipperwillow.

You're not as surprised as I am. I thought you might be coming here next, but I never imagined we could actually meet like this.

"Who *is* this woman, Mrs. T.?" asked Lateesha.

"And how does she know *us*?" added Jamie.

"Children, may I introduce to you Krista, the woman who is writing down our story."

"What?" Gino exclaimed, his eyes wide with surprise. "She can't be here. She's on Earth!"

"Haven't we been going to Earth, Children? So why can't she visit here?"

The children floated around me, and Yoshi reached out to touch my long hair. "She feels real enough," Yoshi said. Mrs. Tipperwillow gave me a wink.

"But how did you find your way *here*?" Lateesha asked me.

My first visit to this lake was many years ago, Teesha. I was deep in meditation when one of my spirit friends broke into the quiet and said 'I have someplace special to show you. Follow me.' He led me to the shores of this lake, and together we swam through the healing green waters. Now every once in a while I come back here on my own.

I'm really so glad we got to meet like this, I continued, *but I should be going now. It is time to get out of bed and into my new day.*

"You're dreaming us?" Jamie asked.

Well, I'm awake and I know I'm in bed, but I'm here as well. You might say I'm imagining.

"But we're *real*," said Aaron.

And so am I! Good bye, everyone! I'll see you in the story!

"Hey, wait a minute, Krista," Gino said as I began to open my eyes. "What's the title of this story we're in, anyway?"

I refocused my inner sight. *It's called "From Here to Earth and Back Again."*

"That makes sense!" he replied and smiled at me with those wild eyes of his.

See you! I thought, throwing off the covers.

◆   ◆   ◆

Minutes later I was in the kitchen making breakfast. "Hi!" said a familiar voice.

Gino, is that you? I asked in my mind.

"Gino!" scolded Mrs. Tipperwillow.

"Sorry to disturb you, Krista. Gino here followed your energy traces and made his own door to get here. Quite a clever boy when he wants to be."

I sensed the other children wandering about the rooms of the house. "Where *are* we?" Lateesha asked, coming into the combined kitchen, living, and dining area, then looking out of the front window.

We're on the Big Island of Hawaii, I thought, just as the others appeared. The children floated through the sliding glass door and out onto the front deck to look at the view.

"They'll want to explore a bit," Mrs. Tipperwillow explained. I nodded, and suddenly the house was quiet. By the time my toast was burnt, they were back.

Mrs. Tipperwillow, I bet the children might like to see the active volcano, Kilauea, which is on the other side of this island. It's been erupting since the 1980's, and you can get closer to the flowing lava than tourists are ever allowed.

The magical sort of cow nodded her large head. "What a splendid idea."

"Yes!" all the children said at once.

"Let's leave Krista to her day now," said Mrs. T., motioning the children out onto the deck. "Sorry to have disturbed you, Krista."

It's no problem, I thought, licking butter off my finger. *See you all later.*

18

Swimmin' with the Fishes

"One moment, children," Mrs. Tipperwillow said, as the family gathered on the front deck of the house. A book appeared between her hooves.

"What's that, Mrs. T.?" asked Aaron.

"Why, a tour book, of course!" she replied, looking at the cover.

"Well, aren't you going to *open* it?" asked Gino, who was impatient to get going.

"No need to, really. Here, Gino. Why don't you give it a go? Just put your hand on the book."

As the boy's hand touched the cover, he began to see images. "What's this?" he asked and quickly jerked his hand away. Just as quickly, his hand was touching the cover again.

"What is it, Gino? What do you see?" asked Lateesha as she came around to his side.

"I see a map of the island we're on, and now I'm seeing pictures of the places we could go! It's kind of like a slide show at school."

"Let me try!" Teesha said, reaching out.

"You may each have a turn," said their teacher, "but one at a time, please."

Gino stepped back, and Lateesha, Aaron, Yoshi, and Jamie took their turns. Gino peeked through the window at me eating breakfast at the dining room table. He turned back to Mrs. Tipperwillow and asked, "Where are we on the map?"

Mrs. Tipperwillow touched the boy's forehead with the tip of one hoof. "Here, Gino." He closed his eyes to see a map labeled "Big Island of Hawaii" with a red star on one portion.

"Aha! I've got it now!" Gino yelled and flew away so fast that he created a little bit of wind in his wake.

Mrs. T. called out, "Gino, we're going together!"

"Oh, yeah, I forgot." He was standing again on the deck, his cheeks flushed from the quick flight. "Well, are you done *yet*, Jamie?" The boy tapped his foot impatiently.

She looked up. "Okay, I'm done!"

The children agreed that on their way to the volcano, they'd stop at some of the places pictured in the tour book. "Then away we go!" yelled Mrs. Tipperwillow, leaping into the air.

The Summerland family quickly flew down toward the ocean, which was sparkling in tropical morning light. They drifted above the shoreline, noticing the fields of hardened black lava and the paths they made from the mountain to the sea.

The group landed on warm sand, and their blanket appeared beside them. "Since we still have our swimsuits on, how would you all like to see some tropical fish?" asked their teacher as she lowered Snoody to the blanket. He squeaked unhappily.

Yoshi bent down and picked up the small creature. "He wants to come with us, Mrs. T. Please! I'll hold him."

"Of course you may. Here's a little carrier for you to wear." It appeared around Yoshi's waist, and the girl carefully tucked the excited snoode inside. The children followed Mrs. Tipperwillow to the water's edge and ran into the breaking waves. They flew beneath the ocean's surface and discovered large batches of coral on the sandy floor. Brightly-colored fish wove in and out of the coral.

Jamie looked around in wonder. *This is almost like what you showed us in Summerland, Mrs. T., but there are even more fish here.*

Two brightly striped Moorish idols swam by, waving their long fins. These were followed by five rounded, bright-yellow tang. Turning around, the children spotted a school of large, rounded purplish fish—triggerfish, Mrs. Tipperwillow called them. Several rainbow-colored fish swam by. The children heard the word *wrasse* in their minds as they noticed these fish. Yoshi pointed at a small black, white, and yellow fish that looked like it was wearing a mask. *What's that, Mrs. T.?*

That's a raccoon butterfly fish. Doesn't it look a little like a raccoon with its mask? The girl nodded.

Aaron thought to his friends. *Come look at this!* Everyone rushed over. They discovered six long, skinny needlefish swimming near the surface. The fish were hard to see because they were nearly the color of the water itself.

Lateesha pointed to a diamond-shaped fish about the size of her hand. It had an unusual pattern of black banding and dark yellow lines on a lighter peachy-yellow background, a patch of light blue above its eye, blue on its blunted nose, and a bright orange stripe on its fin. *That sure is a strange looking fish, Mrs. Tipperwillow. What is it?* Her friends swam over to have a look.

That's the Hawaiian state fish, Lateesha, commonly known as the Picasso trigger fish. And for a small fish, it has a very long Hawaiian name. Can any of you say humu-humu-nuku-nuku-āpu-a'a three times quickly? Mrs. Tipperwillow asked, carefully accenting the sounds.

After some bubbly underwater attempts, the children emerged, laughing. "Humu-humu to you!" laughed Gino as he poked Lateesha. She poked him right back.

The children dove under again and discovered a large green sea turtle floating near them. And two of the large triggerfish were eating kelp that was attached to the turtle's back! The family gathered around for a closer look. *That looks yummy*, Gino thought as he reached out. His hand went through the turtle's shell.

Suddenly, there was a low pitched sound that slid into a higher one. *What's that?* Aaron asked, edging closer to his teacher, his eyes wide. The others stopped to listen.

Oh, aren't we the lucky ones today! Follow me, children ... and stay close, please.

19

Close Encounter

The family flew underwater, further and further out from the sandy shore. In his excitement, Gino had surged ahead. Aaron was close on his heels, both boys following the sound.

Hey, what's this? Aaron asked, coming up quickly on something huge directly in front of them.

Dear me! Mrs. Tipperwillow thought. *Boys, come back now!*

Gino and Aaron turned their heads at the frantic sound of their teacher's inner voice. But it was too late. They had been moving so fast that their momentum had pulled them forward through a gray wall and into a world of darkness.

Where are we? Aaron asked in a frightened voice.… Nothing. *Gino … are you here?*

Feeling something different, the humpback whale stopped its singing.

I'm here, Aaron, Gino answered. *We're inside of a whale, really inside of a whale, just like Jonah in the Bible story. How cool is this?*

But … but … how do we get out? Aaron asked, his thoughts echoing.

Feeling full of confidence, Gino replied. *We just pass through to the other side, of course.* He reached around in the dark. *Take my hand, Aaron. We'll go out together.*

The whale turned abruptly. The boys lost their balance and flopped down on their backsides.

Meanwhile, Mrs. Tipperwillow and the girls had shown up and were staring open mouthed at the gray sides of the giant humpback whale.

It's beautiful, thought Yoshi.

And so big! Jamie added.

Lateesha swam up close and looked into the intelligent eye. *It sees me, Mrs. Tipperwillow! I know it does!*

The whale turned to get a look at the rest of the group. They backed up.

But where's Gino? And where's Aaron? Jamie asked. *I don't see them.*

Mrs. Tipperwillow pointed her hoof at the side of the huge body. *In there, I'm afraid.* The girls' eyes grew wide.

Their teacher turned to look at them. *Long ago, this same thing happened to another tourist visiting from the spirit world. That story came to Earth as many do, through the magic mailbox, and it was written down.*

Jamie pushed her hair back from her face. *But ... how could this happen?*

I don't really know, Jamie. But I have heard great whales referred to as the record keepers of planet Earth, Mrs. Tipperwillow replied. *Perhaps this unusual occurrence has some connection.*

The sort of cow shook her head. *I'm going to swim around our big friend here to make sure the boys aren't just on the other side. Please don't get too close. I'll be back soon.*

We pass right through people on Earth, Yoshi thought, biting her lower lip.

Maybe it's something different about the whale's energy, Lateesha guessed. *I'm going to try something.*

Don't, Teesh! Yoshi cautioned, trying to pull her friend back. *Remember what Mrs. T. said!*

I won't go any closer, I promise. Lateesha pulled away.

The humpback started singing again. A long high note slid into a lower one and it made a beautiful sound. The vibrations thrummed through the girls ... *and* through the frightened boys inside the whale.

20

The Rescue

We can't get out! Aaron whimpered. Both boys had fallen back down after a second failed attempt to get out of the whale.

Now what? Gino asked, as a high tone passed through him. It was followed by a deeper one.

Meanwhile, on the outside, Lateesha was sharing her thoughts with Jamie and Yoshi. *It has got to be about vibration*, she said in her mind.

Mrs. Tipperwillow swam up and Lateesha turned to her. *Mrs. T., I'm glad you're back. I think I have an idea to get the boys out. We have to make an energy doorway.*

You may just have it, Teesh! But first we must ask the assistance of this lovely creature, who otherwise may not appreciate the attempt. The magical sort of cow drifted over underwater to meet the whale eye to eye.

Moments later, Mrs. Tipperwillow returned. *Dear ones, I was able to communicate our desires to Galen. That is the whale's name, you see. He is very aware of the situation and quite adept at moving and shifting vibrations through his song. He promised to aid us. Lateesha, what is your plan?*

Well, I thought that if we all concentrate on Gino's vibrations ... what he is, you know....

And then if Galen can match them, continued Mrs. Tipperwillow, catching the idea.

We can make an energy opening to set him free, the girl added. *The same goes for Aaron.*

Yes, I see ... like to like and one at a time. Mrs. Tipperwillow swam over to relate the plan to the whale. She returned quickly.

Okay, Lateesha said. *Let's start with Gino, and then we'll move quickly to Aaron.*

Yoshi spoke up at once. *Aaron must be really scared. He doesn't know much about being eight years old yet. Can we save him first ... please?*

The nine-year-old nodded. *That's a good idea. Yoshi, since you know Aaron best of anybody, you begin to form up his energy. And then we will join in to make it even stronger.*

Okay, but how again?

Just think of what Aaron is like and put that in a ball. Do you think you can do that?

I think so.

The girls and Mrs. Tipperwillow formed a circle under water. Jamie and Lateesha followed Yoshi's lead as she concentrated on Aaron. Swirling energy began to form in the center of their circle. It became so strong that almost immediately, they could clearly see a fuzzy ball of purplish light.

Okay, you've done it! Mrs. T. thought. She pointed to an area on the side of the whale. *Now Lateesha, move the energy right there.*

At that moment, Galen the whale began to sing. His song was sad and sweet and somehow reminded the girls of Aaron. When the energy in the target area of the whale began to shift, the children and their teacher could see inside. There was Aaron's tear-streaked face. Gino had his head in his hands, and he was crying, too.

Lateesha called out, *Aaron*! The boy looked up. *You can come out now!*

I see you! Aaron jumped to his feet.

What is it, Aaron? Gino asked. *I don't see anything.*

Aaron, tell Gino we'll be right back for him, and walk through the opening.

Okay, Teesha, he replied, and shared what he had heard with Gino. Aaron stood up and moved through the glowing doorway. It faded behind him. Yoshi gave him a tremendous underwater hug.

Wasting no time, Lateesha formed up Gino's energy, which was white with orange sparkles. Jamie joined in to make the sending stronger. Then Galen added his song, which felt bouncy, just like Gino. A second portal opened.

Soon the family was together once again. As they floated on the ocean's surface, the girls told the story of what they had done to rescue the two boys.

"You and your wiggly lines, Teesh," Gino said. "You saved us! Thank you. Thank you all so much."

Gino looked over at the whale floating nearby, and a smile covered his face. "I sure hope Krista is getting *this* story!" he said in an excited voice. "It's *fantastico!*"

Mrs. Tipperwillow cocked her cow head to one side and chuckled. *How quickly fear can turn to adventure in a boy's mind,* she thought to herself.

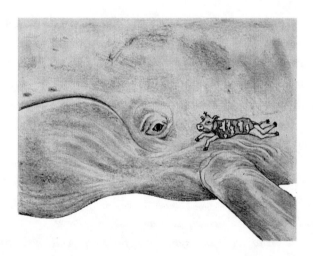

Galen looked out of his huge eye at the Summerland family, and he began to sing once more. The family listened, entranced, as a song of Earth moved through them. Images of their planet's beginnings appeared in their minds—images of fire and floods and ferny forests. They saw animal life beginning with the smallest of ocean creatures, then fishes, amphibians, and reptiles, and finally, the mammals we know today. And the dinosaurs! Oh, the dinosaurs!

The last image Galen sang was of children climbing a play structure in a green park. Some were swinging, some were going hand-over-hand on the monkey bars, and some were taking turns on the slide. The images dissolved, and with a final sounding, slowly, ever so slowly, the humpback whale turned and glided away.

Mrs. Tipperwillow and the children swam toward shore and emerged from the shore break next to a pile of soft blue towels. Drying themselves off, they looked up just in time to see Galen's blow sending water vapor high into the noon day sky. Mrs. T. imagined wearing her favorite flowered "moomoo" … and she was. With a wave of her hoof, the children wore surfer shorts and white tee shirts with "Hawaii" written across the chest. Beneath the writing was a picture of Galen, the humpback whale.

21

From Beach to Volcano

Over the shoreline, the Summerland tourists flew. Soon they spotted the perfect place for a short rest ... an area of green grass overlooking a beautiful white sand beach. Their blanket appeared, and Aaron helped Gino smooth it out on the lawn. Yoshi placed Snoody down next to her. A soft breeze was blowing, and the sound of the ocean was so soothing that one by one the children sank down onto the soft blanket and fell fast asleep.

The magical sort of cow looked out at the waves breaking onto the shore. For awhile Mrs. Tipperwillow watched as happy people ran into the waves and played in the sand. *What an amazing day*, she thought with a sigh. Then, listening to the sounds of voices and the roar of the ocean, she tucked her legs beneath her and slept, also.

It was late afternoon when the children and Mrs. Tipperwillow awakened. A noisy family barbecue was beginning nearby. Someone was playing an ukulele and singing. People were laughing. The smells of grilling chicken, hot dogs, and hamburgers filled the air. The sun was low in the sky as the children and their teacher got to their feet (and hooves) and looked around.

"My, my, we slept quite a long time," Mrs. Tipperwillow said, stretching. "I suggest that we visit the volcano now, and that way we can see it before and also after the sun sets."

"Yes!" Gino exclaimed. He began hopping up and down with his arms high above his head. Aaron copied him. Then the girls joined in.

"What are we doing?" asked the sort of cow, waving her hooves in the air and jumping up and down with the rest.

"It's a little volcano dance, of course!" Gino replied with a kick of his heels.

Finally, with her face flushed from all the jumping around, Mrs. Tipperwillow asked, "Are you all about ready?"

"We are!" yelled the children.

◆   ◆   ◆

The Summerland family lifted high into the sky and drifted away from the shoreline. Soon they found themselves over fields of chunky lava rocks between two huge mountains. Each mountain wore a crown of glistening snow. "On the left is the volcano named Mauna Kea," yelled Mrs. T. above the wind, "and on our right is Mauna Loa."

Lateesha laughed. "Snow in *Hawaii*, Mrs. T.?"

"It is wintertime here, and yes, snow in winter is common at the highest elevations on Earth—even in Hawaii."

Gino turned and began gliding down toward Mauna Kea's summit. *"Can't resist it, can you, boy?"* Mrs. Tipperwillow turned to follow him. By the time the others touched down, Gino was kneeling over the snow, desperately trying to grab handfuls. His hands came up empty. He looked up, shaking his head. "No snowballs fights today, Gino, Mrs. Tipperwillow said with a chuckle. Shall we be on our way?"

"But Mrs. T-e-e-e," Gino whined. "Wait a minute!" He stuck a finger in the air. "We can create our *own* snowballs!"

A snowball whizzed past Mrs. Tipperwillow and hit Aaron squarely on the chest. And the play was on! Soon all five children and one sort of cow were covered with snow. Suddenly realizing they were *freezing,* the children began brushing snow from their bare legs and light clothing. Mrs. T. blinked her eyes twice. Everyone was warm and dry again.

With a nod of agreement, they left the mountain and soon were flying over the waterfront town of Hilo. By following the map in their minds, they discovered the entrance to Hawaii Volcanoes National Park. Traveling through a ferny forest, they saw a sign that read *Thur-*

ston Lava Tube. Gino took the lead as they followed a trail that led to the entrance. They swooped through the long tunnel of hardened lava *and* through several people, who were trying to avoid mud puddles on the tunnel's floor.

Coming out the other side, they floated across the road and down hundreds of feet to land on the floor of a wide, flat crater. There was no flowing lava here, just sulfur steam rising out of the ground in several places. They drifted toward a steam vent to get a closer look.

Mrs. T. clapped her hooves together, and the smell of rotten eggs filled the air.

"Who farted?" Gino quipped.

Mrs. Tipperwillow chuckled. "That's the smell of sulfur coming from deep within the Earth, Gino."

"It stinks!" Yoshi and Jamie said at the same instant.

"But where's the hot lava, Mrs. T.?" Lateesha asked, holding her nose and looking from one edge of the crater to the other.

"Let's fly higher and take a broader look. I'm sure it's here somewhere!"

The light in the sky was fading as Mrs. Tipperwillow pointed to a red glow in the distance which was lit up by the setting sun. "On and on we go!' she laughed and streaked toward the ground with the children close behind.

"Wow!" Gino exclaimed as he landed next to a crack in the blackened surface. A red bubble of lava was growing in the crack. Without any warning it exploded with a pop, sending splatters everywhere.

"If you were in an Earth body, you'd be *fried* by now!" said Mrs. Tipperwillow, cheerfully. "See the splatters all around you there?" Gino looked into his teacher's eyes with little tears forming in his own.

"Are you all right, Child?" the sort of cow asked as the others landed. The lava started flowing out of the crack toward them. They lifted into the air to give the lava room.

"It's just so big somehow," replied Gino. "... So beautiful and so...."

"Powerful!" finished Jamie.

The children looked around. The sun had set quickly, and the few clouds in the sky had turned deep pink and orange. Sensing something Mrs. Tipperwillow exclaimed, "Get back quickly, Children … and up, up *now!*"

The children quickly moved backwards and leapt high into the air. The next moment, a huge spray of bright red lava blasted into the sky. "Woo!" exclaimed Gino as the lava, pushed by tremendous force, rose up, up, up and fell back to Earth just where the children and Mrs. Tipperwillow had been standing. They watched in awe as more lava exploded like fireworks and pushed higher and higher into the sky. As it fell back to Earth, the melted rock slowly spread like thick red and black syrup over the older lava beneath it.

"Children," Mrs. T. whispered, "we are seeing the birth of new land."

Several helicopters arrived and hovered as close to the spewing lava as they could safely get. One copter had "Channel 8 News" written on the side. A cameraman leaned out of the open door. He began taking pictures.

"It looks as if we were the very first to witness a major eruption," Mrs. Tipperwillow said softly. The Summerland group landed on a solid patch of ground near the flow of liquid rock and watched silently as more lava pushed high into the twilight sky.

22

Pele

The family continued watching with all of their attention focused on the eruption. There was a shimmer in the air behind them. An old woman appeared with a thin, white dog by her side.

The woman wore a white dress, and in one hand she carried a wooden staff. Her head was encircled by a wreath of ferns, leaves, and red flowers, and her long white hair flew out from her weathered face in the night wind.

Sensing something, the children and their teacher turned. "Welcome to Kilauea," said the old woman, who was glowing with white light.

"She can see us," whispered Jamie to Lateesha.

"Well, of course I can, Children."

"Who are you?" asked Aaron.

"My name is Pele."

"Goddess of the volcano," said Gino in a hushed voice. "I read about her in my book of legends." The children's eyes grew round as saucers.

"There is no reason to fear, Children. I will not bite you. Come over here! And you must be their teacher," she added, with a nod to Mrs. Tipperwillow.

"So I am...." responded the sort of cow, as she felt the words she could have said leave her.

"Truly, I have a fearsome reputation," continued the old woman, whose face was lit by the red glow of the nearby lava. "But really I am just a kindly spirit who watches over the *'āina*. That means land, Children."

The family edged closer. Pele spoke again. "Soon there will be elders here, Hawaiians who follow the old ways. They will bring me fruit, garlands of flowers, and gin, a type of liquor that I have been known to favor. They will chant of a time when the land was honored, when the connection between human and spirit was understood. They will chant for Pele, who watches over this sacred ground. The chants are prayers ... *very* powerful prayers. Would you like to hear my favorite?"

The children and their teacher nodded. Finally Mrs. T. found her voice. "We would be honored, Madame Pele," she murmured and made a little curtsy.

Pele carefully laid the wooden staff on the ground. A large gourd, which was decorated with red and yellow feathers, appeared on the ground beside her. She picked it up and began hitting the gourd with the flat of her hand. It made a hollow, drumming sound.

The chant began, low and powerful, rumbling and crackling like the sound of the flowing lava nearby. The glow around Pele intensified until there were red sparks flying off around the edges. The chant entered the family, and the children and Mrs. Tipperwillow felt as if their feet and hooves were actually glued to the earth beneath them.

They felt the power of new land being born and the power of sudden unexpected change that cannot be avoided. They sensed giant trees toppling and burning as lava flowed out over the land and into the ocean with a crackle and a hiss of steam. Then the chant softened, and Mrs. T. and the children sensed the wind and the rain running over the cooled lava and new life beginning. Small grasses were pushing through the cracks. These were followed by scrubby trees and then taller ones, which bloomed with wispy red flowers.

The chant ended. Pele's eyes were glowing as she looked at the Summerland family. She reached down to pet her dog, and just like that, she disappeared.

"She forgot her walking stick," whispered Jamie and drifted over to pick it up. Power flowed through the wood, and the children each took a turn at feeling the energies. They looked up to see that the sky was getting lighter. In a puff of red light, the staff disappeared from Gino's hands.

"It just got dark a few minutes ago," Yoshi said, looking at the rising sun. "How can it be morning already?"

"Children," said Mr. Tipperwillow, "we have been treated to magic of the highest kind. I have no idea how long we stood here listening. Do you?"

"It must have been a *very* long time," Yoshi replied, yawning. "Can we go home now?"

"Without seeing any waterfalls?" asked Jamie.

"Why don't we see one waterfall on the way back," Mrs. T. suggested. "I'll carry Yoshi."

The little girl climbed into Mrs. T's arms and held on tight, her head snuggled against the sleeping snoode as they lifted skyward. Yoshi's eyes were barely open as they stopped to see beautiful Rainbow Falls near Hilo. She completely missed the trip through the Back door and the quick flight home.

"You all right, Yoshi?" Aaron asked his "big" sister after she was tucked into bed.

"Ummm," she mumbled and was asleep again at once.

"Waffles for breakfast," mumbled Gino, and he, too, was fast asleep.

Soon soft sighs and sounds of breathing filled the red and white striped tent. The magical sort of cow imagined a little fire in the fireplace. She stared at it for a very long time.

23

Break-fast

Mrs. Tipperwillow was up early. She created a rosy sunrise to greet the children when they awakened. The trouble was, they didn't wake up. *Ah,* she thought, *the dear ones have so much to absorb from yesterday's journey that they are sleeping long to take it all in.*

With a wish, she set the sunrise to stay exactly as it was until all the children could see it. Finally, Yoshi wandered out of the tent, wiping the sleep out of her eyes. She discovered Mrs. Tipperwillow sitting cross-legged and meditating with her eyes closed. Yoshi smiled at the beautiful sunrise. She sat down by her teacher, crossed her legs also, and closed her eyes. One by one, as they noticed the pink light streaming through the tent flap, the other children emerged and joined in the meditation. Aaron was first and Gino was last out of the tent.

Gino sat down. He crossed his legs like the others and closed his eyes. A moment later he took a peek. No one was moving yet. "Well, *that* sure was a good meditation!" he stated loudly. "I'm ready for breakfast … how about you?"

Aaron was up first and followed Gino into the tent. The girls and Mrs. T. settled back into their clear thought place until finally the racket from inside the tent became too loud to ignore. Pots and pans were crashing and banging. A blender was roaring. The boys were laughing. A spray of milk actually managed to travel *through* the open tent flap.

"Hmmm...." Mrs. Tipperwillow murmured, and she opened her eyes as the girls did the same. "I think it's time to see what the boys are up to. Shall we?"

Jamie, Yoshi, and Lateesha nodded, and soon all four were scrambling into the tent, climbing over an overturned kettle, some spatulas, a mixing bowl, and an enormous spoon on the way in. Flour, milk, and several eggs (still partially in their shells) were spilling out of a large bowl.

"Where did you get all this, Gino?" questioned Mrs. T., with a sort of half smile on her face.

The boy turned. His face and Aaron's were both covered in flour, except for mischievous eyes peeking out and red lips.

"Ah, yes ... cherry juice," Mrs. Tipperwillow said with a sigh, as she studied the half empty juice glasses and the broken pitcher and the cherry juice seeping into the rug. "Interesting color choice," she murmured, cocking her cow head and scratching her ear with one hoof. "Did you boys make all this?"

"Yep! We thought we'd make waffles the way they do on Earth, with blenders and flour and stuff," answered Gino, proudly.

"And have you succeeded, young man?"

"Well, not yet, actually. It is *very* hard work!"

"I see. I am really quite impressed by your ability to create, Gino, and in such a short time at that."

"It was easy once I discovered it was *fun*," the boy said with a winning smile.

"Learning is like that," responded the sort of cow wistfully. "Now, I think we'd all like some waffles. Do you have any idea just *when* they might be ready?"

Jamie tripped on a kettle lid and landed on her knees, laughing. "What a mess!" she exclaimed.

Mrs. Tipperwillow stifled a chuckle. She cleared her throat to appear more serious. "We *are* having a bit of trouble getting around in here, boys. Are you as good at cleaning up as you are at making messes?" Gino tried to look hurt, but he couldn't hide the grin that was beginning at the corners of his mouth.

"How about the spilled cherry juice first," suggested Mrs. Tipperwillow. "As interesting as the bright red looks against the peach colored carpet, it *is* rather sticky."

"Okay," replied Gino, concentrating. The spot on the rug and the broken pitcher disappeared.

"Now, how about putting our tent back the way it was and then creating some waffles in the Summerland sort of way."

"Well, I could do that, I guess. Cooking is a lot more complicated than I thought." Gino closed his eyes and Aaron copied him. Gino yelled "Presto-cleano!" The entire mess dissolved. He took a peek and breathed a sigh of relief.

Next, Gino held out his hands and yelled "Binga-boom!" A huge plate of blueberry waffles appeared between his hands. "Mrs. T., could you make the table, please? These are really hot!" The table and six chairs appeared, and the boy put the waffles down.

"Jamie," asked Mrs. Tipperwillow, "would you like to set our table with forks, knives, and plates?"

"Sure," Jamie answered. The place settings appeared.

"Yoshi, can you create some juice? You choose the kind you'd like most." Yoshi closed her eyes and reopened them. Six classes of orange juice sat at one end of the table. Each child took one and sat down.

"Aaron," asked Mrs. T., "can you picture some more napkins just like this one?" A white napkin appeared between her hooves and Aaron took it and looked at it closely. He closed his eyes and said in a loud voice, *Alacazam!*

"You did it, Aaron," said Yoshi. "Look ... a whole pile of napkins!"

"I did it! I really did it!" exclaimed the boy in wonder.

"Lateesha, will you create the butter and syrup, please?"

"Okay!" First a slab of butter appeared on a bright pink plate and then a pitcher of maple syrup.

"Excellent creating, Children! Let's eat!" Everyone sat down.

"The next time you want to cook in the Earth way," said Mrs. Tipperwillow to Gino around a mouthful, "a cookbook sure might make it easier."

"Easier maybe, but not nearly so much fun."

Sitting by his side, Lateesha poked Gino. Jamie, who was on his other side, poked him, too. "Hey you!" he said to both of them and poked them right back.

24

Catch!

"Since it seems we're done here," said Mrs. Tipperwillow, delicately blotting her large lips with her napkin, "how about a game of catch in the meadow?" The children agreed and barely made it to their feet before the table and chairs disappeared.

Out they floated into the new day. The sky was still in sunrise mode, looking exactly as it had when the children first awakened. "Oh, dear," murmured the sort of cow and clicked her hooves together twice. The rosy sky dissolved, and beneath it lay a clear, golden Summerland day.

The children formed a large circle on the grass, and a red ball appeared in the center of their circle.

"I'll start," Jamie said. She concentrated her thoughts, and the ball rolled toward her and floated up into her hands. Jamie threw the ball across to Yoshi, and when it was halfway there, she changed it to a yellow tabby kitten. The younger girl caught the kitten, kissed its nose, and floated it over to Aaron, changing its color to black on the way. Aaron reached for the kitten, petted its soft fur, and looked up in confusion. "It's not a real Earth kitten," Yoshi said. "You can't hurt it, Aaron. Try floating it over to Gino and then turning it back into a red ball again."

"Just picture what you want, the way you did with the napkins," suggested Lateesha.

Aaron turned the kitten around and stared into its green eyes. "You sure?" he asked his teacher. At her nod, Aaron floated the kitten out toward Gino, closed his eyes and ... yes! It became a red ball again.

Gino caught the ball and threw it fast to Lateesha. Halfway there, it changed form but stayed about the same color. "Oh, no you don't!" exclaimed the girl. She turned the lobster with its pinching claws around and....

"Ouch!" Gino yelped as he automatically caught the unhappy crustacean and got pinched for the effort. The lobster disappeared in a puff of smoke, and the other children and Mrs. Tipperwillow howled with laughter.

The girls began a chant of: "What you do comes back to you! Karma! Karma! Karma!" Over and over they chanted the words. Aaron joined in. And Gino did, too.

Soon all the children were jumping up, down, and around the meadow like kangaroos. "What you do comes back to you-o-o-o!" they yelled, bouncing higher and higher into the Summerland sky.

At last the chanting died out, and the children again floated down to the soft green grass.

25

Questions and Answers

Mrs. Tipperwillow gathered the five friends in a circle. "I thought perhaps we could just sit and talk for awhile." She motioned for them to sit down in the grass.

"Sure Mrs. T. What's up?" Gino asked.

"Well, my dears, I thought you might have some questions about our travels thus far. We have had many new experiences. Is there anything you wish to ask me? I will try my best to answer."

The children paused a moment. "Okay, I have one," said Gino. "Did you or Lateesha come up with anything else about why Aaron and I got trapped in the whale?"

Mrs. Tipperwillow looked at Lateesha and raised her cow brow. "Well, I did have one idea, Gino," the girl said, proud to be the one to answer. "Maybe if whales *are* the record keepers of Earth, their energies are really special. Maybe they are closer to *our* energies, even though they are solid to people on Earth."

Gino nodded to himself. "I think I get what you're saying. Whales are halfway spirit. So we can go in, but then we get stuck." He looked at Mrs. T. "Are there others like that? Could we get stuck in another animal if it were big enough?"

"I don't really know the ways of many of Earth's creatures, only that they are able to sense us," said the sort of cow, smoothing out her red checkered dress with one hoof. "But I suppose it *is* possible, so we should take care. Soon we will be going to Africa, and believe me, getting you out of a stampeding elephant would be a lot more difficult than getting you out of a floating whale. And remember that Galen even helped us through his song."

Gino looked at his toes. "Yeah, I know."

"No one is blaming you boys for what happened," said Mrs. Tipperwillow kindly. "It was clearly an accident. But we must be ever more watchful, *especially* in Africa."

"Right," Gino replied. "Can we go now?"

"Not quite yet. Are there other questions?"

"I have one," Yoshi said. "How come *we* could see that timing problem with accidents on Earth when the grown-ups couldn't do it?"

"Ah, yes, *that*," answered Mrs. T., nodding her head. "Children, do you remember what Wallace said to you right before you had your visions?"

"He said that they'd been through the web over and over, but they couldn't figure out what was wrong with *their system*." Jamie nodded to herself. "Yeah, those were his words."

"That's right. As children grow to be adults they tend to rely more and more on *thinking* and not so much on *imagining*. It is interesting that Wallace and his friends forgot to open themselves to the very intuition that the Light Web promotes.

"Also, people who live on Earth and even spirits who used to live on Earth will think of something they don't understand as a problem, rather than as a delicious mystery to be solved. They will assume that they or someone else has done something wrong and then worry or feel guilty or angry about it until nothing clear comes through. You had no worries at all, children. You just opened up and *saw*, brilliantly, I might add."

"And Wallace said we'll have a party sometime," added Yoshi, smiling.

"Yes, he did say that." Mrs. Tipperwillow winked at the girl. "Now is there anything else?"

Gino asked, "Is Madame Pele really a goddess?"

"Indeed Pele is a special spirit," answered Mrs. T. "Many people in Hawaii honor her, as they have for generations. Some fear her power. They believe that she actually *causes* the volcano to erupt and that she can even change the path of the lava's flow. And she has this unusual talent. Pele has the ability to make herself seen by people on the island of Hawaii. She will appear, either as the old woman we saw or as a beautiful young woman, to bring warning of a coming disaster such as an eruption or a tsunami. A tsunami, Children, is a giant tidal wave caused by an earthquake or by a volcanic eruption. Pele's ability to lower the *frequency* of her vibrations so that she can be seen by people on Earth is *very* special." Gino grinned at Lateesha and moved his hand up and down in a wavy pattern.

"But I'd like you all to remember that *you* are special, too. You each have talents and qualities that are quite unique, and you are each a part of God and Goddess, and Goddess and God is a part of *you!*"

On the word "you," there was a shimmer in the air. The children stared at each other's haloes and reached up to feel the energy of their own. Gino was the first to jerk the gold circlet down from above his head and look through it. "You're way too funny, Mrs. T.!" he exclaimed.

26

Teesha's Tale

Mrs. Tipperwillow wiped away a tear of laughter. "Now, next in our travels we will go to a country in West Africa. The name of this country is Ghana, and when we leave Summerland to get there, you can say that we'll have *Ghana way.*"

"That's a good one, Mrs. T.!" Gino said. The sort of cow took a bow. "But before we travel … Lateesha, would you tell us a bit of your story and what you know about your great-great grandfather who lived in Ghana?"

"Sure!" The children moved in close to listen.

"Well, as most of you know," the girl began in her best storytelling voice, "before I came here I lived with my momma and daddy and Nana Maria in Oak Park. That's the town right next to Chicago. Nana Maria lived with us. She helped take care of me since I was little 'cause Mom and Dad both work full time. I had a great little dog named Shaggy. He was white and well … shaggy. He was smelly, too, but that wouldn't make a very good name." Everyone laughed.

"My parents are both lawyers. My dad works for something called the EPA. He writes laws to help protect the land, but he doesn't talk in court. My mom does, though. She helps defend people who are accused of crimes, and she's *really* good. Daddy used to say that he could never win an argument with her because she got so much practice in court everyday. Sometimes I got to sit in the courtroom and listen to her." Lateesha got a far-off look in her eyes.

"One time, Mom told me the story of her great grandfather. That makes him my great-*great* grandfather, see? He was born in this small village in the middle part of Ghana. That's a country in West Africa, on the bottom bubbly part that sticks out. Mrs. Tipperwillow, will you make a map so I can show them?"

"I think this will do." A map of Africa appeared on the ground in front of Lateesha.

"Thanks. Right there, see?" Teesha pointed. Her friends nodded. "Ghana used to be called the Gold Coast because gold was mined there. Maybe it still is. I don't know.

"Anyway, my great-great grandfather was a young warrior in his tribe. I think he was maybe only fifteen years old. One day, his village was attacked by people from a nearby village who wanted their land. The other tribe won, and my great-great grandfather and his friends were caught. And then they were sold to the British as slaves."

"You mean that people from the villages sold each other?" Gino asked. "That's really weird."

"I know it is, Gino. Anyway, my great-great-grandfather was sent on a ship to England. Then they put him on *another* ship to America, where he was sold again to someone who grew tobacco in Virginia. That's where he met my great-great-grandmother. And then they fell in love."

"There's more to the story," Lateesha added, "but my parents said they didn't want me to waste my life being angry. If I hadn't passed to Summerland so quickly, I think they would have told me more later on. They just wanted me to be happy," she said with a sigh, "… and I was."

"But now you have *us* to play with!" Gino said and reached over to pull one of Teesha's braids.

"Oh, you!" Teesha said and tickled Gino under his arms.

"Oh, no you don't!"

"Children, Children!" said Mrs. Tipperwillow, chuckling. "Shall we go now, or do I get *my* chance to tickle you?"

"You don't have any fingers!" Yoshi said. "How could you tickle any of us?"

"Oh, I have my ways!" replied the magical sort of cow, with a wild look in her eyes.

27

Ghana Way

With the tiniest wink of the sort of cow's eye, Mrs. T. and the girls were wearing bright dresses of red, orange, and yellow. The boys were dressed in white slacks and shirts in the same fabric and colors as the dresses. The children looked down and ran their hands over their clothes, which were made of sewn patches of woven cloth. "This is called *kente* cloth, Children," said the magical sort of cow, smoothing out the fabric on her dress, "and these clothes are a specialty of Ghana. Are you ready for our grand African adventure?"

"We are!" yelled Aaron.

The group lifted into the golden sky, and in moments they were floating by the Back door. It opened. They stepped across … and right into the middle of a noisy celebration!

The sounds of singing, the beat of drums, and the tinkling music of xylophones filled the air. Dark-skinned people dressed in bright colors were dancing down the street that was shimmering in the hot mid-day sun. The women wore scarves wrapped around their heads. Nearly everyone was smiling and laughing as they danced past.

"Wow! This is great!" exclaimed Lateesha. "Can we dance, too?"

"Well, of course, we may!" said Mrs. Tipperwillow. The Summerland family joined in, swinging their arms up and down with the others, surprised that somehow they already knew the steps. Lateesha was especially skillful at weaving her body in rhythm with the dancers. Finally, Mrs. Tipperwillow and the children moved to one side to watch. At the end of the line of dancers, six men were carrying a large box. The box was shaped and painted to look just like a giant running shoe.

"What kind of a party is this … a *shoe* party?" said Gino and headed right over.

"Wait, Gino!" Lateesha yelled. "I think it's a…."

"Coffin," the boy finished, quickly removing his head from the closed box. "Oops!"

Gino noticed a familiar face in the crowd. A white-haired man was hovering above the heads of the other people, and he was staring straight at Gino. The man cocked his head toward the giant shoe. Gino grimaced. "That's you in there. Uh … sorry about that."

The boy drifted back to his friends. "It's a funeral celebration," he said. "Mrs. Tipperwillow, do you know why the man's body is in a shoe?"

"I believe I do, Gino. When people in this area of Ghana are nearing their time of passing, they have coffins designed to symbolize what they did in life. Perhaps this man was a fast runner."

"Or maybe he owned a shoe store," Jamie suggested.

"…. Exactly! A librarian might be buried in a coffin shaped like a giant book, or a mechanic in a wooden car."

Gino laughed. "Or a chicken farmer might be buried in a giant *chicken!*"

"It's entirely possible," replied Mrs. Tipperwillow, cheerfully. "Now, there's someone who lives nearby whom I would like you all to meet. Come along!"

The family rose quickly into the blue sky. Moments later, they were flying over the shoreline. They swooped down over the giant palm trees edging the water. A tall man was standing underneath one palm, and he was beating a kettle drum.

Mrs. T. glided toward him and floated up to place her arm around the man's broad shoulders. "This is my friend, Kofi," she explained. "He was one of my children many lifetimes ago, but he has never forgotten his old teacher."

Kofi looked straight ahead, his eyes glazed. "Mrs. Tipperwillow!" he said aloud. "Is that really you?"

"Yes, my dear boy." This sounded so strange to the children that they started to giggle, for Kofi was *so* much bigger than Mrs. T. "And this is my current family," she stated proudly, and she introduced Jamie, Gino, Yoshi, Lateesha, and Aaron to *her boy*. "Lateesha's great-great grandfather lived in Ghana centuries ago," Mrs. Tipperwillow continued, "so we have come here to explore."

"That is a fine thing," the man replied.

"Are you blind?" asked Lateesha.

"I am that," Kofi said, "but it has been a blessing of sorts. Because I was born blind this time, my other senses have been stronger, and I am able to hear beyond what most people do. But here, let me show you something. Listen closely."

The man began beating on his drum. "It sounds like words almost," observed Gino.

"I think I can understand it!" exclaimed Lateesha, as the drum pounded the same rhythm over and over ... two short taps, followed by two more short taps, and then six taps, played on different parts of the drum to create different tones. "It says '*Welcome, welcome, Mrs. Tipperwillow.*' Am I right?"

"You *are* right," Kofi replied. "For many generations, our people have passed the art of drum-talking from father to son. Messages have been sent by drum from clan to clan over great distances. Before there was the telephone or the telegraph, there was the drum."

Kofi beat out another message. *"My new friends, would you like to eat with me?"* Everyone understood the drum language this time.

"We would love to, Kofi," answered the magical sort of cow, "but of course, we will have to create our own Summerland version of your food."

Kofi picked up the staff lying beside him on the ground and tapped the staff in front of him as he walked a short distance to a square build-ing with walls made of concrete blocks. The children and Mrs. T. followed. Outside of the building (which the children assumed was Kofi's house), there were eight plastic chairs and a long wooden table. On the table rested a bowl with something gooey looking inside of it.

"This dish is called *fufu*," Kofi explained and touched the bowl with his long fingers. "It is made from cassava root, and I have mashed it with plantain, which is a type of banana that grows here. Fufu is a staple of my diet. Do you think you can create this for the children, Mrs. Tipperwillow?"

"I shall certainly give it my best effort," Mrs. T. answered, frowning slightly. Six small bowls appeared on the table with a mashed something inside of them. The children and their teacher sat down by Kofi. The man began eating with his fingers and seeing no spoons, they did the same.

As the children tasted Mrs. Tipperwillow's creation, they sneaked peeks at each other, trying to hide their smiles, for the concoction tasted exactly like mashed potatoes mixed with ripe bananas. They washed it all down with mango juice, which did indeed taste like ripe mangos.

"Delicious!" Gino said and was glad he didn't have to explain exactly *what* was delicious.

During their meal, Kofi asked Lateesha about her ancestor. She explained what happened to her great-great grandfather and how he got to America.

"Ah," said Kofi. "Then perhaps you would like to visit the old fort on the Cape Coast where he was held before being sent out on the ship to England. All the men taken as slaves were imprisoned there until the ships came for them. It is a rather dreadful place with several ghosts roaming around for those who can sense them."

"Maybe just a quick flyover?" asked Mrs. T. She looked with concern at Lateesha, who nodded.

The family said farewell to Kofi and were soon flying west along the coast. "There it is!" yelled Lateesha, pointing to the ancient white fort, which was resting on the edge of a cliff overlooking the ocean.

"Teesha, where are you going?" called Mrs. T. as the girl swooped down toward the fort.

"I have to see where he was held. I can't explain it ... I just have to!"

"All right then, we're coming!"

The nine-year-old flew into a central courtyard, and without stopping, she headed down a wide, dark staircase. At the bottom, through a heavy wooden door, lay the dungeon ... and two ghosts! The ghosts walked into a corner and disappeared.

"Hello...." Lateesha called, her voice echoing.

"Here we are," said Mrs. Tipperwillow, as she and the other children landed.

"The energy is terrible here, just like it was in the Tower of London," whispered Yoshi, looking around at the large empty room made entirely of gray stone and the two narrow windows near the ceiling that admitted feeble light.

Lateesha shook her head to clear it. "I can't believe my great-great grandfather survived this place for the three weeks he was held here. They hardly gave him any food or water, and he was locked up with lots of other boys and men. There was almost no room even to lie down, and it was filthy in here. Men were sick and coughing, and many of them died. Other men came and dragged the bodies away, and they didn't care at all." Teesha's eyes filled with tears. "I can *feel* it. It's almost like I'm remembering."

"That's called ancestor memory," explained Mrs. Tipperwillow.

"Let's get out of here," Lateesha said abruptly.

"My thought, exactly," said Mrs. T. "Come along, Children." Quickly they flew up the staircase and soon were floating high in the clear African sky.

28

On Cloud Nine

Out of nowhere a fluffy white cloud appeared. "What's that doing here?" Yoshi asked, as the group drifted in the sky toward the lone cloud.

"I thought we could just sit a spell and recover from our trip to the dungeon."

"On that cloud?" Jamie asked. "Clouds aren't solid enough to sit on, Mrs. T. They're just air with lots of water in them."

"I bet that this is a *special* cloud," Gino said and floated over to touch it. Sure enough, it felt like a soft, fluffy mattress.

Gino flew up, up, up, and then drifted down dramatically, his legs sticking out in front of him. But instead of landing softly ... he fell right through. "Mrs. T., you *fooled* me again!" he wailed, flapping his arms like wings in his teacher's face.

The magical sort of cow poked him playfully. "Got you!" she said in a sweet little voice. "Now, let's try this again, shall we?"

The small cloud pulled itself together again. It floated close. The children each reached out and tested the cloud for cushiness. It was *very* cushy. They jumped on and settled in, pulling parts of the cloud around themselves to form pillows.

Mrs. Tipperwillow began speaking. "This cloud shows how some religions on Earth portray heaven ... with lots of angels just sitting around on clouds all day. So here we are! How do you like it?"

Gino answered first. "I think we need *harps*!" He clapped his hands twice and opened them. Between his hands, a long piece of wood with strings attached shivered into sight. The girls giggled.

"That's not a harp," Lateesha said.

"Well, I guess I never paid too much attention to what a harp looks like. Mrs. Tipperwillow, will you make me a harp? Oops!" Gino said, instantly realizing his mistake. "No, no! Don't make *me* a harp! Create a harp for me, please," he said with sudden politeness.

Mrs. Tipperwillow smiled mildly. "My child, what *are* you so worried about?" A small harp appeared between Gino's hands. "Play away!"

Gino plucked the strings for awhile and then looked around at his friends, who were patiently waiting for him to stop. "This would make a really *boring* heaven," he said finally. "How could people believe something so … well … stupid?"

"I suspect, Gino, dear, that after a challenging lifetime this view of afterlife is comforting for some people. Now let me ask you all something. How many of you thought that after you came to the spirit world, you might be doing this very thing?"

First one and then another hand went up. Last of all and with an embarrassed grin, Gino raised his hand, too.

"In the absence of understanding, Children, all *sorts* of stories get started. Some stories claim that there is nothing after death. Some stories create a fiery hell to punish bad people. And some stories equate a good afterlife with doing nothing but sitting around on clouds, just like we're doing here."

"I'm glad it's the way it is," said Aaron. "I like feeling free and having fun and creating stuff and flying." His friends nodded their heads in agreement.

"It seems you enjoy being eight years old, Aaron," said his smiling teacher.

"Yes, it's really cool," replied the boy, using Gino's favorite word.

29

Ancestor Memory

"I suspect, Lateesha," Mrs. Tipperwillow said, "that you would like to visit the village where your grandfather grew up."

"You heard my thought, Mrs. T. I know it was in the center of Ghana someplace, but I don't even know the name of his village, and this is a *really* big country. How will we ever find it?"

"The answer, Teesha, is that you carry the location with you all of the time."

"I do?"

"Indeed, my dear, you do. Each one of you has all the information of who you have *ever been* in the energy around you, and this includes the memories of all your ancestors. This is true for people living on Earth as well."

"But that's too many, isn't it?" asked Yoshi, scratching her head. "That sounds *really* confusing."

"I know, dear. That's why people usually block out these memories. It would be too confusing, especially for those living on Earth."

"But I think I can do it!" Lateesha exclaimed. "I think I can find my great-great grandfather's village now!" The girl closed her eyes and lifted off the cloud cross-legged. She began drifting northward. Very quietly, Mrs. Tipperwillow and the other children followed her.

The Summerland tourists passed from the coast and soon found themselves over a huge rainforest. A few really tall trees stuck above a canopy of shorter ones, and the forest was so dense that it was impossible to see the ground. As their flight continued, the trees beneath them began to thin out. They came to a drier area.

"This is it," said Lateesha, opening her eyes. Her friends followed as she glided down to land in the middle of a village. Small square houses made of dried mud with thatched grass roofs surrounded a dusty central area.

Women were walking here and there. Some carried baskets of fruit and vegetables on their heads, and some had babies tied to their backs with colorful fabrics. At one end of the village, a group of boys kicked a ball between them, creating little clouds of dust as they played. Chickens plucked the ground, looking for seeds and insects. A few goats wandered between the houses.

"I can remember living here," Lateesha said quietly, "even though it wasn't me and even though it was all those years ago. It looks pretty much the same as it did then. I remember playing here as a child and how proud I was to receive my first spear."

"Yes," said Mrs. T., patting Lateesha's hand with her hoof. "All of you and everyone who has ever lived have these magnificent connections all over the world, through time and space, through all of your lifetimes and through all of your ancestors' lifetimes. It really makes you one big family, don't you see?"

"But if we're all so connected, then what is the fighting about?" asked Aaron.

"What indeed?" asked Mrs. Tipperwillow, turning the question back to the children.

"Land and greed," suggested Teesha, thinking of her ancestor's story.

"And being proud and stubborn," said Gino, nodding to himself.

"And being hurt and angry, too," added Aaron.

"And religion," Jamie said. She turned to look at the new eight-year-old with suspicion in her eyes. "So, Aaron, what happened to you?" The boy shrugged his shoulders.

"This is a discussion for another time," said Mrs. Tipperwillow firmly. She rose quickly into the air.

30

Over and Under

The children lifted off to join their teacher high in the sky. "Now, how would you all like to see some wild animals?" she asked.

"Yes!" they shouted and followed closely on Mrs. Tipperwillow's hooves as she flew north at top speed. Moments later, the children slammed into their teacher and into each other as they pulled to a sudden stop.

The sort of cow pointed. "Look there, Children! Below us is the Molé (she pronounced it *mo-lay*) Game Reserve. It is the largest game park in West Africa with nearly four hundred miles of protected land where animals can live without being hunted by humans.

"Gino, *come back here, please*," called the sort of cow as the boy streaked toward the ground. A moment later, he was back.

Mrs. Tipperwillow's eyes were smiling as she looked at her "wild child" and announced, "Children, I think it might be brilliant to tour this park from a flying carpet." A large fringed carpet appeared nearby and floated right over. Woven into the center was a picture of stampeding elephants.

Gino shouted, "*I get it already!*"

"Climb aboard!" ordered Mrs. Tipperwillow with a laugh. And they did.

The carpet carried the Summerland family slowly over the park. As they looked down, they spied many kinds of animals. There were herds of African antelope, a family of baboons, and a pride of lions resting under a tree.

In the open grassland, they spotted four hyenas bent over, eating a dead antelope. Flying over a large lake, they noticed several hippopotamuses, including one baby, floating in the muddy water. The beasts lifted their rounded heads as they sensed the Summerland tourists above them. There were alligators, too, who snapped their wide jaws as the family swooped down for a closer look.

The magic carpet floated out over the plain again, and the children and Mrs. T. spotted a large group of wildebeast and then a herd of running elephants. Drifting near, the others looked from the elephants to Gino and back. "I didn't *do* anything!" Gino yelled, as the huge animals thundered past.

Chuckling, Mrs. Tipperwillow dissolved the carpet beneath them and called the children into a circle. "Hold hands and close your eyes," she whispered mysteriously. "And don't peek until I say." There was the feeling of wind and then…. "You may open your eyes now."

"My eyes are open, but it's *very* dark. Where are we?" asked Yoshi.

"Everyone, keep on holding hands, and follow me!"

As their eyes grew accustomed to the dark, the children found themselves in a wide tunnel. Men wearing lighted helmets were operating big machines and moving large rocks toward the tunnel's entrance, which could barely be seen in the distance.

"That looks like *very* hard work," Aaron said. "What are they hauling those big rocks for?"

"Maybe they are digging a tunnel for cars to go through," Gino suggested.

"I think I know," Lateesha said, "but it's not what I expected."

Teesha's friends heard the word she was thinking and without warning, the Summerland tourists stood in a large workroom. A man wearing heavy gloves and goggles was pouring hot, buttery liquid out of a large vat and into a rectangular tray.

"Gold!" exclaimed the children.

Mrs. Tipperwillow nodded. "Oh, my, yes, and isn't it lovely in its liquid form?" A block of the hardened metal was sitting on a table nearby. "I believe that one gold block could buy your parents a very nice car."

"Wow!" exclaimed Yoshi. "Ghana must be a really rich country then, Mrs. T."

"Not exactly, my dear. A few people own the rights to the gold, and they might not even live in this country. Here people are considered wealthy if they have enough money to own a small house, a car, and a television set. Many others just live from day-to-day, trying to survive. Come, I'll show you."

Flying high over Accra, the capitol city of Ghana, the tourists from the spirit world saw streets lined with palm trees, tall buildings, houses, apartments, and cars. A short distance away, they discovered scores of tiny shacks topped with broken metal roofs. They drifted lower for a closer look. A group of thin children dressed in torn clothing ran between the shacks, apparently playing a game of Hide and Seek.

"One day," said Mrs. Tipperwillow, "this will all be changed … when the people of Earth learn to live without fear and without greed."

"Will that ever happen?" Aaron asked, shaking his head sadly as he looked at the scene below.

"Yes, it will, Aaron … ab-so-tively and pos-so-lutely!"

The hot sun was shimmering near the horizon when Mrs. Tipperwillow turned to look at her children. "Dear ones, we have seen a lot today. How about returning to Summerland? And … once we're home, I will be more than happy to make you some of your new *favorite* treat, Kofi's excellent pudding! I know how much you all enjoyed it!" She smiled broadly.

"Uh … uh …" Gino stammered, "I was just thinking about how refreshing a fruit smoothie would taste, because it's so hot here and all."

"We could make it with mangoes and bananas and pineapple juice!" added Jamie.

"Well … if you'd prefer that … of course."

Soon the adventurers were sitting in the cool green meadow outside of their own striped tent and slurping the last of their icy smoothies.

"Are you *sure* you wouldn't all like some of Kofi's pudding?" Mrs. Tipperwillow asked hopefully, as a bowl of the mashed stuff appeared between her hooves.

"No! No thanks!" Gino replied, perhaps a little too quickly. "I'm *way* too full now."

"Way too full … way too full," his friends repeated, shaking their heads furiously as they patted their bellies.

31

Indigo

Early the next morning, Mrs. Tipperwillow drifted toward the tent to see if the children had awakened. She discovered Gino sitting in a patch of yellow daisies. "Why won't you talk to me?" he was asking the flowers. "You talk to Mrs. Tipperwillow. She said so."

"Oh, good morning, Gino," said the sort of cow, gliding up. "Quiet today, are they?"

"I guess," replied the boy, frowning.

"Flowers can be a persnickety bunch. Sometimes they just yak and yak, while at other times they won't let out a peep. It seems you have found them on a persnickety sort of day."

"Mrs. Tipperwillow?"

"Yes?"

"How come you never get angry with me ... when I rush ahead and stuff? On Earth, it seemed like somebody was mad at me all the time."

"All the time.... Is that so?" Mrs. T. sat down next to the boy and put one arm gently around his shoulder. He leaned into her side.

"You are a very special boy, Gino, full of fun, imagination, and the desire to explore. And you have a great and loving heart. I suspect that some people just don't know how to relate to someone with so much energy. I believe on Earth you would be called an Indigo Child."

"That sounds good."

"Indeed it is, my dear ... indeed it is. Indigo Children are the ones who break through old ways of doing things that don't work anymore. With their boldness, they are helping to bring new ideas to the Earth, and like you, they are full of energy and just want to be treated fairly.

Indigos love to explore and create, and they are very easily bored ... *just like you.* And they often know things without being taught. Do you recall following Krista from the healing lake to the house in Hawaii? How did you know to do that, Gino?"

"I just knew, Mrs. T. I saw a sparkly trail of light moving away, and I remembered what to do."

"That is the way of it, my boy. Sometimes the knowing is just there. During your last lifetime, did you ever feel like you'd lived before? Many Indigo Children do."

"Some things seemed familiar ... like the smell of meat in the butcher shop where my mom shopped. And I *really* liked drum music. I even got a drum for my birthday two years ago. Mom said it nearly drove her crazy sometimes." He sighed. "Do you think I was remembering my African lifetime, Mrs. T.?"

"Yes, Gino, I believe you were."

Gino sat up straight and tapped his thighs like a bongo drum. "But-why-are-we-called-Indigo-Children?" He tapped this on his thigh.

"That's an easy question to answer, Gino. All of you Indigos have some of that dark bluish-purple color in the energy surrounding your bodies, in your auras. "Do you remember what we talked about at the pizza restaurant in Venice?"

"You mean the *clairs*?"

"That's right, Gino. The color indigo connects to insight and inspiration, to deep and sudden knowing, to...."

"To clairvoyance, right?"

"Indeed it does. Do you begin to see how you Indigo Children will help change the world? You have the ability to tap very easily into the Light Web we've visited and to pull out new ideas. And many of you know from an early age *exactly* what you want to do when you grow up. You also tend to remember what you've learned from different lifetimes, so you can inspire others with what you know. It's really *quite* exciting."

"When I go back to Earth next time, will I be an Indigo Child again?"

"Of course you will ... a lovely, brilliant Indigo Child." Mrs. Tipperwillow squeezed the boy's shoulder. "I hope you know Gino that even though I tease you sometimes, this old cow just loves you to bits."

Gino snuggled close. "I love you, too, Mrs. T."

"Now," said the magical sort of cow softly, "shall we check and see if your friends are awake?"

32

Aaron's Story

The girls and Aaron were just awakening when Gino and Mrs. Tipper-willow entered the tent. Aaron floated out of bed and over to touch his teacher's arm.

"Are we going to go where I lived today?"

"Yes, Aaron, we most certainly are. Children, let's sit together by the fire a bit, and Aaron, you can tell us what you remember of your life in Jerusalem. Maestro Gino, would you?"

Gino glanced at the empty fireplace and casually flicked his hand. The children and Mrs. Tipperwillow sat down on the rug before the crackling fire.

Running a hand through his dark hair, Aaron began speaking. "Well, I was just little, you know. I remember sitting in my high chair. Mommy and Daddy were talking and laughing at the kitchen table. The walls in the kitchen were light green. They laughed a lot, but sometimes my uncle would visit." Aaron's smile faded. "He almost never laughed, and even if he did, his laugh had a mean sound to it. He wore different clothes, with big brown splotches."

"Camouflage, I bet, like they wear in the army," Gino guessed.

Aaron shrugged. "Anyway, Uncle Benjamin was angry all the time. So when he came to our house, I would climb up on Daddy's lap and push my head against him, trying not to hear. Sometimes I would cry. Then Mommy would take me into my room and hold me."

"You were clairsentient for sure," Jamie said.

"But why was your uncle so angry?" Lateesha asked.

257

"I didn't understand, but he used words like *war* and *fight* and *revenge*."

"Oh," the children said at once.

"I wished my parents would make him go away, but they didn't. They said he was *family,* but they didn't like the way he talked either. Sometimes they tried to tell him how they felt, but he wouldn't ever listen. He just left earlier ... and that was all right with me." Aaron shook his head.

"Then there was Sarah." A smile slowly spread across the boy's face. "Sarah was my babysitter, and she took care of me when my parents were working. They both worked at the same place, and you had to take a train to get there. I know because they took me to work with them once, and I remember the *chugga-chugga* sound the train made. They worked at a place that made newspapers, and there were all of these big, noisy machines." Aaron got a faraway look on his face.

"Anyway, Sarah was so nice. She never got angry with me. She would bring over warm cookies to share, and she would take me to the park in my stroller everyday."

The boy stopped. Everyone looked at him, waiting. Tears formed in his round, gray eyes. "I don't know what happened. I was in my stroller, and Sarah was taking me to the park. She was singing me my favorite happy little song. We were next to a big building, I think, and people were walking toward us on the street. Then I...." His voice trailed off. "Then I woke up in a bed. There was my angel looking down at me, and she was all covered in white light. She said 'Welcome home, Aaron, dear,' without even opening her mouth."

"That was your guardian angel," Yoshi said. "That's when you came to the nursery in Summerland."

"You don't remember anything else?" Gino asked.

"Well, there was a noise, I think ... maybe."

"Maybe you blew up!" Gino blurted, and he was immediately sorry that he had said anything.

"I ... I.... *What?*" Aaron asked, choking on the words. He climbed into Mrs. Tipperwillow's lap. "I did, didn't I? I blew up," he said finally, holding his teacher close. "And Sarah, too," he added with a little sob.

"My dear boy," said Mrs. T. in her most soothing voice, "that is indeed what happened."

The boy sniffled a bit and then straightened. "It was all that hate like my uncle had, wasn't it? And there was a feeling of fear in the city. It was like a big scary ghost following everybody around."

Mrs. Tipperwillow sighed, shaking her head. "War is such a waste. Aaron, do you still feel like going to Jerusalem today, or would you rather wait a bit longer?"

Aaron brushed away a tear. "I want to see Mommy and Daddy. I want to make sure they're okay now."

"Then this might be a fine time for you to visit your parents, as they gather with friends and relatives to honor your life."

"You'll get to see everyone you loved," Jamie said, remembering her own life celebration, "and you'll get to send them your love, too."

"That sounds good," the boy replied. "But isn't it too late? I've been here *so* long."

"Time is different here," Gino replied, "and anyway the magic door can take us to any *time* we want. Jamie, tell Aaron about the energy ball you made to send your love in."

"What a grand idea!" Mrs. Tipperwillow exclaimed. "Let's go outside for a small demonstration."

Aaron climbed off his teacher's lap, and the family floated through the tent flap and out into the green meadow.

They formed their circle. "Watch closely, Aaron," Gino said. "This is really cool."

"Ready, Jamie?" Mrs. Tipperwillow asked.

"I think so," answered the girl, concentrating. A huge, fuzzy ball of pink light appeared in the air above them.

"Look!" Aaron pointed as the ball drifted down. Suddenly the light was all around them. "Oh!" exclaimed the newest eight-year-old.

Gino clapped his hands. "Didn't I tell you?"

"I really *feel* you, Jamie … and so much love! I feel that, too! Can you show me how?" Aaron asked in an excited voice. "I want to do the same thing for my family."

"Sure," Jamie agreed. She showed Aaron how to imagine his energy gathering at his heart and how to bring it out from himself as a ball of light that he could move around with his thoughts.

Later, as Aaron's energies floated down to cover everyone, all sadness was forgotten. "I'm ready, Mrs. T.!" he said, cheerfully.

"Children, I think this journey should be Aaron's alone. Will you please entertain yourselves while I take him back?"

"Sure," answered Lateesha.

"Maybe the rest of us should skip going to Aaron's city today. Then we can just head for the big theme park when you get back." This was Gino, of course.

"Jerusalem is a beautiful and interesting city," Mrs. Tipperwillow said. "So why don't Aaron and I explore the city today after we see his family. Then on another day he can show you around himself." Aaron nodded.

"See you later, Aaron," said Yoshi, as the boy and Mrs. Tipperwillow dissolved into thin air. "Have a wonderful trip!"

◆   ◆   ◆

"War shouldn't exist," Gino said, staring at the spot where Aaron and Mrs. T. had been standing.

"No, it shouldn't," agreed Lateesha. "But we have to start by getting rid of hate and fear and greed."

"And everybody has to decide to forgive each other," added Jamie, "for whatever hurt them."

Yoshi looked down and squeezed her eyes tight. Then she reopened them. "I will work very hard to understand and forgive you, Hiromi," she said softly to herself. "I promise."

33

The Garden

"I have an idea," said Lateesha, sticking her forefinger in the air. "Let's make a Peace Garden to surprise Aaron when he gets back!"

"With lots of different flowers growing together," said Jamie, as she picked up the idea. "Like people of all kinds living together in peace."

"With lots of grass and paths to walk on and places to sit," added Lateesha, looking in the distance as if she could already see it.

"And a pond," suggested Gino.

"With ducks swimming in it!" added Yoshi.

"I know how we can shape it!" exclaimed Lateesha. "Yeah … this is gonna be great!"

The children moved out into the meadow, looking around for the perfect place to carry out their plans.

◆   ◆   ◆

No one was in sight when Aaron and Mrs. Tipperwillow touched down. "Where are they?" the boy asked, as he peeked into the empty tent.

Then Aaron heard Yoshi's voice in the center of his head. *We're up here!*

"They're up on the top of the hill," Aaron said, pointing. "Look!"

The sky suddenly turned to dusk. Multicolored lights flashed a signal as Gino, Lateesha, Yoshi, and Jamie rose dramatically into the air.

"Children, will you join us in the tent, please?" asked their teacher as she opened the tent flap and stepped inside with Aaron.

"Coming!" they answered in unison. A moment later, the four children tumbled into the tent.

"Wait 'til you guys see what we did!" exclaimed Gino, his hair sticking out wildly from the quick flight.

"It's a surprise!" said Yoshi, who was barely able to contain herself.

A wide smile covered Lateesha's face. "We've been working ever since you left!"

"You're *really* going to like it!" Jamie added.

"My, my, Children," said their teacher. "I don't know *when* I've seen you all so excited. We would love to see what you've done. But first, would you mind if Aaron tells his story?"

Jamie, Lateesha, Gino, and Yoshi look at each other and then at Aaron, who was bursting with excitement himself.

"Sure, Aaron," Gino said. "Our surprise can wait until you tell us about *your* trip." Mrs. Tipperwillow sent a quiet "thank you" to Gino. He nodded.

34

Coming Together

The children formed a semi-circle on the soft rug. "Gino, would you?" asked Mrs. Tipperwillow, tilting her head toward the fireplace.

"Can I try, Mrs. T.?" Aaron asked.

"Why, of course you may, Aaron. What a grand idea!"

The boy stood, and as he had seen Gino do so often, he raised his arms dramatically. He pointed to the fireplace and loudly proclaimed, "Alacazam!" His friends applauded as a blazing fire appeared. Aaron sat down again, blushing with pride.

The others looked expectantly at the boy. He began his story.

"Well, first we came to the Back door ... but you know *that* ... it is the same one we always go through. When the door opened, I walked through right into *my* house. There was a party going on for me. Mommy and Daddy's friends and some neighbors were there. Grandma Ruth was there and Uncle Benjamin was there, too. He's the angry one I told you about. People brought all sorts of food. And everyone was saying what a sweet little boy I was, and what a shame it was, and how sorry they were ... and stuff like that. For a party, it was pretty sad." Aaron sighed and looked over at Jamie.

"Then I did what you showed me, Jamie. I floated to the ceiling and made a big ball of Aaron, and I put all my love into it. When it was really, really strong, I told it to move down to cover everybody in the room. And it did!"

"Wait 'til you hear what happened next! My mom looked up and smiled. My dad was talking to our neighbor, but he stopped. His mouth opened and his eyes got *really big*. Everyone in the room felt me. I watched their faces, and I'm sure of it. Then my uncle, if you can believe it ... I couldn't ... he made this weird noise, and he just started to *cry*. Then he hurried outside, because people were staring at him. I followed him. As he walked away from our house, he shook his head and said to himself, 'It's always someone's children. That's it. No more fighting for me ... no more hating. I've had all I can take.' And ... and ... that's what happened!"

"Wow!" said Jamie. "He made his decision to change because of *you*, Aaron."

"But wait ... there's *more*! Mrs. Tipperwillow took me back into my house, but now it was in the future. She told me so. My parents and Sarah's parents and some of our neighbors and Uncle Benjamin were sitting around the kitchen table. They were talking about doing something special to honor Sarah and me and all the other children who died because of war.

"Then Mrs. T. took my arm, and she told me to close my eyes real tight. When I opened them again we were further ahead in time. We were in a big room with lots and lots of chairs, and there were lots and lots of people, too ... maybe even a *hundred*! My dad was on a stage talking to everyone about buying the place where we blew up and buying the lot next to it, too."

"Mrs. Tipperwillow told me to shut my eyes again, and when I opened them, we were floating above the spot where I died. Big machines were clearing the land. Then Mrs. T. did something and everything started moving faster and faster!"

"Like a movie on fast forward," Gino suggested.

"I guess. Anyway, the land was smooth, and lots of people came with shovels and rakes. Then a big truck came with the rolling part going around in the middle...." Aaron moved his hands in a circle to demonstrate.

"A concrete truck?" asked Gino.

"Yeah, like that. And another truck came with rolls of grass. Everybody worked so hard, Mommy and Daddy and our neighbors and lots of people I didn't know. My uncle probably worked the hardest of anybody."

"There were people dressed in lots of different ways, too. Mrs. Tipperwillow told me that some of the people were Christians and some were Jews and some were Muslims from Pala.... What was that Mrs. T.?"

"Palestine, dear."

"Yeah, like that ... and that the Jews and Muslims had been fighting and killing each other for such a very long time, but these people were working together because they didn't *want* war anymore. When they were working, more people stopped to look, and they started to help, too. Anyway, more trucks brought lots of flowers and some other stuff, and finally the garden was done."

Gino and the girls looked at each other, their eyes wide.

"What?" Aaron asked as he looked from one to the other.

"Never mind, Aaron.... You go ahead," said Lateesha, barely able to contain herself.

What is it? Aaron asked again, feeling the tension in the air.

"You finish *your* story first," Yoshi said. Gino's hands were tight on his crossed legs.

The boy shrugged. "Okay. So then it was done, and there was this beautiful garden with rounded paths and two bridges and water you can walk over. There was grass to sit on between the paths, and pretty flowers were growing all along the walkways. The paths formed a funny shape. Mrs. Tipperwillow called it a 'peace symbol.' Is that right, Mrs. T.?" The sort of cow nodded. "And in the very center was a tall pole with a metal bird. A 'peace dove' is what Mrs. T. called it. The bird turned around and around when the wind moved it.

"And outside by the street, there was a sign that said: *Aaron and Sarah's Garden. Two Children Who Died. Let There Be Peace.*"

All of the other children were busting with excitement now ... except for Yoshi. Out of nowhere, she burst into tears.

"Yoshi, what's wrong?" Aaron asked in a worried voice. "It's a happy thing."

"I know. It's the *best*. It's just so … so *wonderful*," she sobbed.

"Okay, Aaron, it's time to show you *our* surprise now," said Gino taking his friend's arm and pulling him to his feet. Yoshi stood and wiped an arm across her eyes to stop the flow of tears.

"Let's go see what you all have been up to," said the magical sort of cow.

Outside the tent, the sky turned to daylight once more. Up into the air flew the four children. They hurried to the top of the hill with Aaron and Mrs. Tipperwillow close behind.

Everyone stopped abruptly and floated in the air above the children's creation, which was glistening in the golden light of a perfect Summerland day.

At first no one spoke. Finally Mrs. Tipperwillow said in a soft voice, "My goodness, Children. Look what you have done."

Aaron stared down, his eyes wide, his mouth open. "I don't believe it!" he exclaimed. "This is just like my garden in Jerusalem! How did you know what they were making?"

"Oh, no, Aaron, don't you see?" said Jamie. "You went into the *future*. This was our idea first! It's in our story on the Light Web already, and your parents' wish to do something special for you brought the garden from the web, through the magic mailbox, and into their thoughts!"

Aaron's mouth formed a round "O." Then, with much excitement, Aaron and Mrs. Tipperwillow floated down for a personal tour of the garden.

"Even the peace dove in the center is the same," Aaron said, looking up at the bird spinning slowly at the top of the concrete pole. He looked at the circular moat. "But when I saw the garden, there weren't any ducks in the water."

"I bet there *will* be!" Yoshi said.

"There's one more thing that *has* to be different Aaron, Gino said. "Can you find it?"

"Everything looks the same," answered the boy, as he skimmed over the paths. "Wait a minute … this strange purple and white flower. I don't remember seeing this."

"Right!" said Lateesha. "There's no way this flower could be on Earth. We saw it on *Mars*."

Aaron laughed. "I remember! We saw this when I was a baby and we went back in time."

For minutes (or was it hours?), the family wandered over the paths and across the bridges of their peace garden, feeling the happiness of a dream come true. And so it was on this beautiful Summerland day that the children came to truly understand the power of love and imagination.

35

The Final Hoorah

Feeling just the tiniest movement of air by his pillow, Gino opened his eyes, sat up, and picked up the rounded, black felt hat. He ran a finger over his name, which was embroidered in gold scrolling letters on the back, and then he touched the two black plastic ears before putting the hat on his head and snapping the elastic band under his chin.

"Goody Morning!" trilled a familiar voice. Gino looked toward the entrance of the tent. But instead of Mrs. Tipperwillow, a familiar looking mouse just her size was standing there. Snoody peeked out of a pocket in the mouse's jacket.

The other children awakened to discover *their* hats as Gino jumped out of bed and headed for the mouse. It held out its arms for a hug. "Cool costume, Mrs. T.," said the boy as he moved out of his teacher's arms. "I bet I know where *we're* going today!"

"I just bet that you *do*," said Mrs. Tipperwillow from inside the mouse suit.

The rest of the children climbed out of their beds and surrounded their teacher. She took off the mouse head and held it under one arm. "Well, my dears, would you all like some breakfast before we head off for our grand theme park adventure?"

"Mrs. Tipperwillow, we're in our spirit bodies," Gino answered. "We don't *need* to eat!" He hopped up and down. "Can we go now?"

With a nod from the other children and a wave of their teacher's hand, the group was dressed in jean shorts and turquoise t-shirts. A picture of a castle adorned the front of each shirt, with the theme park name underneath.

Mrs. T. replaced her mouse head. "It's on to California!" she chortled, and almost before they knew it, they were walking through the main gate of one of the best loved theme parks in America.

"This way first," said Mouse Tipperwillow, taking Gino's hand and moving through the crowded street *and* through the people on the crowded street, as well.

"Up-up-up!" cried their guide suddenly, and the children and the magical sort of mouse landed two by two in small cars shaped like elephants which were flying around in a circle.

"Gino!" called his teacher from the next car, "I thought you especially would appreciate this ride. You can be inside an elephant here and not worry about getting *stuck*."

Very funny, Mrs. T, Gino replied, as he sat through a boy about five, who didn't seem to realize he was sharing space with another child in his spirit body. The ride ended, and the Summerland family floated out of their seats and into the sky to get an overview of the park.

Gino pointed. "I want to go there!" he yelled as he streaked away.

"E-e-e-e-e-e!" the children and Mrs. Tipperwillow screamed as the roller coaster sped them up and down and through a mountain. They exited laughing and a bit dizzy, and they chose a calmer ride next. This ride took them underwater in a small submarine. "Look at all these phony fish!" Aaron exclaimed. "They're cute but not like the real fish you showed us in Hawaii, Mrs. T. Those were the best!"

The Summerland group lifted into the air again and drifted on the light spring breeze until the girls noticed a white building with lots of spires and golden designs all over it. "Let's try that one!" suggested Lateesha.

Walking through a long line of people entering the large double doors, the children and Mrs. Tipperwillow took seats in little boats traveling along a hidden track. They moved into a big room between colorful scenes representing different areas of the world. Groups of large dolls, which were dressed in the costumes of each country, turned their heads and raised their arms and legs as the same song played over and over and over again. At the ride's end, the Summerland family emerged into bright sunlight.

Lateesha, Jamie, and Yoshi put their arms around each other's shoulders and belted out the theme song as the boys lagged behind. Gino whispered to Aaron, "That sure was *boring*."

"No, it wasn't," Aaron replied, disagreeing with his friend for the very first time. "It's about how we're all connected, even though we dress in different ways and live in different places. I think it's *important*."

Gino shrugged. "Well, the idea is good." He looked up. Some distance ahead a large mouse was just disappearing into the crowd. "Mrs. Tipperwillow, wait for us!"

"What is it, Gino?" answered a familiar voice right behind him. Gino turned to see *another* mouse, this one with a snoode in its pocket. "Do you mean to tell me there's another like me in this park?" said *this* mouse, hooves on its hips. "Someone should talk to the management!"

Gino looked from his costumed teacher to the other mouse. Only the tips of its ears were showing as it moved away. Everyone laughed.

All through the long day, the Summerland family wandered through this most magical place, exploring *every* street and taking *every* ride. Sometimes they shared cars with others, and sometimes Mrs. Tipperwillow created their own cars at the end of the rest.

"Boo!" yelled Gino to the ghosts that floated around inside a big old mansion.

"Boo!" all the children yelled, as they floated out of their seats and into the center of a large, open chamber. One by one, the Summerland spirits imagined themselves wearing sheets and flew between the holographic ghosts in the hall yelling "Boo!" and trying to look scary.

"Very nice, Children!" called Mrs. Tipperwillow, who had finally tired of her mouse costume and was wearing a denim skirt with the theme park sweatshirt *and* the snoode around her neck, of course. "Bravo!"

Early on, the children had decided that their last ride should be the very best of all. Lateesha was the only one who had been to this particular park, and she steered them away from her favorite until the very end.

They stepped ahead of a long line of people and found themselves in partial darkness. Mrs. Tipperwillow created their very own boat, and out they drifted in water under what looked like a starry night sky. "Isn't this pirate ride awesome?" Lateesha asked. Her friends were so busy looking around that no one answered.

They traveled under a bridge as one pirate looked down on them and waved his sword. A balcony appeared. Serving girls wearing aprons and carrying plates of food were being chased around by another pirate. There was fire, confusion, singing, and a cave filled with treasure. The ride ended. The Summerland tourists followed the crowd to the street.

"Again, Mrs. T.!" Gino yelled.

"Sure!" she yelled back. The sort of cow turned and rushed back through the exit. The children followed close on her hooves. "Who wants to be pirates and who wants to be serving girls?"

"Pirate!" yelled Jamie.

"Me, too!" said Aaron.

"Me three!" added Lateesha.

"I want to be a pirate, too, but isn't that too many pirates?" asked Yoshi.

"You can *never* have too many pirates," said Mrs. Tipperwillow, seriously. The four were suddenly dressed in pirate costumes. "And how about you, Gino?" she asked.

"I'll be a *sweet* serving girl," said Gino in an imitation, girl's voice, "and I bet you can't catch me!"

"I bet we can!" yelled Jamie.

In a blink, Gino was dressed in a long, puffy skirt and blouse, with an apron tied around his waist.

"And when we do ... I am going to give you a *big fat kiss!*" yelled Lateesha.

"Oh, no, you *don't!*" Gino turned to make his getaway, but he was hampered by the red wig which had just appeared on his head and was falling down over his eyes. A platter of plastic food attached itself to one of his hands. "Mrs. T-e-e-e!" he whined, adjusting the wig with his free hand and trying to shake the plate off the other. "Whose side are you on, anyway?"

"I'm on the side of fun, of course!" The sort of cow winked, and the platter of food disappeared. She twirled around and was dressed instantly in an outfit matching Gino's.

And the chase was on! The pirates dashed through the ride, skimming the water, flying through tunnels, then rushing high into the air chasing the serving girls (although honestly, they seemed more intent on catching Gino than Mrs. Tipperwillow.)

Finally, the pirates surrounded Gino. One was in the air above him, one below, and one to each side to foil any getaway attempt. The other serving girl stood off to one side.

"Aaron, help me!" Gino pleaded.

"I can't," Aaron answered, adjusting his three cornered hat. "I'm a pirate now."

"All right, Gino," said Lateesha, as she came close. "Are you ready for a *big fat kiss?* I'll go easy on you and just kiss you on the cheek!"

Gino squished his face and closed his eyes tight as Lateesha floated over and kissed him soundly. She put one hand up to his ear and whispered, "If we were on Earth and if we were older, I'd *marry* you." Gino opened his eyes wide. His face turned red as a beet.

"Well," said Mrs. Tipperwillow, saving the day, "isn't anyone going to try to kiss *me?*" She turned to make her getaway, and all the pirates rushed to surround her, leaving Gino floating in the air alone with a *very* strange look on his face.

The play continued longer than long ... so long, in fact, that the moving figures of the pirates and the serving girls ground to a halt, and the music stopped. Row by row, the lights flickered off, and the family floated outside to discover that the sky was already dark. Suddenly, fireworks of red, green, blue, and white began exploding in the night sky to the "oohs" and "ahs" of the many people crowding the streets.

"A perfect end to a perfect day," thought Mrs. Tipperwillow, as she looked from the fireworks into the glowing faces of her children.

36

Home Again

Summerland seemed so quiet after the excitement of their trips to Earth, and the children settled back easily into life in the spirit world. Since Aaron hadn't explored much of Summerland, the children and Mrs. Tipperwillow introduced him to their beach for a fine day of play. And on another day, with Jamie as captain, the family flew in the purple and white snow boat up to the top of their mountain for a snow date.

This time, Gino was the first to lie down and move his arms up and down to create an angel in the soft snow. When their guardian angels showed up, Aaron was not at all surprised that it was Sufy, who had stood by his crib when he first arrived in the nursery and who had comforted him earlier in Jerusalem, who came to visit him now.

It was Gino, to everyone's surprise, who suggested a trip to the Library of Lives to show Aaron some of his different lifetimes on Earth.

"You never know *what* you'll find there," Gino said in a fatherly voice, putting an arm around his friend's shoulders. "Maybe you were a king or a real live pirate ... or a giant!"

"Or a sneaky spy!" added Lateesha.

"Or maybe you were a weepy little princess," Yoshi said. Everyone turned to look at the girl. "Well, you never can *tell*."

Before they left on the Sky Train, Mrs. Tipperwillow gathered the children around her. "I will go with Aaron, since this is new to him. I have an assignment for each of you. Study at least five of your lifetimes, and see if you can find the major theme for each one. I will help Aaron with his assignment."

"What do you mean by *theme?*" asked Yoshi.

"Ah, yes," said the sort of cow. "Look at each lifetime to the end, and see if you can discover the biggest thing you learned from each one."

"You mean like learning to cook?" Jamie asked, thinking of her mother's excellent cooking.

"Not so much, Jamie. What did you learn about yourself and about getting along with others? What feelings did you explore? Remember, too, all of you, that you may have done things that hurt other people badly or even killed their bodies. If so, look at why you did these things. Can you forgive yourself and the other people who hurt you?" Yoshi nodded her head in understanding.

"Believe me when I tell you that this is the *most* important lesson anyone on Earth or in spirit can learn. Whether you're eight years old or a hundred and eight years old, *this* is the big one. Forgiveness leads to joy. It is forgiveness that will change the world."

37

Lifetimes

There were so many stories to tell from this trip to The Hall of Records that the children spent several long evenings around their fire describing what they had seen and learned.

Going back to look at his life as a butcher, Gino discovered that after his wife died in childbirth, he raised three children all by himself and as his son said at his funeral, "he was always slow to anger and quick with a kind word."

"It is not what you do that matters so much," explained Mrs. Tipperwillow, "but *how* you do it."

Yoshi explored a lifetime when she was a princess. She was separated from the common people and had no friends her own age.

"If clothes could make a person happy, I would have been the happiest little girl alive," she explained one evening, staring at the fire. "But I was so lonely and bored, and so I grew up to be an angry old woman. The worst thing is having no one who loves you."

Jamie discovered that she was once a famous male artist. (We won't say which one.) He loved to create village scenes in bright colors, had a large group of friends, and was always laughing in a big booming voice. "It was a good life," Jamie mused, "because I didn't take things too seriously."

In one of her lives, Lateesha was a spy for the king of Spain and very good at disguises. Because of his job, and because he knew *he* couldn't be trusted, he grew into a person who never trusted anybody else. He died unhappy and alone. "I learned from that lifetime that telling lies and pretending to be something you're not will destroy your happiness," said Lateesha, shaking her head.

Aaron saw a life where he had been falsely accused of a crime and was thrown into prison. It took him a long, long time, but finally, he was able to forgive those who put him there and to find peace for himself.

"Even though I died in prison, I died happy. I learned that happiness is in here," Aaron said, touching his heart, "not on the outside."

On their last evening of discussions, Lateesha began describing a lifetime she spent as a burly longshoreman in New York City, working on the piers, loading and unloading cargo from ships.

"It was a good life," she explained. "I was this big, strong man named James. When I got home to my wife and three girls after work, even though I was really tired, I was gentle as a kitten. I would always read my girls a story before bedtime."

"Hold it!" Gino said. "Your wife's name wasn't Mary Rose, was it? And your children … were they named Lydia, Anna, and Grace?"

"How did? Oh, Gino … you? *You* were Mary Rose?" She let out a whoop. "No wonder!" She looked at Gino's reddening face. "I always felt I knew you from somewhere."

Gino studied his toes. "Yeah, me, too … I guess."

With much excitement the children tried to figure out if there were any other life connections between them. It seemed that Yoshi and Jamie had both lived in Paris during the French Revolution. But it was a crazy time of fighting, beheadings, and the like, and apparently they hadn't known each other. No other connections were found.

As the children got more and more tired, their conversation got sillier *and* sillier. Jamie claimed that she was Yoshi's parakeet during the princess lifetime and that she flew out of her cage one day to be eaten by the family cat. Yoshi said that in one of her lives, Gino was a yappy little terrier named Theo, who belonged to the neighbors and kept her up all night with his barking. At this, Gino began barking, then chasing around on all fours, finally returning to paw at Yoshi's leg.

"Good boy, Theo, good boy," Yoshi said, as she patted his head, and their friends broke down in laughter.

38

The Fashion Show and the Party

Early one morning, the girls and Mrs. Tipperwillow exited their tent house to find a huge pile of costumes stacked nearby. "Are these from the museum in London?" Jamie asked. Not waiting for an answer, she pulled out a long black satin dress with lace around the neck and a stiff, scratchy underskirt.

"Indeed they are, Jamie," answered the magical sort of cow, "and with Summerland magic, they will fit each of us *perfectly*."

She clapped her hooves together twice. There was a wiggle in the pile, and another wiggle in the dress that Jamie was holding. "And away we go!" exclaimed Mrs. Tipperwillow with a laugh, as she reached for a shimmering sequined dress.

The girls and their teacher tried on one fancy outfit after another, which were all popular during different time periods on Earth. They took turns swooping and twirling down the red carpeted runway Mrs. T. imagined in the meadow.

Gino and Aaron, who were not at all interested in the fashion show, were some distance away, racing tiny cars around the circular track they'd created. Finally, the laughter and applause became too much for the boys, and they wandered over.

Mrs. Tipperwillow was wearing a short lavender dress with a long fringe at the dress's hem that shimmered over her cow knees as she danced.

"This dance is called the Charleston," she explained. "Women and men danced this way in the 1920's. Gino, my boy, will you join me and kick up your hooves for a spell?"

Without waiting for an answer she pulled Gino toward her, and he slammed against her chest. Then he tried his best to copy her movements.

"Knee up, step back ... now you've got it!" Mrs. T. chortled merrily, as the girls and Aaron applauded.

"Bravo!" they yelled. "Bravo!" The dance ended with Gino making a dramatic bow.

"I created you a costume, Gino," Lateesha said a bit shyly, holding out a stack of brightly colored clothing.

"Should I be scared?" he asked, holding up diamond patterned tights and making a face.

"It's a jester costume, silly, like people wore in the olden days to clown around for kings."

A smile crept to the boy's face. "You're right. It is ... and in my favorite colors, too!" In a flash, Gino was transformed into a court jester. He wore orange and yellow tights, an orange and white striped vest with a puffy white shirt underneath, and soft orange shoes which curled up at the toes. His yellow hat had four points. One fell toward the back and one toward the front, and two more fell like dog ears on either side of Gino's face. There were golden bells on each point, which tinkled merrily as the boy shook his head.

"All right!" he yelled and began by pulling up into the sky and doing a series of hand-over-hand flips, first forward, and then backward, which ended in a triple mid-air somersault. As he landed, Gino clapped his hands dramatically. Five red balls appeared and floated in front of him. "This is hard," he admitted moments later as he tried to juggle the balls with his thoughts. They disappeared. Next a Hula Hoop popped into sight. Gino pulled it over his head and wildly swung his hips and waved his arms in the air.

"Gino," said Mrs. Tipperwillow, chuckling, "I'm not really sure they had those in the olden days, but it does make a *fine* addition."

Soon, with a little help for Aaron, the other children created jester costumes for themselves and joined Gino clowning around in the meadow.

They were all having so much fun that they almost missed the sound of a familiar bell out by the mailbox. "I'll get it!" yelled Mrs. Tipperwillow. She hurried over.

"Tearing open the bright red envelope as the children gathered around, their teacher removed a black card with a twinkling web of light spreading across it. It was an invitation.

Mrs. Tipperwillow turned the card over. "Children, this is from the Web Workers' Guild. We are all invited to a party in your honor. It is to be held in the park between the Hall of Records and the Grand Council Chamber—that's where Wallace had his growing up ceremony, if you will remember."

"When is this party, Mrs. T.?" Gino asked, looking over her shoulder.

"About half past now, I'd say."

"Oh, gosh ... we'd better hurry then!" Jamie exclaimed. The children rushed into the tent, wishing they would find a big closet of clothes to choose from ... and they did.

◆   ◆   ◆

The party was "magnificent," as Yoshi said later. By the time they arrived, the grassy park was full of people, who applauded loudly as the children and Mrs. Tipperwillow landed. Wallace, who Yoshi thought looked very handsome in his navy blue suit and red tie, greeted his Summerland family and introduced each of them to the nearly one thousand web workers who were floating or standing nearby.

Then pictures appeared in the air next to the children, showing each of their visions on that momentous day when they had discovered the trouble with time. There was more applause.

Next, Wallace presented each child with a gold lapel pin, engraved with a picture of the Light Web on the front and their names on the back. "I present you with these solid gold pins," he said solemnly, "which represent your honorary membership in our Light Web community."

Following the ceremony, there was a fine picnic and dancing in the street to an unseen band.

Home again at last, the children slipped into their warm bunks and drifted into sleep, each wearing a gold pin affixed to the chest of their flannel pajamas.

39

Visitors

Days rolled into weeks or maybe even months or a year. It's so hard to tell in Summerland, where there are no clocks, and night only comes when night is created. Lately, the family had been spending more time at home, and the children and Mrs. Tipperwillow had been busy entertaining.

Jamie's grandfather came for a visit, and Jamie was happy to introduce him to her friends. "We saw you when you were eight years old!" Aaron said in an excited voice, as he and the others told Grandpa Reed about their adventures in London.

On another golden day, Sarah came to visit Aaron, carrying a plate of warm peanut butter cookies. Aaron was surprised to see her as a grown woman instead of a teenager, and *she* was surprised to see that Aaron was no longer the baby that she had cared for.

Wallace showed up one day, too, coming straight from the Light Web after work. Yoshi was in her big brother's arms in a second.

Even Master Matsuyama, the meditating man they had met on Mt. Fuji, stopped by one day for a visit with Mrs. Tipperwillow and the children. He had indeed passed to spirit at four o'clock *exactly*, just as he had said he would. But he had even surprised himself, for his body, instead of being left behind, had simply disappeared with his spirit. Only rainbows remained in the space where he had been meditating.

"That's what I want to do when I leave Earth next time!" Gino proclaimed. The other children agreed that this was a great idea, and that it was not nearly as *messy* as dying in the ordinary ways.

Each of the visitors was treated to a special Summerland meal created entirely by the children's thoughts and then to a tour of their Peace Garden at the top of the hill. Sarah had already visited their garden in Jerusalem, but she was totally surprised to learn that it was created here first.

"This *must* be in the Light Web!" stated Wallace, as *he* floated over the garden. The children rolled their eyes. "Oh, yes, how silly of me.... It's in our *story*," he said, turning bright red under his beard. "Perhaps we will put your idea into other places in the web as well," he added quickly. Aaron explained that the garden was already on Earth, in his hometown of Jerusalem, and he invited Wallace to come with the family when they toured the city. Wallace agreed to take time off from work and join them.

40

Jerusalem, Israel

Through the Light Web, Wallace received a message from Mrs. Tipperwillow. She and the children were about to leave for Israel. Wallace left work immediately. He found the children and his old teacher waiting for him outside their tent house. Moments later, the Summerland family was on its way.

Stepping through the Back door, the children, Wallace and their teacher found themselves floating above the golden hills of a large city. Mrs. Tipperwillow and Aaron took the lead as the group drifted down toward the walls surrounding the Old City of Jerusalem.

Everyone agreed that Aaron was an excellent tour guide as he and Mrs. T. showed his friends the city in Israel where he was born.

"This is one of the oldest cities on Earth, and it was made out of the desert," Aaron explained. "People have been living here for 6,000 whole years. Isn't that right, Mrs. Tipperwillow?" She nodded her large head.

"Let me see if I can get this right," Aaron continued. "There are Muslim mosques and Jewish syn-a-gogues and Christian churches and … Arm … what is that, Mrs. T.?"

"Armenian, dear…."

"Yeah, that's it … *Armenian* churches in Jerusalem."

With Mrs. Tipperwillow and Aaron in the lead, the Summerland family spent the afternoon flying to see the eight gates in the old city wall and floating through them to explore the different areas where people lived and worshipped God in their own ways.

At last, they visited the most famous of the old city walls called the Western Wall and behind it the beautiful golden domed mosque called The Dome of the Rock.

"This is a really special place for Muslims and for Jews, too," Aaron explained to his friends, as they landed on a crowded street in front of an ancient stone wall. "This wall right here is the only part left of a temple that was destroyed long, long ago. Jewish people pray by this wall because they think God can hear their prayers better here.

"So this is what they do," Aaron continued. "They write wishes and prayers on little pieces of paper. Then they stick the papers in the cracks in this wall, and then they ask God to make their wishes come true."

The Summerland tourists moved up take a closer look. Sure enough, little pieces of paper were stuck everywhere between the grey stones. The family noticed that some of the people lined up along the wall were praying and that other people were adding more slips of paper to the wall.

Aaron flew upwards and motioned to his friends. "And look up here! This is called the Dome of the Rock. The Muslim people believe that this is where Mu-ham-mad.... Did I get it right, Mrs. T.?" She nodded. "Okay ... that this is where Muhammad flew up to heaven on his winged horse to talk to God. This beautiful gold domed mosque is *their* special place.

"Some Jews and some Muslims get angry with each other because both religions want this place just for themselves. And some people get *so* angry they make bad things happen." Aaron sighed. "And sometimes people like me and Sarah get killed."

Aaron looked down, frowning. Directly below the Summerland family, two men in Israeli Army uniforms stood on a street corner with rifles in their hands. Four more officers were patting people down, searching for guns or bombs before they would allow anyone to get close to the wall. "I want to show you our garden now," choked the boy, wiping tears from his eyes.

◆   ◆   ◆

The family rose higher into the air and headed north. By the time they landed next to a large, newly planted garden, Aaron was smiling again. The sign at the entrance said:

Aaron and Sarah's Garden
Two Children Who Died
Let There Be Peace

"Yep, it's the same as your garden in Summerland," Wallace said. "This is *so* exciting!" he added, as the group floated along the circular paths.

"And look, Aaron," said Yoshi, pointing, "there's ducks now!"

When the family once again was floating high over the golden hills of Jerusalem, Lateesha stopped suddenly. She cocked her head to one side. "The energy in this city is different from the other places we've seen."

"How do you mean, Teesh?" Gino asked, coming to a stop behind her.

"This city is important somehow," she said as she stared down. "It's almost like Jerusalem is at the center of a big wheel." She nodded her head. "Yes, that's it! When people stop fighting and killing each other here, over religion or land or whatever, the same sort of thing will start happening all over the world at the same time. I can't explain, but that's just how it feels."

"My friends and I have been learning about the energies of different places on Earth," Wallace said, "and we've come across this very same idea. You're a natural, Lateesha!"

"But a natural *what* is the question!" Gino grabbed one of his friend's tiny braids and gave it a tug.

41

Decisions

So many good times and so many stories ... life in Summerland is all of these. But as with life on Earth, finally, even the best stories move over to make room for new ones.

It was evening, and dusky light fell through the tent flap. The children sat by the fire that Aaron had just created.

"Dusk so soon?" questioned Mrs. Tipperwillow, entering the tent as the children turned toward her. Aaron was up and in her arms in a flash.

"Can I stay here with you, Mrs. Tipperwillow?" he asked as he snuggled against her belly.

"Well, of course you may, Aaron dear."

"But I want to grow up, too," he proclaimed. "I want to be ten!"

"Just as you wish," answered his teacher kindly, as she and Aaron joined the others by the warm fire. "I do believe I sense a whole *flock* of butterflies coming," she said warmly, wiping a tiny tear from her eye with the tip of one hoof.

"We have had such a great time here in Summerland with you," Jamie began, "and we have learned so much, too. But I want to go back now and be born again, so I can teach what you showed us. I want to be a part of all the wonderful changes that are taking place. Maybe I'll even write a book one day," Jamie said, with a dreamy smile on her face, "and it will be read all over the world."

"I'm sure it will, Jamie," replied Mrs. T., her brown eyes glistening.

"And I decided to work on the web with Wallace," Lateesha said, casting a quick, sad glance at Gino. "I like the idea of different energies passing from here to Earth and that I can help create the pictures and the ideas to send. That will be *really* fun."

"You'll be good at it, Teesh," said Gino, who was being serious for a change. "You and your wiggly lines," he added, wiggling his fingers *just* a bit.

There was silence. Then Yoshi spoke in a confident voice. "I want to grow up now. I want to work in the Summerland nursery, helping babies and little kids who are afraid and hurting like I was. I want to help them feel happy again. Then I'll bring them here to you, Mrs. Tipperwillow. And I'll visit a lot. I promise."

"That will be lovely, Yoshi."

"I have to stay in the spirit world until Wallace is ready to go back, so we can go to Earth at the same time and be best friends, just like he said," Yoshi finished. The others nodded, remembering the day Wallace left them and his promise to Yoshi.

The family stared at the fire in silence. The silence got longer ... and *longer.*

"Well," said Mrs. Tipperwillow finally, "that takes care of all of you, I guess."

"Hey, no it doesn't! What about *me?*"

Mrs. T. laughed. "Well, yes, Gino, what *about* you? I bet you have some big plans. Will you stay in the spirit world, or will you be born on Earth for another lifetime?"

"I want to go back and be a kid again, but this time I won't be so *stupid* and get hit by a car while I'm chasing a ball." The boy was silent again.

"Well?" asked Lateesha. "Stop teasing us, Gino! What do you want to do in your next lifetime?"

"Did you decide to be a glassblower?" questioned Jamie.

Yoshi chuckled. "Or maybe ... *Superman?*"

"With a cape!" added Aaron, remembering Gino flying overhead in the restaurant in Venice.

Gino shook his head, a secretive smile on his face. "I have my plans," is all he would say and strangely, not one of the children could hear what he was thinking. Only a glint in Mrs. Tipperwillow's eye showed that *she* had picked up his thought.

"You're getting very good at protecting your thoughts so we can't hear you," Yoshi said finally.

Gino laughed. "I heard you all knocking, too. It's like you're all outside of a door saying, 'Let me in! Let me in!' But really, I don't know if I can even do what I'm planning yet, so I don't want to say anything and maybe spoil it."

No one could disagree with this logic, even though they were all *very* curious.

42

Goodbye

Suddenly Jamie blurted out, "I don't ever want to forget you, Mrs. Tipperwillow! No matter where I live or what I do with my next life, I want to remember you ... and all of the rest of you, too." Jamie looked around at each of her friends. Her throat caught, and a little sob escaped her lips. Soon tears were streaming down the faces of all five children and one magical sort of cow.

The family stood up and hugged each other until the tears stopped. "My, that was a *fine* cry," Mrs. Tipperwillow said, wiping an arm across her eyes. "Good job, everyone. Shall we go outside now, say our blessings, and call in the nighttime?"

"Mrs. T.," Jamie said, "I want to remember our blessings, too, so I can say them with my own children one day. Do you suppose I'll be able to?"

"Oh, yes, and you'll have help remembering not only our blessings but all of your adventures here in Summerland."

"How's that?" asked Gino, scratching his head.

"Our stories!" exclaimed Lateesha.

"That's right, Teesh," replied their teacher. "One day you may each find yourselves in a bookstore or perhaps in a library on Earth. Or maybe your parents will come home with a book as a present for you. No matter what your names, for they will be different, no matter if you've been a boy here and you're a girl there or vise versa, no matter the color of your skin or how old you are ... one magic day, you will see the words, *Mrs. Tipperwillow* on the cover of a book, and it will be like a bell sounding."

"Like a cowbell!" Lateesha exclaimed. Her friends all laughed, and Gino laughed the loudest of all.

"Then when we read our stories...." Jamie began.

"The stories about us...."

"Yes, Aaron, the stories about us," Jamie continued, "we will remember everything."

"Oh, I should expect so!" trilled the magical sort of cow. "Now," she said, taking Gino's arm, "shall we go outside?"

The children and Mrs. Tipperwillow gathered in the meadow outside of their red and white striped tent. They formed their circle, holding hands and hooves tightly. Then, for what might have been their very last time together, they repeated [and dear ones, you may join us now if you so choose], "Blessings to all we've ever been and to all we'll ever be. Blessings to all we've ever loved, to the Earth, to spirit, and to dreams." Together they called in the nighttime chanting, "Softly, softly into night, softly, softly goes the light. Goodnight! Goodnight! Goodnight! *Goodnight!*"

THE END.... (Of *This* Story)

An Ordinary Day

It was an ordinary day on Earth, a Saturday, and it had been raining all afternoon here in Dearborn, Michigan. Frank, the father of three children, was taking a day off from his job at the factory where he was the foreman. He was wearing his comfortable weekend clothes, sweatpants, a sweatshirt and slippers, and he was sitting in his favorite leather chair reading the newspaper.

His two older children, Frank junior, who was seven, and Amy, who was five, were in the kitchen helping Mom prepare dinner for Grandma and Grandpa, who would be coming over later. Frank's job for now was to watch over little Tony, a happy two-year-old, who was playing with his new toy truck on the living room carpet.

Frank looked lovingly at his son. Then, for probably the thousandth time in the last twenty years, sadness came over him. "There was so much traffic on our street that day," he thought, "so Mom sent me out to watch him play in the front yard. If only I had been closer, if only...."

A pan crashed to the kitchen floor. "Are you all right in there?" Frank called, his thoughts broken.

"Fine!" yelled his wife, Judy. "It's impossible to cook with these two wild chefs without *something* happening!"

Little Tony looked up at his daddy and tilted his blond head to one side. "Sometimes," Frank said sadly, "you remind me so much of my youngest brother."

At these words, the toddler dropped his truck and pulled himself to his feet. Then raising his hands high above his head, he turned in a circle, doing a little dance.

Frank's eyes grew wide, and his mouth dropped open. *I remember that.*

The toddler stopped dancing and stared intently at his father. A tiny laugh escaped his lips, and he clapped his hands. Then, with one chubby finger, he pointed to his chest.

Frank squeezed his eyes shut. When he reopened them, he was staring into his little boy's eyes with tears in his own. He cleared his throat and said the one word his son was waiting to hear....

"Gino!"

1

A New Beginning

It was a glorious day in Summerland, golden like any other. Four children were hunkered down behind a sand dune, talking softly and occasionally peeking over the top toward the shoreline.

"Shhh ... here they come," whispered ten-year-old Aaron to his friends. Ali, who was nine and Aaron's best friend, signaled Shanthi, who was eight, and Carlos, who was six, to *stay down*.

There was a shimmer in the air, and suddenly, a tall girl with long yellow hair and a bright red swimsuit stood by the ocean. A blue-and-white surfboard was tucked under one arm. She looked down in surprise and shifted the board under her arm. "Boy, this sure is a real clear dream," she said to herself.

Looking around, she spotted someone coming down the beach. It was not a person, though, but sort of a two-legged cow, and it was wearing a pink and black striped swimsuit. It waved one arm in greeting as it floated over, touching down on delicate hooves.

"Welcome, Dana! My name is Mrs. Tipperwillow. I will be your guide here in Summerland." The girl blinked her eyes several times to see if the cow would disappear. It didn't.

"I hear you like surfing," said the sort of cow, and a surfboard appeared under her arm, too.

"I've always wanted to surf," Dana replied, a little shyly. "My Uncle Dick is a surfer. But I got sick before I had a chance to try it."

"Well, I've never gone surfing either, but that doesn't make any difference here in Summerland. We'll be brilliant!"

Mrs. Tipperwillow ran into the ocean, jumped on her board, and paddled out. The girl followed.

Perfect little waves began rolling into shore. Dana pulled herself to standing position and rode one in easily. Mrs. Tipperwillow wasn't so bad herself, as she took the second wave.

Dana laughed as they paddled out again. "This is so much fun! I feel so free!"

Mrs. Tipperwillow looked back at the girl, and over the ocean's roar she yelled, "Just wait until you try flying!"

Meanwhile, from behind the sand dune, four heads peeked out a moment. Then the children scooted down again, giggling and waiting for their cue.

A Final Note from the Author

As I was getting close to finishing this story, I had a problem. The endings had already come through, and I'd written them down, but I couldn't picture what was happening in an earlier chapter.

One afternoon, I was doing dishes at the kitchen sink when someone said, "Hi, Krista!" I recognized the voice. It was Jamie. I felt the other children with her, and I also felt confusion, as if they wanted to ask me something but were not sure they should.

Finally Gino blurted out, "We have a question for you. Will you answer it?"

That depends. What's your question?

"Do you know how our story ends yet?"

Yes, I have the ending, I said in my mind, being careful not to think of it.

Yoshi asked, "Are you sure you got it *right?*"

Well, it came through really fast and clear, Yoshi. So yes, I think I have it right. But wait! Where are you in your story? Did you get a message in your mailbox from the Light Web Council yet?

"Yeah, and we went to our party," answered Gino. "It was *fun.*"

Well, maybe you can help me. Right before you got the invitation to your party, I sensed you boys running tiny cars around a circular track. But what were you girls doing? Were you reading to each other from a story book? That doesn't seem right.

"I bet you were using your mind instead of your listening," Yoshi said in her small voice.

Yes, I have to be careful about that.

"What happened," Gino said, "is that Mrs. Tipperwillow and the girls were trying on all those clothes from the museum in London, while Aaron and I were playing with the cars. That part's right."

Of course! That's where it fits. Thank you. I think I can take it from here.

"So will you tell us how our story ends now?" Gino asked in an excited voice.

Oh, I don't think that's such a good idea, Children. Maybe if I tell you, you'll do what I say, not because it is your choice, but because I told you what would happen. And suppose I'm wrong? The ending of your story is yours, and even if I can see it, I won't spoil it for you.

Suddenly I felt Mrs. Tipperwillow appear. "Are the children bothering you, Krista?"

No, Mrs. T., not really, but they asked me a question I don't think I should answer. Then I explained to her in my mind what had happened.

I could sense the small smile playing on her lips as she replied, "I *quite* agree with you, Krista. We'll be going now, and I will be sure to keep these rascals from looking over your shoulder as you type the ending."

I sensed them leave at once, and all was quiet again.

Months later, the story was finally complete. I was relaxing in the living room reading a book when I heard whispering.

"Krista? Can you hear me?"

Yes, Yoshi, I can hear you.

"I have to be quiet," she said softly. "The babies are sleeping. Lateesha took me to see the ending of our story in the Light Web, and I just wanted to tell you ... *you were right.*"

A Final Message from Mrs. Tipperwillow

Throughout the centuries, so many of you have come to me. I've sat with you, played with you, hugged you, and taken you flying. I've shown you creations wondrous to behold and reminded you that *you* are grand creators, too.

If these stories ring a bell in your hearts, then greetings, my dear children, from your friend in spirit, Mrs. Daisy Tipperwillow.

May your hearts be glad and your creations sound. May you remember how deeply loved you are ... each moment and forever.

Visit our website at www.tipperwillow.com

978-0-595-44671-1
0-595-44671-X

Printed in the United States
118919LV00004B/97-273/P